Suspicions

Also by Sasha Campbell

Confessions

Consequences

Published by Kensington Publishing Corp.

Suspicions

Sasha Campbell

Kensington Publishing Corp.
http://www.kensingtonbooks.com

DAFINA BOOKS are published by
Kensington Publishing Corp.
119 West 40th Street
New York, NY 10018

All Kensington titles, imprints and distributed lines are available at special quantity discounts for bulk purchases for sales promotions, premiums, fund-raising, and educational or institutional use. Special book excerpts or customized printings can also be created to fit specific needs. For details, write or phone the office of the Kensington Special Sales Manager. Kensington Publishing Corp., 119 West 40th Street, New York, NY 10018. Attn: Special Sales Department. Phone: 1-800-221-2647.

Dafina and the Dafina logo Reg. U.S. Pat & TM Off.

ISBN-13: 978-0-7582-4198-6
ISBN-10: 0-7582-4198-4
First Kensington Trade Edition: May 2011
First Kensington Mass Market Edition: May 2014

eISBN-13: 978-0-7582-9215-5
eISBN-10: 0-7582-9215-5
Kensington Electronic Edition: May 2014

10 9 8 7 6 5 4 3 2 1

Printed in the United States of America

This book is dedicated to my *true* friends who have stood by me through thick and thin. Your friendships mean more than you could ever imagine.

Acknowledgments

I gotta thank William and Natilee for being my Chicago connections. Thank you for answering all my questions about the Windy City and making me feel like I was right there.

I want to thank Selena for coming up with a much more appropriate title. You knocked it out of the park again!

Shout-outs to all the fans who read *Confessions* and took the time to e-mail and let me know just how much you enjoyed my first book. I hope this one gives you the same reading pleasure.

I love hearing from my readers. You can visit me at www.sasha-campbell.com. Please join my Facebook page, where there's no telling what I might say.

1

Tiffany

"*Guuuurrrrrrl*, I met this dude from Jamaica last weekend. Trust and believe me when I tell you, he was a straight-up Mandingo!"

"Peaches, sit still before I burn your ear!" Damn! How was I supposed to style her hair if she kept moving? Besides, I don't know what made her think I wanted to listen to her talking about getting some from a dude she barely knew.

"Oops, my bad!" Peaches chuckled. "It's just not often that I find a man with some good dick."

"Ooh! I know that's right," cackled some toothpick with a jacked-up weave, sitting in the chair beside her. "I haven't had a man with anything worth talking about in a long time. They either can't get it up or when they do, it ain't worth my time."

While everyone on the salon floor started talking about men's private parts, I simply pursed my lips and kept on flatironing Peaches's hair. I don't know why my clients always think I want to hear about their sex lives.

"Shhhh-shhhh! I don't know if y'all heard this or not, but . . . Tiffany don't know nothing about getting laid."

I grabbed a comb and pointed it at Debra, ready to cuss her behind every which way, but decided not to waste my breath. She's the newest stylist at Situations, and unfortunately my booth happened to be right next to hers, which meant she had eavesdropped on one too many of my conversations. In fact, it was a bad habit I was determined to break. "Debra, nobody asked you to be spreading my personal business," I mumbled. What she needed to be worried about was that no-good baby daddy of hers.

Debra gave an innocent look, then had the nerve to wave her hand like she was dismissing me. "I don't know why you getting mad. You should be proud to let everyone know you're not getting none."

"Not getting none?" Peaches's head snapped in my direction, her bubble eyes were big as saucers. "What's up with that?"

Now all eyes were on me. Damn, why she all up in my business? "I'm just not out there trying to give it up to everybody." I wasn't yelling, but I had definitely raised my voice.

Debra started laughing. "Everybody? Hell, you haven't given it to anybody."

I gave her a nasty look. With God as my witness, before long, she and I were going to have it out. "Some of us were raised to hold on to our virginity for the right man while others weren't." I don't know why I was even trying to explain to a bunch of chicks who wouldn't understand that some of us didn't believe in giving it up to every Tom, Dick, and Jerry they come across.

"Okay . . . lemme get this straight. You saying *you're* a virgin?" Peaches asked for clarification and swung her seat all the way around so she could look at me dead in my mouth. Thanks to Debra, they were all trying to get in my business.

"Did I stutter? I'm saving myself for the right man," I replied with a mean glare. "Now turn around." I was done discussing my personal life. Unfortunately, Peaches wasn't finished yet.

"Hold up, Tif. What about that cutie pie who picked you up the last time I was here?"

I glanced around to see if anyone else was listening. The last thing I wanted was one of these trifling females in the salon to try and push up on my man. "What about him?" I said with attitude.

"I *know* you gotta be getting some of that." She said like she'd caught me in a lie. "*Sheee*-it, I would."

"Puhleeze," Debra cackled. "Tiffany ain't gave him shit!"

"You lying?" Peaches's mouth was hanging open, then all of a sudden she and Debra looked at each other and burst out laughing. "Dayuumn, Tiffany. I ain't mad atcha!" I was seconds away from telling Peaches to get the hell out my chair because I didn't give a damn if she believed me or not, but she was one of my best clients and times were hard.

The skinny chick sitting in Debra's chair threw her hands up in surrender. "Hell naw! I heard it all."

The conversation wasn't anything new to me. My girls had always thought it strange that I was 27 and still a virgin. All of them couldn't wait to fall in love and have sex, while I had the willpower they didn't have to say no. I won't say it had always been easy, but it was either wait or deal with Ruby Dee. My mother was one woman you didn't want to mess with. If she said keep your legs closed, then you better do it. Her fist was the only chastity belt I had ever needed.

I glanced around the floor, then took a deep breath before I said, "Why is it if a woman says she's a virgin, she has to be lying?"

"Damn, Tiffany, it's not like it's a bad thing. It's just, well . . . almost unheard of," Debra said on the defense.

When Peaches finally stopped laughing, she said, "Also, there is this thing called *being horny*. Hell, I lost my virginity when I was fourteen."

And that's why she has four kids. I reached for a brush. "So what? Everybody ain't like you. My mother taught me that what I have is precious and I needed to make a man earn the privilege after he makes me his wife." I probably sounded like I thought I was all that, but so what. Women needed to have more respect for themselves.

Debra sucked her buck teeth like a horse. "I know that's right, girl! Make those niggas beg for it." That wasn't at all what I meant, but I doubt Debra would know the difference.

That anorexic-looking chick with the jacked-up weave had the nerve to give her two cents. "You a better woman than me, because there ain't no way in hell I would marry a man before I knew what he was working with. I think about all those women back in the day who couldn't have sex until after they got married only to find out that not only couldn't her husband fuck, but his dick wasn't even circumcised."

"Ugh!" Peaches was laughing so hard, she practically fell from my chair. "I couldn't even imagine. Call me a ho if you wanna, but to me it's just like sampling a piece of meat in the deli. I need to know what I'm getting before I spend my money!" She flinched. "Ouch!"

"That's what you get for moving. I told you to sit still," I replied and tried to keep a straight face. That's what she gets for being all up in my business.

Now everybody wanted to get in the conversation. They were now shouting back and forth across the room with the chicks sitting in the waiting area. I half listened as I worked on my client's head. I've heard this topic time and time before, and I'll admit there have been times when I wondered what it would be like being married to Kimbel, and what if he doesn't satisfy me. But on the other hand, as my best friend told me, you can't miss what you've never had.

Ms. Conrad lifted the hooded dryer from her head. I should have known her nosy behind was listening. "I'ma tell y'all, I was married to my husband for twenty years before he decided he wanted his freedom. Charles was the only man I had ever been with, so I had no idea what I was missing. But leaving me was the best thing he could have ever done for me. I now got a man in my life who makes my toes curl."

"Shit, I know that's right. This dude I was with last night had my toes curled and me calling out his name!" screamed some tall chick sitting in the lobby.

Ms. Conrad glared at her. "That's the problem with all you young folks. You're too busy trying to get yours. Relationships are supposed to be about a lot more than just sex."

Debra waved a hot comb in the air as she spoke.

"True, but sex is important. If the sex is bad, then so is the relationship." She shook her head. "Tiffany, I don't see how you can do."

Toothpick chick gave me a curious grin. "So is your fiancé a virgin, too?"

Damn, they're nosy. "Nope, but he knows I am and he respects that." I wasn't about to tell them Kimbel spent half his time trying to convince me to give it up. Part of me felt the only reason he proposed so soon was because he knew that marrying me was the only way he was going to get some. But Kimbel was rich and he could have any woman he wanted, yet he picked me, a little girl from the projects who grew up in a single-parent home. I truly believed he wouldn't have asked me to be his wife if he didn't love me.

"How long y'all been together?" Toothpick asked.

"Six months. He proposed on Valentine's Day." I held out my hand so she could see the three-carat solitaire surrounded by emeralds that I wore proudly on my finger.

She barely looked before she frowned. "And you think your man's been faithful all this time?" As soon as I nodded, she started laughing. "Honey, puhleeze! Just 'cause you're not fucking doesn't mean he ain't. He's a man, and a man's got needs that someone else is more than willing to fulfill."

I hated bitches like her. I shook my head. "I trust my man."

"I trust mine, too . . . as far as I can see him. Because the second you turn your back, there's some hoochie trying to ride his dick. My baby is fine; therefore, I keep his ass on a short leash."

Debra started yanking the weave out her head. "That's because Ricky ain't no good. Ursula, shut up."

She rolled her eyes. "Whatever, you know what I'm saying is true."

Ms. Conrad came to my defense. "All of you need to quit. There is nothing wrong with this young lady saving herself for the right man."

Peaches turned on the chair again. "Yeah, but how do you know he's the right man until you find out what he's working with, and, better yet, if he can work it?"

"I know that right!" Toothpick high-fived Peaches and ignored the pissed off look on my face.

"Just because we don't have sex doesn't mean we don't do other things." I don't know why I felt like I needed to prove something to these ghetto chicks up in here.

Peaches glanced over her shoulder and gave me a strange look. "Things like what? And I hope you're not talking about oral sex. Because last I checked that was considered sex as well."

"No, it isn't," Debra said, and tossed a sponge roller at her.

"Yes, it is. There was a news report on *Dateline* a while back about all these high-school kids giving each other head because it's supposed to be cool. Kids think it's okay to have oral sex."

While they debated the issue, I tuned them out and thought about what they said. I would never admit it to any of them, but there were many times when I was tempted to give in to the moment and let Kimbel have exactly what he wanted, but every time I was that close to spreading my legs, I heard my mother's nagging voice in my ear, saying, "Why buy the cow if the milk is free?" But I'm not going to lie. These heifers in the salon had me thinking. It had been six months since we started dating, which meant Kimbel hadn't had any in half a year. I was confident he wasn't getting any. Some might call me arrogant. Others might call me stupid, but I trusted my man. However, the last thing I wanted was for him to get tired of waiting, then go out and get him some from one of those trifling chicks in the streets. Now, don't get it twisted. I wasn't about to give up my virginity before saying, "I do." Nevertheless, my mama ain't raised no fool. I was just going to have to prove to my man that what I have would definitely be worth the wait.

2

Chauncey

"*Oooooh!* That's it! Right there."

Grinning, I gazed into Patricia's eyes. "Boo, I aim to please," I purred, making sure my voice sounded as smooth as melted butter. Reaching for the warm oil, I drizzled it along the length of her legs, then massaged every drop down to her cute little pinkie toe.

"Mmmm." Her eyelids rolled shut and my lips curled upward. This was just too easy. All it took was me licking my lips like LL Cool J and rubbing on a woman's feet and I had her juices flowing immediately. A brotha had mad skills, and right now I had Patricia exactly where I wanted her—on the verge of an orgasm.

I focused my attention on the peanut butter brown beauty. Massaging one foot and the other, then worked my hands up her calves. She groaned and I increased the pressure. I wanted my hands to feel better than any foreplay she'd ever experienced.

"Ooh, yeah, Chauncey, damn that feel ssssoooo good!" she moaned.

Grinning, my hands were just creeping up to her inner thighs when I heard this loud voice behind me.

"Damn, Chauncey! How much longer 'fore it's my turn?"

Before I could answer, Patricia's eye snapped open and her head rolled to the woman standing impatiently to her right with a hand planted at her thick waist. "Don't be trying to rush him. My money is just as green as yours and the rest of these chicks up in here." She pointed at the women sitting on the fake leather couch in the waiting room in front of a large flat-screen television. "You're just gonna have to *wait* like the rest of them," Patricia replied, then closed her eyes and leaned back in the chair.

I gave the angry female my signature smile. "Beverly, I'll be with you in just a few. You know I like to make sure all my clients get their money's worth."

My comment pleased her because she smacked her full lips. "I just bet you do," she mumbled under her breath yet loud enough for me to hear. Momentarily pleased, she turned and moved back to take a seat in the waiting room. I'm a man who loves a female with a big ass, so there was no way I could miss the sway of her succulent hips in low-ride jeans. I don't know how long I was staring before I heard Patricia clear her throat. My head whipped around to meet her frown.

"Now . . . where were we?" I said with a wink.

She turned up her lips. "Before we were rudely interrupted you were giving me my massage."

"Oh yeah." I rubbed her legs and it wasn't long before she was moaning on her chair again. A few minutes later, I rose. "I'll be right back."

"Mmmm," Patricia purred. "Don't keep me waiting too long."

I moved over to a heating unit in the corner, removed a hot towel, then carried it over and placed it across her feet. "How's that feel?"

"Ooh-weee! Chauncey, you've got skills!"

I gave her another shit-eating grin, then signaled for Beverly to come on the floor. I poured hot water in the bowl beside Patricia's, then added some foot soak salts.

"Chauncey, I've been waiting all week for this."

Beverly had a lazy eye, so I never knew which direction she was looking. It took everything I had to focus on the left eye when what I wanted to do was follow the direction of the other up toward the ceiling. "I'm glad to hear that. How you been? How's your daughter liking the new daycare?"

Her face lit up. Apparently it blew her mind that I had remembered. "Fine. That's all she talks about."

"That's whassup." I learned that if you want to keep your clients loyal, you have to build a personal relationship with them. All you have to do is show them you care. I instructed for her to place her right foot in my hand. Beverly started laughing like she was trying on a glass slipper. I stared down at her feet and it took all I had not to do a double take. It didn't matter how often she came in, I still couldn't get used to her having some big-ass Fred Flintstone toes. The bottoms of her feet were so hard and crusty, one would have thought she had used them to peddle her car over to the salon. "Damn, boo, you got some pretty feet."

She smiled just the way I wanted her to, then dropped her eyes and tried to act shy while I removed the polish from her toes. "You think so?"

"Most definitely, I bet your man likes to suck your

toes," I flirted. She grinned and licked her lips—the way females do when you tell them exactly what they wanted to hear.

Patricia's nosy behind glanced over at Beverly's feet and then at me with her brow raised and snorted. "Be for real."

It took everything I had not to laugh. What can I say? I aim to please. And so far my fat pockets proved that I knew what I was doing. How's the saying go? The proof is in the pudding. Before I had even graduated from beauty school I knew that I would make more money doing female pedicures than I ever would cutting a nigga's head. "What would you like me to do today?"

The look Beverly gave told me that whatever was on her mind had nothing to do with her feet. Maybe it's the freak in me, but I like a woman who made her intentions known. I allowed my eyes to run freely over her body. Beverly had a slamming shape. A wide ass and big breasts perfect enough to hold in the palm of my hands, but there was no way I could go out with her. Not with her wandering eye. I wouldn't know if she was looking at me or the dude sitting at the next table.

Beverly slipped her feet in the water, then shrugged. "I don't know . . . What do you think?"

I splashed water across her legs with my hand as I spoke. "How about bronze polish? I think it would bring out the gold tone of your skin."

She batted her eyelashes. "You really think so?"

"Oh yeah. And how about a white flower on the big toe with a stud in the middle?"

"Whatever you think." She giggled.

"I got you, boo." Art décor was extra. The more I

did, the more I got paid, and I was definitely making my money. In a few more months, I would be able to finally get a crib of my own, because living at the YMCA was cramping my style.

My boys thought I was a joke and said that only a fag would be interested in working at a beauty salon doing pedicures, but I was determined to prove them fools wrong. I've got a sister and I know there are things women don't mind spending money on— clothes, hair, and nails. Half my boys were struggling to pay their child support while I had built a clientele, and never walked around with less than a couple hundred in my pocket. Who's the man now?

I had only been working at Situations six weeks, and already the other nail technicians were complaining because I had all of their customers wanting me to sit between their legs and play with their toes. What can I say, except that I know what it takes to make the ladies happy.

The bell over the door chimed and I cursed under my breath when I recognized the chick coming through the door. Tameka. I instantly felt a migraine coming on. Ever since she found out where I worked, she'd been dropping in every couple of days, and when she did, she always did something to piss me off. She was a fatal fucking attraction. As soon as she stepped through the door and spotted me rubbing Beverly's feet, I had this feeling she was about to start some shit. My shoulders sagged with relief when she moved into the small shop off to the side where the owner of the salon sold hair-care products, hoop earrings, and all that other stuff females thought they needed. Hopefully, Tameka would pick up whatever she had come for and keep it moving.

We dated for a hot second. Tameka wanted a commitment and I didn't. Hell, I wasn't offering that to nobody. Commitment was just one thing I wasn't having. Love either, for that matter. The last time I trusted a female and let my guard down, it cost me five years of my life.

I will never forget that day. I was at this club downtown located a couple of blocks from Harpo Studios. My boy and I were out celebrating my twenty-first birthday when these females stepped into the joint. Now, they all looked good, but it was the one in the middle who had my attention. She was chocolate just like a Hershey kiss and just the way I like them. Keke was chewing gum and had a walk that told you she knew she was the shit; and as good as she looked, she had every right. Those jeans were hugging everything the good Lord gave her plus some. She had her hair pulled up in a ponytail with the cutest bangs that made her look young enough that I should have known better. Instead, I found out the hard way.

"Chauncey!"

I heard one of the stylists call my name. I looked over at Tiffany, who tilted her head toward the door. As soon as I saw Tameka standing there, the question "What the hell you want now?" slipped out my mouth.

"Chauncey! Don't play like you don't know."

"What the hell she doing up in here?" Debra yelled. She and Tiffany were stylists, and they'd seen Tameka clown the last time she had come into the salon when she tried to make it known to every female in the room she and I were screwing.

"Beverly, I'll be right back." I handed her a magazine, then moved toward the lobby. "Tameka, you need to get out of here."

"I ain't going no damn where until you tell me whassup!"

The salon grew silent. All eyes were on us.

I stood in front of her and smelled the scent of Juicy Fruit on her breath. One thing I had liked about Tameka was she had excellent hygiene and was a beast in bed. But when she started shopping for wedding gowns, I knew it was time for a brotha to bounce. "Ain't shit up with us. I told you, it's over."

"You weren't saying that last week when you were lying all up in my bed!"

The roomed erupted with "oohs" and "aahs," and by now the females had come out from under the hair dryers to hear what was about to go down.

"Don't try to play like I wasn't honest with you. I told you I wasn't looking for nothing serious." Tameka was like all the others who thought they had what it took to change a brotha's mind. I had yet to meet a woman with pussy that damn good. I ain't gonna lie, Tameka is a cutie. She's about five-three, mocha, with a tiny waist and ass for days. She has a short curly afro that looks good on her, and if she wasn't so ghetto, maybe I would have kicked it with her a little longer. But one thing I don't do is loud-ass women.

She smacked her lips. "Okay, so I guess you now gonna deny saying you loved me?"

Her comment made me laugh. "I never said that. You got that shit twisted. I said I love what you do for me." I'm not one to put my business in the streets, but if she wanted to go there, then so be it.

"I know you ain't passing up a top-of-the-line dime." She planted her hands at her hips.

I reached inside my pocket. "Here's two nickels. Now get the hell up outta here."

"Who the fuck you think you talking to!" She got all up in my face and then started to scream at the top of her lungs, making a scene. The chick was straight gutter and I had no one to blame but myself. I was ready to wrap my hands around her neck and choke the shit out of her when I spotted the owner, Noelle Gordon, coming out from her office in back. Oh snap!

"What's going on out here?" she demanded to know.

I tried to speak but my stomach was in a knot, which gave Tameka a chance to put her two cents in.

"Not that it's any of your business, but I'm trying to have a discussion with my man," she yelled, snaking her neck as she spoke.

Noelle's eyebrows curled. "I don't know who you are, and with that attitude I don't want to know. However, I do know this is a place of business, *my* business, and I would appreciate it if you'd get out of here before I have to call the police."

Noelle is a full-figured sistah and the look in her eyes said she was ready to take Tameka down if she even dared to look at her cross-eyed. Already, I could see my lucrative career going out the window.

"Noelle, I got this." Before Tameka could respond, I took her by the arm and led her out the salon. As soon as we were outside the door, she snatched her arm back.

"You ain't got shit! I don't appreciate you playing with my emotions, Chauncey."

Through the storefront window I saw them nosy chicks inside, watching like it was a soap opera. "Listen, I didn't play with your emotions. I told you straight up I wasn't looking for anything serious. It's not my fault you took it there."

Tameka just stood there with her hands on her hips and suddenly her bottom lip quivered. "I love you."

I simply shook my head. "I'm sorry, but I won't lie to you." Next thing I know, she hauled off and landed a slap across my face. Inside, the salon erupted with laughter. It took everything I had not to hit that chick back. My mother taught me to never touch a female even if she wasn't acting like a lady. "We done! You hear me. Don't bring your trifling ass around here again! Otherwise, like my boss said, we're gonna call the police."

Tears started running down her face. "Yeah . . . all right . . . but this shit ain't over. You gonna regret fucking with my emotions." With that, she turned and walked to her car.

As I watched her leave, I began to wonder that maybe it was time I made some changes in my life. All the hitting and quitting was starting to become a problem. I thought being honest with a chick from the jump would save a lot of unnecessary heartache and pain. Instead, females seemed to find my lack of interest in a commitment as a challenge. My skill in the bedroom was something I was not going to apologize for. I listened to the women in the salon every day complain about men who weren't satisfying them. I was fortunate enough to not be one of them. What I had was an addiction. Just like drugs, liquor, and potato chips. A female couldn't seem to have my good loving just once. They craved my touch, my tongue, and my magic stick. But just like a crackhead, I left females feenin' for more. That's why chicks like Tameka tried to put salt in my game.

I didn't know it before, but I knew it then. I was

going to have to make some changes, because females coming on my job, I wasn't having that. Thanks to Tameka, my tips for the rest of the afternoon were now going to be half of what they would have been. Females knew I was too fine to be single, but that doesn't mean they want it rubbed in their face either. And that's exactly what Tameka just did. Damn! Patricia was one of my biggest tippers.

I stepped into the salon. Noelle cut her eyes at me.

"We'll talk later," she said, then moved back to her office.

Tiffany took one look at me and started laughing. "You need to keep that chick on a leash."

That wasn't a bad idea. I shook my head and gave a half laugh to hide my embarrassment, then moved over to the chair where Patricia wasn't looking too happy. "Sorry about that." I took my seat on the floor in front of her. "How about white tips to show off your cute toes?" I stared up into her eyes and moistened my lips with my tongue. Patricia's frown quickly curled into a smile.

"Whatever you think, Chauncey."

"I got you, boo," I said, and reached for the clear polish. In a matter of seconds I had smoothed things over.

As God is my witness, unless I'm feeling the next female, there ain't no way in hell I'm letting another get that close to me again.

3

Noelle

I'm one of those women who had sense enough to know when something was wrong. Well . . . something wasn't right with my marriage. I could feel it. Grant was too busy, or maybe I was the problem. Either way, I needed to slow down, take a deep breath, and fix whatever caused my marriage to sour, because I was smart enough to know I had a good thing.

Part of the problem was that while I was so consumed with making Situations, my full-service beauty salon, a success, I forgot about what's most important in my life: Grant and our marriage. No matter what, from this day forth, I'm going to take the time to show my man how much I love him.

My husband worked hard and brought his paycheck home. Not too many of my friends could say the same thing about their husbands. That's if they even had one. He was a good man and had every right to feel like a king when he stepped into his castle. And as his queen, it was my job to serve my husband's needs.

Just this morning it hit me, it had been ten days since we last made love. Sistah girl wasn't having that. I learned from my mother that if you weren't taking care of your man, then you better believe someone else was. Just the thought of some hoochie trying to get her claws on my husband was enough to make me want to yank off my earrings and go grab a jar of Vaseline. I never believed in sharing and I'd be damned if I was about to start now, which was why I had cleared my schedule for the afternoon and asked one of my stylists to cover any walk-ins. Most of my clients would probably be pissed, but some things were much more important. My husband, for instance.

In our twenty-year marriage, we had been relatively happy. Of course, we had our share of ups and downs, and even split up for about three months after a year of marriage. I was at fault. That was a selfish time in my life when I thought I was missing something, only to find out that I already had everything any wife could possibly want or need.

The timer went off and I rushed to the stove, opened the oven, and stared down at two charbroiled T-bone steaks. Perfect. Just the way Grant liked them. Reaching for an oven mitt, I removed them from the heat and put them on top. I glanced up at the clock. Grant had called just as he was leaving the office to let me know he was on his way home. Any minute and I should hear my husband's car pulling up in the driveway.

Reaching up, I removed two piping hot sweet potatoes from the microwave, split them open, and laved them with butter. I stuck the steam basket filled with fresh broccoli in the microwave so the second I heard Grant's car, I could hit the timer.

I smirked happily as I glanced around at my fabu-

lous kitchen with cherry cabinets and granite counter-
tops, admiring the room. I had to thank God because I
was truly blessed. I have a beautiful 3,200 square foot
home located in historical Bronzeville with every
modern amenity possible, an Acura TL in the garage,
and a successful business. There was no way I was losing my husband. I dreaded that one day he would come
home and tell me we had grown apart or, even worse,
he was bored. So I'd given it a lot of thought and I finally figured out what we needed to get our marriage
back where it used to be.

A baby.

Having another baby was the perfect answer. I couldn't
help but smile at the thought of all the fun Grant and I
would have creating another child. Our son, Scott, was
18 and spending his first year away at the University of
Wisconsin. Over the years, there had been other kids,
foster kids, but I had always wanted a daughter of my
own, one with Grant's gold-green eyes and my mocha
skin. Grant will probably think the only reason why I
wanted another baby was because my best friend,
Whitney, was pregnant with her first. And yeah, that
might be part of it, but deep down I had always wanted
a little girl. Unfortunately, time was of the essence. I
was going to have to convince him quickly, because I
would turn thirty-nine on my next birthday.

The second the garage door rose, my heart started
pounding like crazy. Grant was home. I hit the timer on
the microwave, then rushed over to the dining room
table and lit the three candles that made up the center-
piece. After checking the bottle of wine sitting in a
bucket of ice and making sure it was cold, I hurried
into the living room and turned on Whitney Houston's
new CD. Her voice was nothing like it was back in the

day, yet it didn't matter. Whitney had a sultry new sound that I couldn't get enough of hearing. I barely had time to strike a seductive pose when the side door opened and Grant stepped into the kitchen.

"Hey." First, he looked surprised; then his juicy lips curled into a smile that showed off his deep dimples I loved so much. Did I mention how sexy my husband was? He had a medium build. Grant gained a little extra around the middle over the years, but he was still fine. I watched those golden-green eyes drop to my chest. "Wow!"

Inside, I was shouting, *Cha-ching!* That was just the reaction I had wanted. One thing I could bank on was that my husband loved my body. I was a full-figured diva and wherever I went, heads turned, both men and women. Not only was I beautiful, but I was confident inside my body. I may be big, but I had style and knew how to select outfits that played up my thick hips and generous cleavage. I looked down at my costume and chuckled softly. I had almost forgotten I was wearing a skimpy maid's uniform that left very little to the imagination. I even had on a bonnet and a tiny white apron. "Sexy, what took you so long? Dinner is starting to get cold," I added with a playful pout.

"Then give me a few minutes to change and I'll be right down." Grant walked over to me. "Damn, you're looking and smelling good." He pressed his succulent lips to mine.

"Thanks, baby. Now, go change." I smacked him across his butt.

"I'll be right down." He glanced over his shoulder at me, smiled, then hurried up the stairs to the master suite we shared.

My eyes followed as he left the room. The second he

was out of sight, I frowned. I didn't miss the beer on his breath. Lord knows I wanted to ask Grant where the hell he'd been besides work. My husband taught English at Kenwood Academy. School would be out in three weeks, and I knew he was trying to grade research papers for all eight of his classes and had been working longer hours; however, he hadn't said anything about going out for drinks. Usually he told me when he was hanging out with his boys. So what was he trying to hide? Let me tell you, it took everything I had to hold it together. *Not tonight, Noelle.* Maybe I was just jumping to conclusions. My interrogation would only start another argument, and that was not at all how I planned to spend our evening. Tonight was going to be perfect. It had to be. My marriage was everything. There was plenty of time to ask about the beer later, or maybe not at all.

I quickly set the table and carried over all the food. I was putting broccoli on our plates when Grant stepped through the door. The moment I stared up into his almond brown face, I remembered all the reasons why I first fell in love with this man. Grant was fine back in the day, and twenty years later he still could turn heads.

"Sweetheart, you didn't have to go to all this trouble," he said with a nervous smile. His eyes darted around the room, taking in the dim lights and scented candles.

I swayed my hips over to him. And since he stands at six-two and I'm six inches shorter, I lifted on my toes and kissed his succulent lips. He had gargled. Yum, did he taste good.

"Damn, baby, you look good enough to eat." His golden gaze dropped down to my cleavage. The twins stood to attention. My nipples hardened under his intense stare. "Why don't we take this to the bedroom?" he suggested, then kissed me twice more.

I was tempted, but I had gone to way too much trouble. "Not yet, Romeo. There's plenty of time for that later. Now sit." I moved over the bucket, reached for the bottle of wine, and popped the cork.

"Noelle, what's the occasion?"

"Nothing . . . just thought we'd eat in the dining room for a change. It seems like the only time we ever use this room is during the holidays. All this table does is collect dust." I waited until he took his place at the head of the table before I came around and poured him a glass of Moscato.

"Thank you, baby." I poured myself a glass and took a seat; then we bowed our heads so he could say grace: ". . . and Lord, bless the hands that prepared this food. Amen." Grant dug in and his moans told me the food was good. Soft music, good food and wine, I had set the perfect mood.

"How was your day?" I asked, because I read in *O* magazine it's important for couples to share their day-to-day lives together.

He gave a pained look. "Kids. Some days I love teaching; others, I want to hit some of them upside their hard heads. Girls coming in with tits and ass showing, and got nothing but attitude. I don't know what happened to parenting."

I shook my head, feeling his pain. I never could understand how he could do it. There was no way in hell I could have tried to teach someone else's badass kids. "I know. I hear the women in the salon complaining all the time about the girls their sons bring around. Not that the boys are any better."

"Mmmm, baby, this is good," Grant said after taking

a bite of his steak. I made sure it was medium, warm with a slightly pink center, just the way he liked it. "No, in my opinion, the boys are worse. When I was growing up, my mother would have knocked me clear into next week for some of the shit these kids say and do."

"I know that's right," I replied with a chuckle. My mother-in-law, with her bougie behind, was no joke. While we ate, Grant and I talked about my day at the salon. At the back of my mind, I wanted to ask him about the beer, but I left it alone. We were having too good an evening to ruin it.

The song ended and an old mix CD I had in the five-disk changer came on. I started rocking my hips the second I heard Atlantic Starr's "Secret Lovers." "Ooh, Grant, remember that used to be our song?"

"It sure was." He rose from the chair and took my hand; we moved into the living room and Grant held me in his arms. I rested my head on his chest, smelling Jay-Z's new cologne, 9IX. I had bought it for him for Father's Day.

"Noelle, this is nice," he replied as we swayed to the music.

"I know. We need to do this more often."

"Yes, we do." He pressed his lips to my forehead, cheek, and lips. "How about we go up to bed and do a different kind of dance?"

He ain't said nothing but the word. We moved to our bedroom, dropping articles of clothing along the way. By the time I was lying flat on my back, Grant was slipping his boxers off. I stared down at his erection standing at proud attention. My husband doesn't have the biggest dick in the world, but it was perfect, just like the rest of him, and he definitely knew how to work it.

Grant kneeled down on the floor beside the bed and slid my hips down toward the edge. "Open your legs," he ordered.

Desire throbbed through my body. My baby was about to do what only he knew how to do. Have his just dessert. I opened wide and he grabbed on to my thighs and pulled me into position. The first lick from his velvety tongue about sent me in convulsions. He always knew how to find my spot. Sensations began to build with each stroke. I grabbed his head, loving the feel of his thick curly hair between my fingers. My hips began to rock and move frantically. How could I have gone more than a week without him? Grant had skills. I held him in place as I rubbed hard against his tongue until I finally exploded. He continued his magical strokes until my breathing slowed.

"Mmmm, come here," I purred and pulled him up beside me on the bed. There was no way I was letting him go unsatisfied. "That felt so good." I wrapped my arms around his neck and pulled him down for a kiss. The kiss was so deep I started squirming. "Baby . . ." I whined.

"What?"

"Hurry up."

"Tell me what you want."

"You, Grant. I want you to make love to me." I was slick, wet, and ready.

He straddled me. "How bad do you want it?" The intensity of his expression made me shiver.

"Real bad," I whimpered. "I need you." Grant entered me slowly. So slow he was driving me crazy. I wrapped my legs around him and pulled him deeper. "Ohhhh." I exhaled. That felt good. His strokes were slow and controlled. He pulled almost completely out before sliding deep inside again. I thrashed around on the bed because he was torturing me, or better yet punishing me. I would never deny my husband what was rightfully his, because I definitely didn't want him making love to anyone but me. Soon he picked up speed, plunging deep inside, and I moaned loud and clear.

"Noelle," he hissed as he tried to maintain control. I tightened my walls around him, and it wasn't long before he was screaming my name and stroked hard and fast until we both came together. I laid there with him in my arms, rubbing the sweat on his back and raining kisses to his cheeks. This was the way I wanted things to always be between us.

"Grant?"

"Yeah, baby."

"I . . . I want another baby."

Grant jackknifed straight up in the bed. "Excuse me?"

He heard me. That was just his way of avoiding the question. "Grant, I didn't stutter. I want another baby."

He gave a strangled laugh. "I thought we were through taking in foster children?"

I shook my head. Okay, maybe he truly didn't get it. "No, I don't want someone else's baby. I want a daughter of my own."

Grant started laughing. "You're kidding, right?"

"Why would I be kidding?"

"Because we're too old."

"Speak for yourself. I'm not even forty yet, but I can't say the same about you." I poked his beer belly for emphasis. He quickly sobered.

"Noelle, what I'm saying is . . . Scott is gone, and for the first time in eighteen years we have the house all to ourselves. Why would you want to change that?"

"You know I always wanted a daughter of my own. Foster children were great, but I've always wanted to have another baby. It just never happened for us, but I would like for us to try again even if I have to be artificially inseminated."

Sighing, Grant rolled over in the bed and rose. "I really don't want any more."

"Why not?"

He swung around. "Why do you think? Because we can finally enjoy our lives. No more babysitters and screaming kids. For once I can run around my own house naked." My eyes dropped to his dick. Yes, and he looked good doing it. "Sweetheart, I don't want another child. All I want to do is to enjoy my wife."

"Baby—"

Grant held up his hand. "Baby nothing. How about we go on a trip? I hear Aruba is really nice this time of year. How's a week out under the tropical sun sound?"

A vacation did sound like a good idea. We hadn't had one in years. "How about it? School will be out soon for the summer and I'm sure Tiffany can take care of the salon for a week."

Grant started rubbing my ankles. He knows that does things to me. "Well . . . it does sound like fun."

"Of course it is. Noelle . . . I don't want another baby. I want just you. Only you." He kissed my lips.

"Okay, I guess." Maybe he was right. Maybe a baby wasn't the answer. All I could do was hope a vacation would bring us closer again.

4

Candace

"How about me taking you to dinner after you get off tonight?"

I glared up at the tall light-skinned brother standing on the other side of the desk with the balls to ask me out. *No, he didn't.*

Okay, let's look at this picture: We were at the Southside Medical Clinic on 95th and Thursday evening was free clinic night, or better known as STD night. Dude was here because he got a call from one of our nurses informing him that someone he'd had sexual contact with had contracted a sexually transmitted disease. The only reason why I was there was because I worked as a receptionist.

"Yo, sexy. You wanna have dinner or what?"

It took everything I had not to blast him for even thinking I'd been interested in even walking his infected ass to the door. "Nah, boo." He looked so surprised by my answer, it took everything I had not to laugh. *Are you serious?*

As soon as he returned to his seat, Brenda, one of our licensed practical nurses, moved over beside me. "Did he just ask you out?" she whispered.

"Girl, yes." I rolled my eyes and reached for the next patient's file. "He's got some balls."

"Yeah, but you don't want what's growing down there."

I practically choked with laughter. Homeboy looked me dead in my face, so I swung my chair around and got back to work, checking patients in.

I've been working for the clinic for going on two years. It was barely above minimum wage, but it definitely beat a blank. The best thing about working there, and the main reason why I hadn't already quit, were the benefits. With a 3-year-old, I definitely needed something.

I called the next patient back, then glanced down at her patient history and cringed. She was being treated for genital warts. When I first started working here, I watched a tape they kept in the education department on sexually transmitted diseases. Warts were nothing nice. The patient was 33. I couldn't understand how someone her age could be so careless. Watching those videos and working at the Southside Medical Clinic had been a rude awakening for me. I learned that when you have unprotected sex with someone, you're sleeping with them and everyone else they have slept with. That shit was reality and ain't nothing to take lightly.

The rest of the evening went smoothly. I hated Thursday nights because it would be close to eight before I finally got out of there. Then I had to be in at nine tomorrow.

I had just sent another patient back to see the doctor when I happened to look up and see Pierre step into the clinic. At one time, I thought he might have been my prince, but he never gave me a chance, not that I was complaining.

"Hey, Pierre."

"Hey, Candace. Can you let Gloria know I'll be out front waiting?"

"Sure." I watched him leave, admiring the way he moved in jeans, then shook my head. He was proof that everything that looked good isn't always good for you. He dated Gloria. An *America's Next Top Model* wannabe. I worked the front desk while she worked the back office, processing insurance claims. Several months ago, I had just met Pierre at the candy store on the corner when he dropped by the office one afternoon to ask me out to lunch. My daughter Miasha was sick, so I had to leave early and declined. Gloria's sneaky ass stole him from me while my back was turned. I didn't know it then, but she had actually done me a favor. Since we're contracted by the city, we have access to the State of Illinois Heath Department's database. I looked Pierre's ass up in our computer and discovered he had been a patient three years ago. Treated for chlamydia. Why in the world would Gloria want a man who didn't even care enough about himself to use a condom? I wasn't giving my coochie up to just anybody. Now, don't get me wrong; I wasn't like my girl Tiffany, saving myself until I get married. I respected my girl's decision; however, there was no way in hell I'd marry somebody before I knew what he was working with. On the same token, I wasn't trying to sample every piece of dessert in the bakery window either. But when I do, trust and believe, I make sure he uses a condom. When the relationship's over, I wanted it to be the end. I don't have time for someone from the health department calling to tell me someone I screwed had been treated for an STD and I needed to come in. I had more respect for myself than that.

I guess having a strong man in my life made a big impact on my life. I am the daughter of a Baptist preacher. Although my father is Mexican, he was raised in black churches. That's how he met my mama. Papa said he fell in love the moment he heard her singing in the choir. Together they built Lift Every Voice, which is one of the largest churches on Chicago's south side. For years, my whole life was about going to church at least four times a week. I believe in worshipping God, but almost every day of my life can be a bit much. Nevertheless, my parents had been together thirty years, and I wanted the same thing and refused to settle for anything less. That's why me and Miasha's daddy weren't together. Speaking of Tyree, I reached inside my purse for my phone and sent him a text message. Daycare was due and he still hadn't given me his half. It didn't make any sense that every week I had to track his ass down just to get paid.

"Excuse me, miss, but how much longer before I get to see the doctor?"

I glanced up at this cute white guy with the prettiest light gray eyes and grinned. "Not sure. There are three people ahead of you. You just have to wait your turn."

His eyes darkened with concern. "You don't understand, I need to see the doctor *now*. I've got to get home before my wife does."

"Your wife?" I said, looking at Brenda out the corner of my eyes. "If anything, your wife should be down here with you."

He looked at me like I was crazy. "Have you lost your mind? I'm not telling my wife about this. You know how many times she told me if I messed around I better not bring anything home? Well, that's why I'm here." No. He was here because he didn't have enough respect for his wife to use a condom. "Listen . . . I've been avoiding my wife for two weeks, but tonight she's not taking no for any answer!"

Brenda moved up to the desk. "So what do you want us to do?"

He glanced over his shoulder and made sure no one was listening before saying, "Can I get a prescription, or better yet something I can give her while she's sleeping?"

"In her sleep? Dude, you going to have to talk to the doctor about that." It disgusts me every time a married man comes up in here. If he had been home like he was supposed to be, then he wouldn't have to be at some free clinic getting a shot in his ass.

Most of the patients at our clinic were disgusting. Every evening I went home and took a hot shower like I was afraid I might catch something from this place. But I must say, getting a job at the clinic was the best thing that could have ever happened to me. It was an eye-opening experience that taught me to respect myself.

I was so happy when the last patient took his STD-carrying behind out the building. As soon as the door shut, I grabbed the bottle of Lysol and sprayed the lobby.

"That's not how you catch gonorrhea." Gloria cackled as she moved to the front office.

I rolled my eyes toward the ceiling. "Whatever, I'm not taking any chances." As fast as STDs were spreading around the city, you would have thought it was the flu.

"Have you seen Pierre?"

I took in her big bubble brown eyes, small nose, and

thick painted lips. At five-eight, she could have been cute if she wasn't so damn skinny. "Yeah, he said he'll be waiting out front."

"Thanks. That man is sooo good to me." She grinned like her man was really all that, then swung her purse over her shoulder. "I'll see you tomorrow."

I watched her leave, hoping she contracted something a shot in the ass couldn't cure. I used to feel sorry for Gloria, but not anymore. She's one of those women who's looking for love in all the wrong places, and sleeping with any man who looked in her direction. That chick was in love if her date treated her to dinner and a movie. Seriously, Gloria's been with more men than I can count, and I'd only been working at the clinic almost two years. I watched her leave and shook my head. She was the epitome of everything I never wanted to be.

I took the 95th Street bus to Halsted, then walked to my parents' house. Pappa hated me being out on the streets at night. I agree. The neighborhood was nothing like it was when I was a kid. Drugs and crime were everywhere. But I didn't have a car. Not anymore. The one I had broke down a month ago. Engine locked up. No oil. Can you believe that shit? I guess I should have asked someone what that knocking sound was. Luckily for me, my job was barely three miles from my apartment.

I stayed long enough to talk to Mama and promised to pay my daycare bill on Friday when I got paid. I was sick of having to make promises I couldn't keep. If Tyree would take care of his responsibility, I wouldn't have that problem. He thought since my mother was watching her granddaughter, she shouldn't charge me.

Business is business, but he wouldn't know anything about that.

My apartment was only two blocks up from my parents' house, but my father always insisted on taking us home when I worked late. I loved my father. We had always been close. I had three brothers, but I was his only little girl.

"I really wish you'd move back home with me and your mother. I hate that you don't have a car," he said when we were a block from his house. I'd been hearing the same thing for almost a month.

"I'll buy another car in September." I was waiting to buy one when I got my student loan check.

"If you won't accept a gift, I could buy you one and you can pay me back?"

I looked over at my father with his golden brown face and fine salt-and-pepper hair. How I loved that man. "No thanks, Papa. You do too much as it is."

"There is no such thing as doing too much for your kids. You remember that." He pulled in front of my building and was putting the car in Park when I heard him growl, "What the hell is he doing here?" He then started muttering under his breath in Spanish. A Mexican immigrant, he had been raised to never speak his native language in America, but it was times like this he forgot. I knew who it was just by the look on my father's face. Only one person made Papa mad enough to cuss. I looked over at the door to my apartment building and there was Miasha's daddy standing out front smoking a cigarette. Tyree was obviously waiting for me.

"What does he want?" Daddy couldn't stand him ever since the day he had found out I was pregnant and Tyree refused to marry me.

I took a long breath before I reached for the door handle. "Who knows."

"You want me to stay?"

I immediately shook my head. The last thing I wanted was for the two of them to get into it. I needed money, and making Tyree mad was not the way to get it. "No, Papa. Tyree's probably here to see Miasha."

"She's asleep."

"Then he can carry her up to bed." I kissed his cheek, trying to smooth things over, then signaled for Tyree to come help. He put his cigarette out with his foot, then hustled over to my father's Buick.

"Good evening, Mr. Santiago."

"Hello," Papa mumbled, then watched as Tyree picked his granddaughter up from the back seat and carried her toward the building. I waved at my father, then hurried to open the door and climbed up to the second-floor apartment. While Tyree put Miasha to bed, I thumbed through my mail. Of course, there was a disconnection notice for my electricity and my house phone. I was so sick of living this way when I shouldn't have to.

For two years, I had been caught up in the excitement of being with a thug and believed all the bullshit he sent my way. Tyree used to have chicks calling my house, and some nights he didn't even come home at all. By the time I realized he was simply running game and was full of shit, I was already pregnant with Miasha. For my baby's sake, I tried to hang in there a while longer because I wanted my child to have a father around, the way I had, but things just went from bad to worse when one of his hoochies came onto my porch with her belly sticking out farther than mine.

"Yo, she's out like a log."

I swung around and glared at him with a hand at my hip. "Tyree, what do you want?"

"Damn, can't I come and see my daughter?" he said on the defense.

"You know she goes to bed early."

"Then maybe I came to see you." He smiled at me, then looked longingly at my breasts. I immediately crossed my arms over my chest.

"To do what? Give me daycare money? I told you to take that by and give it to Mama." I don't know why men were so hardheaded.

"Damn, I was busy. I thought I'd drop it off with you instead, if that's okay with you?" He reached inside his pocket and pulled out a wad of money. I rolled my eyes because he was always trying to floss. I don't give a damn how much money he has in his pocket if he doesn't have any intention of giving it to my daughter. He peeled off five twenties, then returned the rest to his pocket. He then gave me that look and took a step closer. At one time I was so desperate for money from him that I was willing to do whatever it took to get it . . . plus a little extra. Well, not anymore. Not since I started working at the clinic and decided to go to school and make a better life for me and my daughter. There was no way I was giving him some for money that was rightfully mine and Miasha's.

What I should have done years ago was put child support on his ass. But Tyree didn't like to work, so all the judge could have done was carted his ass off to jail. One thing about Tyree, he knows how to hustle, and because of it, he always had money in his pockets. As long as I don't get the courts involved, he would at least continue to make that money so he can help me financially with Miasha. It would be nice, though, if the help was consistent.

He stared at me with those pretty brown eyes of his and the two of us making love invaded my mind. Tyree's got skill. If I wasn't striving for something better, I would have taken his hand and led him to my bedroom. Instead, I ignored that horny look in his eyes and pushed him away. "Uh-uh, don't even think about it."

He had the nerve to look offended. "Damn, Candy! I ain't had none in a minute."

I dropped a hand to my hip. "You right . . . a minute. Because knowing you, an hour ago you were banging someone else." I walked into the kitchen and grabbed an apple from the fruit bowl. I was suddenly hungry. The lasagna Mama packed me for lunch was long gone.

Tyree followed, then moved in close, leaning over, and had me wedged between him and the counter. "I miss being with you." Before I could turn away, his lips covered mine and he was prying my lips open with his tongue. I resisted for a few seconds just so he wouldn't think for a second it was ever going to be that easy, then I allowed him to slip his tongue inside. I could feel an erection through his loose-fitting jeans. Like I said before, Tyree had it going on in the sex department. It was the commitment part that he seemed to have a real problem with. "I wanna be there for you and Miasha." He tried to kiss me again, but I turned my head and he got my cheek instead.

"You know how many times I have heard this same song and dance," I began with a frown. "Kiss me again and I promise you I'm going to bite a hole in your bottom lip." I was mostly angry at myself for enjoying how good he made me feel.

"Candy, I'm serious. I love you and my daughter, and I'm ready to settle down with one girl and that girl is you," he added with a grin.

I stared up at his sexy honey-brown face and looked directly into his big brown eyes. At one time I wanted that more than anything, but not anymore. I was tired of being his fool. "Sorry, but Miasha needs a *real* man in her life."

"What the fuck that 'posed mean?" I could see that look of jealousy in his eyes that I had seen too many times over the years. Tyree could mess around, but let me think about trying to be with someone else and suddenly it was a problem.

"Just what I said." I pushed him away from me.

"Shee-it! What you think I'm going to let you bring some other muthafucka around my daughter?" His words were clearly meant to scare me. Tyree's known me long enough to know I don't scare that easy. Some of the dudes I dated he had been able to punk, and others, I just never bothered to let him know about. However, none of them had been worth keeping around and introducing to my daughter.

"There ain't nothing you can do about it if I do."

"Just watch me." He warned, then stormed out the door. One thing about Tyree, I've learned to take his threats seriously.

5

Tiffany

Fridays are always hump night at Situations. By the time I finished my last client's head and left the salon, it was after ten. I was dead tired. I planned to go home, take a hot shower, and curl up under the covers before I had to do this all over again in the morning. However, when I pulled into the driveway of the three-bedroom home I shared with my fiancé, sleep was the last thing on my mind. Kimbel was home! I wasn't expecting him until tomorrow night, but I ain't mad that he was already at home waiting for me. My heart started pumping wild and I had to take a deep breath to calm my excitement. We'd been together for almost six months, but every time I arrived home to find him already there, waiting, it had this kind of effect on me. Kimbel was like no other man I had ever dated, and there was no doubt whatsoever I was in love with him.

I pulled my Honda Accord into the garage, then lowered the door and went inside to find Kimbel on the couch watching the game. "Hey, baby." I wrapped my arms around his neck and gave him a kiss. "What are you doing back so early?"

Kimbel was an athletic recruiter for Northwestern University. Monday, I had dropped him off at O'Hare Airport for Minneapolis.

"The workshop didn't last as long as they thought, so I took the first available flight back. Come're, baby." He pulled me onto his lap and kissed me some more. "I missed you."

"I missed you, too." I was lucky. I had a wonderful man who was not only handsome and rich, but he loved me. I couldn't wait for the day I would become his wife.

"Let your man show you how much he missed you." Words were no longer needed. He laid me down on my back and rolled on top of me. The kisses got deeper and I opened my mouth and let him have complete access. He slipped his tongue inside and I met each stroke. *Oooh*, he had my body tingling. His tongue traveled down to my neck and I flinched because I couldn't help it. I'm ticklish there. Kimbel pulled back and smiled down at me. "I know your spot." I didn't miss the humor in his voice.

"No, you don't." I laughed, running my hands along his hard chest.

"Oh, but, boo, I do."

He started kissing my neck again; then his fingers reached for the buttons on my blouse and released them. Kimbel then unsnapped my bra. "You are so beautiful." I arched off the couch the second he wrapped his lips around my nipple.

"Oh, Kimbel, that feels sooooo good." Not that he didn't already know that. My man knew what I liked and always did whatever it took to get me there. Desire flew through my body. He sucked deeply, drawing my nipple into his mouth. My knees grew weak and I grabbed his shoulders to steady myself. He reached for my jeans and unzipped them, and I raised my hips and helped him slide them down. Not my panties. I knew better than that. Just my jeans. Anything else and it was a recipe for trouble. Especially since he had me throbbing between my legs and my panties were wet.

Kimbel rose and removed his shirt and jeans, and I stared at my sexy man. Former professional football player. It'd been two years since he played for Philadelphia, but you couldn't tell by looking at him. He worked out every morning. Everything was hard and firm, including his penis. I spotted the head peeking out the top of his boxers. He noticed me staring at him and gave me a mischievous smile, then slowly slid his boxers down his hips. His penis sprang free. Goodness, he was blessed, which was why I needed to put a stop to this kind of behavior.

"Okay, enough. Pull your boxers back up," I ordered. He sighed loud and deep, then reluctantly did what I said. I know he was getting tired of me telling him no. After the way the girls were talking in the salon the other day, the last thing I wanted was for my man to start creeping with someone else. "Come're." I said with a crook of my index finger. The least I could do was let him dry hump my leg.

Kimbel moved over to the couch, then laid on top of me again. I wrapped my legs around his waist while he grinded against me. I closed my eyes and enjoyed the taste of him as his tongue slipped inside my mouth again. "Mmmm, you taste good." He always did. Kimbel was always chewing gum or sucking on mints, ensuring that his breath was minty fresh. I was a lucky woman.

I met Kimbel about six months ago at this club called Presidents on 75th Street. I love light-skinned men, so I was instantly attracted to him. I was out with my girls when I noticed Kimbel standing at the bar.

"Who's that?" I asked Carolyn.

She looked over in the direction, then smiled. "That's Kimbel Morgan and Chicago Bears' Lance Briggs."

All night I made it my business to get his attention, and just when I was ready to give up, Kimbel came from behind and tapped me on the shoulder. I tried to play it cool while inside I was shaking with excitement. "Hey, sexy. I spotted you across the room and had no choice but to come over and introduce myself."

"Is that right?"

"Definitely," he said with a sexy grin, showing all his pretty white teeth.

We spent the rest of the evening with each other and at a coffee shop afterward. Kimbel was a total gentleman. Afterward, he didn't try to get in my pants. Instead, he took my phone number, kissed me good night, and promised to call me the next day. That lasted for about a month before he asked me to stay the night with him. I was still living with my mother at the time, and there was no way in hell I was going to be able to tell Mama I was staying the night with a man. She already knew we were seeing each other because I had taken Kimbel to meet her. After his visit, Mama lectured me on abstinence like I hadn't been listening to that mess all my life. That night he asked to make love to me. I immediately shook my head.

"I can't."

"Why not?"

I was so nervous I was afraid I was going to throw up. "I'm . . . a virgin."

He was quiet for so long tears flooded my eyes. I knew at any second he was going to tell me it had been fun, but he didn't have time. "A virgin, huh?" His lips curled upward. "Wow! I've never dated a virgin before."

"I understand if you don't want to see me again," I replied, trying to make dumping me easier.

"Not see you? What makes you think I would want to end my relationship with you?" He pulled me tightly in his arms.

"I just thought—"

Kimbel pressed a finger to my lips. "Well, you thought wrong. I can only respect that."

I ended up calling Mama and lied when I told her I was staying with my best friend, Candace. Kimbel spent the entire night kissing and holding me, and I think that was the moment I realized I loved him. After a while I got tired of lying to my mother about where I was staying. Kimbel asked me to move in and I stood up to Mama and told her I was in love. She called me every kind of Jezebel. To shut her up, I had to make an appointment with my gynecologist. He did an exam with her standing in the room, staring at my coochie with my legs in stirrups. It was the only way to reassure her I was indeed still a virgin.

Five months later, I still managed to hold on to what I was saving for my husband on our wedding night. In all honesty, it hasn't been easy. Kissing and grinding always had me wet, but we never went any further than that ever, so I was surprised by Kimbel's question that snapped me out of my trip down memory lane.

"Baby, let me eat your pussy."

"Excuse me?" I shot up on the couch, waiting for the man I loved to repeat himself.

"Baby, I want to taste you down there." He slipped his fingers inside the elastic band of my panties. I tried to slide away but not before he ran his fingers along my damp panties, tickling my sensitive area.

"No," I replied, but it sounded more like a purr than a protest. His thumb caressed my clit and I couldn't help but to moan. "What are you doing?"

"I just want to taste you . . . that's all, baby . . . I promise." He was breathing heavily. His tongue trailed across my breasts while he pushed my panties down past my knees. But when I thought he was going to linger there longer, he continued downward. For the life of me I couldn't understand what had gotten into him tonight, but whatever it was, I couldn't stop him. It was my chance to let him find out that what I had was going to be worth waiting for.

"Open your legs," he murmured, then dropped down off the edge of the couch and knelt on the floor. Kimbel grabbed my ankles and slid me down to the edge. Desire throbbed through me because I knew what he was about to do. Read about it. Heard about. Wondered about the day I would allow Kimbel to do me, but I never thought I would let him before we were married. But like the girls said in the salon, oral sex wasn't really sex. God, I hope they were right. His fingers stroked me, then he rubbed my clit. "Oooh!" I hissed. That felt so good.

He grabbed my thighs and the first stroke of his tongue made me arch off the couch. "Oooh, my goodness!"

"You like that?" he asked, and lowered his head so his breath feathered against my flesh.

"Yesssss!" His lips sucked my clit and I moaned and jerked off the couch. Kimbel's hands clamped on to my thighs and held me in place. If I could have gotten free,

I might have tried. What we were doing was wrong. What had Mama taught me all these years? But even knowing that, I couldn't stop even if I wanted to, and Lord forgive me, I didn't want to. His mouth was hot and felt so good. He parted my lips and slipped his tongue inside. My head rolled back against the pillows. My hands traveled to his head holding him firmly in place. I could feel my heart beating fast and the blood flowing and something inside me started to build. Who would have known it would feel like this? Heat spiraled through me. Something was about to happen, and whatever it was, it felt so good I knew it was wrong. I clenched my teeth. "No." I tried to push Kimbel away, but he held on.

"Baby, please let me make you come."

"No," I moaned. I was breathing as hard as he was. I wanted him. Wanted whatever it was my body was craving, but I couldn't take that risk.

"Tif . . . please."

This was way out of control. It took everything I had to push his head away. Swallowing, I managed to whisper. "I think we need to stop."

"What?" he laughed. "You're kidding, right?"

I sat up on the couch and looked at him like he was the one who had lost his mind. "No, I'm serious. You know how I feel about sex before marriage."

Kimbel took several deep breaths, then rose from his knees. "Okay . . . fine . . . then do me."

I gave him a weird look. "Do what?" Instead of answering, he slid his boxers down to his thighs and his penis stood to attention.

"Suck my dick . . . come on, Tif. I'm hard as hell."

I looked him directly in the eyes and realized he was serious. I was willing to do a lot of things, but that wasn't one of them. *Good girls don't suck dick. Only hos do things like that.* Mama had been preaching that to me since I turned 12. I shook my head. "I can't do that. You know how I feel."

"You didn't have a problem with me doing you." Kimbel actually sounded upset.

I gave him a stern look. "That's different. And I didn't ask you to do that."

"You didn't stop me either." He turned away from me.

Goose bumps rose on my arms. I loved this man, but as much as I wanted to, I couldn't. "Listen, baby. Why don't we both get dressed and talk about this?"

"I've been waiting patiently, trying to respect your wishes, but how long do you expect a man to wait. It's been six months, dammit!"

"I know, I know, baby, but we're getting married in a month and you won't have to wait any longer." I was practically pleading with him to continue to be patient with me.

"Yeah . . . whatever. You don't want to do it? Fine. I won't ever ask you again." He pulled up his boxers, then reached for his pants and slipped them on, followed by his shirt. I rose and wrapped my arms around him and tried to kiss him, but he didn't kiss me back.

"Kimbel, please don't be mad," I whimpered. He sure looked angry. I'd never seen him act like this before. "It's going to be worth the wait . . . I promise."

"Yeah, that's what you say." He went into our bedroom with a huff, then came out a few seconds later with car keys in his hands. I put down the magazine I was pretending to thumb through.

"Where are you going?"

"Out to have a drink with my boy."

Kimbel knew I hated when he hung out with PJ.

Even though he was married, PJ messed around on his wife. That was definitely not the type of influence Kimbel needed. "Instead of walking out on me, we should talk."

"We're done talking. You said no and I respect that. I'll see you later." He leaned over and kissed my cheek, then headed out the door. Within minutes I heard his Jaguar pull away. I sat there for the longest time scared to death. In my head, I could hear that stupid conversation the other day at the salon. Those heifers had me thinking again. If Kimbel wanted a blow job, how long would it be before he found someone who was willing to do what I wouldn't?

6

Candace

I had stepped into Situations and was heading over to Tiffany's booth, when something—correction—*someone* caught my eye.

"Who's that?" Obviously—my question wasn't quiet, because some nosy female sitting on the couch to my far right whipped her matted head around, looked my way, and smiled.

My girl Tiffany glanced up from her client's hair and followed the direction of my eyes. "Oh, that's Chauncey," she replied, eyes beaming like she knew something that I didn't.

"Chauncey? When he start working here?" I came into the salon at least once a month to get my hair and nails done, but I'd never seen him before. Trust me, a man that fine . . . I would have remembered.

"He's been here almost two months. Remember, you canceled your appointment last month."

She was right, which was the reason why I desperately needed some serious work on my toes. The polish was chipped and my heels were so crusty I put a hole in my pantyhose this morning.

All the seats in the waiting room were taken, so I stood over near Tiffany while she put a relaxer in some chick's hair. The whole time I was watching him out the corner of my eyes.

"He's fine, ain't he?" Tiffany teased.

Fine wasn't the word. He was sexy as all get out, but I wasn't about to let her know that. "He's aw'ight," I replied, trying to act like he was no big deal. Trust me, the last thing I wanted anyone to know was that I was truly feeling a dude that I hadn't even met yet.

I leaned against the wall and watched him talking to the owner at the rear of the salon. It was hard to be discreet, yet I couldn't stop staring. Chauncey's back was turned and I admired his wide shoulders and the way he filled out a pair of loose-fitting stonewashed jeans. They weren't sagging to his knees like Tyree wore his pants; instead, they hung from his waist just right.

He had beautiful dreadlocks that were worn pulled back with a leather band. I could only imagine how they looked swinging around his shoulders. He was about five-ten and weighed at least two hundred. His biceps were large with tattoos that covered the length of both arms. I was dying to know what they said. After a while I felt stupid standing there saying nothing while I stared across the room at some dude who looked too much like a thug for my taste. After Tyree and a handful of others, I decided that I had a habit of picking the wrong men. Well, no more. Tonight I had a blind date with a fourth-year medical student whom one of the nurses at the clinic had hooked me up with. At first I was skeptical about going out with a man I hadn't even seen, but Brenda had brought in a photo of her nephew and he was a cutie. Not as fine as the dude standing across the room, who was now talking to some fat chick, but good-looking enough for me to go out with him and see where the evening might lead. Brenda told me he was 30 and ready to settle down and start a family. That was enough for me.

"You still going out tonight?" Tiffany asked as if she had been reading my mind.

I nodded and briefly gave her my attention. "Yep, he's picking me up at seven."

"Make sure you call me afterwards with all the details." Tiffany sounded more excited about my date than I was.

"You know I will." She and I had been best friends since eighth grade. Tiffany and her mom, Ruby Dee, had been members of my father's church for years. Her mother never allowed Tiffany to have many friends. The only reason why I was allowed to hang with her was because I was the preacher's daughter and her mother thought I was a good influence on Tiffany. I used to laugh about that. I guess she didn't know that preachers' kids were some of the biggest freaks.

I glanced down at my watch, then over at Chauncey. He washed his hands and moved back onto the floor. Damn, I loved me a bowlegged man. He smiled, and all I could do was stare at him with my mouth open. He was gorgeous. *No more thugs. No more thugs.* The sooner I got my toes done and got the hell outta Dodge, the better. "Where's Julie?"

Tiffany didn't even bother to look up. "Quit."

"Quit?" I asked as if I had heard her wrong. When she confirmed with a nod, I leaned in and whispered, "Then who's doing my feet?"

She pointed across the room. "That fine-ass specimen standing in the back. Tif, guuurrrl, he's good, too! Why you think the lobby is full? All those chicks are waiting for him to put his hands on their feet."

I looked over at Chauncey again. For a second, I thought he was moving to the barber chair in back. Instead, he had taken a seat on a stool in front of the foot spa and was playing with that fat girl's feet. My mouth went dry. A man doing pedicures? What the hell? And not just any man, but *that* sexy creature standing a few feet away. "Oh, hell no! There's no way I'm letting a man do my pedicure." Not the way my toes were looking. You would think I've been running around barefoot in the jungle, carrying a spear.

Tiffany chuckled and shook her head like she was trying to figure out how I could pass up letting a man that fine play with my toes. "Suit yourself. Cheryl will be in on Thursday if you want to reschedule."

Damn! I was tired of slicing my leg in my sleep. I needed my feet done today. Tiffany and I were planning to go out Saturday night, and I was dying to wear a new pair of Baby Phat sandals I bought at River Oaks Mall last month. For a quick second, I thought about going to the nail salon down the street and decided against it. Unlike other salons, Situations had a satisfaction guarantee policy. If cutie-pie jacked up my feet, Noelle would refund my money. *I guess I don't have much of a choice.*

"He's good." I guess Tiffany could tell I was skeptical. "Trust me. All them chicks ain't here to see me," she reminded me, just in case I didn't hear her the first time. I looked at the women eagerly waiting, and the two already sitting in the massage chairs.

"I guess," I mumbled under my breath, then took a

seat in the reception area. One female's mouth was watering as she stared at Chauncey's ass.

"Guuurrrl, I heard that feet ain't the only thing he's good at," she mumbled to the chick sitting beside her.

I rolled my eyes. Some females don't have nothing better to do than spread rumors. The last thing I wanted was a man everybody was trying to get with. I bet you money Chauncey's been seen at least once at the clinic. You better believe tomorrow morning I planned on running his name through our computer. Speak of the devil . . . he was walking toward me. Lord have mercy! He had the prettiest caramel skin and the most beautiful set of eyes. I couldn't decide if they were gray or light brown.

"Which one of you sexy ladies is next?" Chauncey licked a juicy top lip that was covered with a thin mustache. I had to take several deep breaths to regain my composure, then slowly raised my hand. He nodded, then motioned toward the empty chair on the right. "After you."

Suck it up, Candace! I took his cue and moved onto the floor. It took everything I had to ignore his appreciative smile as I passed in black slacks, white blouse, and black leather mules, wishing I had worn the red wrap dress and stilettos I had pulled out my closet this morning. I'm a 36-28-38, which means I've got perfect breasts, a small waist, and a black woman's ass. I loved to be admired and will tell a brotha in a second, "You can look, but you can't touch."

I took a seat and our eyes collided. "How are you doing today?" he asked.

"Fine." I started chanting in my head. *Stay focused. You didn't come to conversate. You came to get your toes done.* Chauncey was gorgeous, but he's still a man just like all the others, at least that's what I was trying to convince myself. Men who looked like him trapped you with their good looks and charm, and once they've stolen your heart, dropped you like a bad habit. I slipped off my shoes, rolled up my pants legs, took a seat, then lowered my feet in the tub. To make sure he knew what time it was, I reached for a book out of my purse.

"How's that water feel?"

Almost as good as that warm tingling feeling he was causing between my legs. My feet felt so good I wanted to moan, but I forced myself to nod since I definitely didn't trust myself to speak.

"Sit back and enjoy. I'll be back in a second." He programmed the massage chair, then walked over to pick up some sterilized utensils. I took advantage of the opportunity to watch him move. Oh, did he have a swagger that was out of this world. His walk reminded me of my baby's daddy, which was an *oh-hell-no!* moment. Chauncey was definitely not the type of man I needed in my life. I forced myself to dig deep and remember what I had gone through with Tyree.

Tyree had been locked up long before Miasha was even born, and ever since he was paroled, he been dropping by almost every week. However, every time he came through, he seemed more interested in climbing back in my bed than spending time with his daughter. I need stability in my life. And Tyree was definitely not the one.

Chauncey took a seat on the stool in front of me. "What can I do for you?"

"French tips would be fine."

He smiled up at me, batting his thick, long lashes, and I felt my stomach quiver. "Your man ever tell you

you have pretty feet?" *Oh Lord, no, he wasn't trying to go there.* "Baby, they look good enough to suck." Was he actually flirting with me?

I glanced over at the female in the next chair. She looked like she wanted to slap me because he was talking about my feet and not hers. I cut my eyes at her because she needed to mind her own business. As desperate as she looked, she probably would have asked, "When and where you want it?" A female like me simply had more respect for herself than to fall for that shit he was dishing out. "Are you going to do my feet or what, 'cause I can just come back another time?"

For a brief second I thought Chauncey was going to tell me to do just that and I would have slapped myself if he had. But as quickly as the frown appeared, it left and his smile returned. "Damn, boo . . . relax . . . I got you."

"I ain't your boo." I hardened the tone of my voice. If I could keep this attitude up until I got out the salon, I would be fine at least until I got home and grabbed my vibrator from the nightstand. His smile was sexy and the way he talked was a downright turn-on. *Why he gotta be so fine?*

I opened my book and tried to focus on reading. I love me some James Patterson, but it was hard to focus when a gorgeous man was handling my feet. He rubbed hot oil on my legs all the way up past my knees. Ooh, Chauncey had mad skills! I couldn't help but wonder what else he was good at. Maybe I should have paid closer attention to what they were discussing in the lobby.

I looked up from my book and my eyes locked in his gray depth. I kid you not, while Chauncey rubbed oil on my calves, he stared up into my eyes with his lips parted and a look on his face that said, "You know you want some of this." And no matter how hard I tried to look away, I couldn't. This man had a sex appeal about him that was dangerous, to say the least.

"You want your nails shortened?" he asked, then licked his lips.

"Uh-huh." I nodded my head like an idiot. *Snap out of it!* I went back to reading my book while he doctored my feet. I had managed to read two pages when I heard him ask me a question.

"What's your name?"

I frowned because he had interrupted my flow, but the sexy smirk on his beautiful face made it impossible to stay mad. "Candace."

"Nice to meet you, Candace." I could have sworn there was a twinkle in his eye. I nodded, then went back to reading again.

"So what you do for a living, Candace?"

I lifted my gaze to meet his. "Why? You looking for someone to pay your bills?" Shit, I had to ask. Most of the men I knew were always looking for a handout.

He laughed. "Actually, I don't believe in taking money from a woman. I just asked because you stepping in here looking all good in that outfit."

"Really? You don't take women's money? I find that hard to believe since you work here. I'm sure your pockets are full of tips."

"It comes with the job. Trust me . . . anything I get from a female is because I earned it. I believe in putting in my work."

"I know that's right!" cried the overweight chick in the chair beside me. Why was she so loud? She rolled up a ten-dollar bill and slipped it into his shirt pocket but not before grazing her thumb across his pecs. "Lord, you should be outlawed!" she added with a giggle.

I started reading my book again, ignoring both their asses. The last thing I needed was to be competing with another woman for a man's attention, not that I had anything to worry about. I was short, petite, and sexy. I was confident in my own skin, and that's not something every woman could comfortably say about herself.

Chauncey finished up that chick's feet, and while she threw herself at him I concentrated on my book. I was so into the mystery that I didn't even realize he was scraping the heel of my foot. Dead skin flew all over his lap. I was so embarrassed for coming in here like that.

"So, Candace . . . you got a man?"

I looked up from my page. "Nope, but I'm seeing someone." Technically, I was seeing someone, starting tonight. Hopefully there would be a lot more after that. Chauncey licked his lips again. I was ready to reach in my purse and hand him some ChapStick.

"So I guess there's no chance of me taking you out to dinner?"

I laughed. "Damn, smooth. Is that how you do it?"

He looked confused. "Do what?"

"Make your tips by asking females out while you're playing with their feet. I saw how you were looking at that chick sitting under the nail dryer, staring up at her with your pretty eyes while licking your lips."

"So you like my eyes?" he asked with a confident smirk.

Why was he twisting my words around? Okay, so

maybe I do think his eyes are sexy, and maybe he does remind me of Michael Ealy from *Barbershop 2*, but I'd been damned before I tell him that. "All I'm saying is that I'm not in the mood for some muthafucka running game. Been there and got the stretch marks to prove it." He shook his head and had the nerve to start laughing. "What the hell is so funny?"

"You, sexy."

The way the word *sexy* rolled off his tongue caused me to squeeze my thighs together while I watched as he walked over and retrieved some hot towels. He laid them across my legs and I exhaled. Chauncey signaled for the next customer to take a seat and I sat there pretending to read my book, but really, I was flabbergasted. I couldn't believe how quickly he had given up. Most dudes kept asking me out until I either said yes or cussed them out.

When Chauncey came back a few minutes later to paint my feet, he didn't even bother to strike up a conversation about anything other than if I was happy with his service, and I must say, he did one helluva job. I paid him. Gave him a reasonable tip because I was paying him for his service, not his looks, then moved over to the foot dryer and listened to him laughing with another client. Chauncey was definitely a hit with the females. Like I said, he wasn't at all what I needed in my life.

I got up to leave and Tiffany signaled for me. "Get on over here and let me see your feet." I came over still wearing those disposable flip-flops. "Ooh, I love the way he put a pink rhinestone at the corner of your big toes."

"Yeah, I do look kinda cute," I giggled, then wiggled my hips to the beat of the music all the way out the door. For some reason, I couldn't help it, I had to take one last look. I glanced through the glass and found Chauncey watching me. He was staring so hard I was trapped in his spell. He stole my breath away. I don't know how long I would have stood there staring through the window if someone hadn't tapped me on my shoulder.

"Uh, excuse me." My head whipped around to stare at some chick with a unibrow, waiting impatiently to get inside the salon. With that thick bush, she looked like one of those aliens from *Star Trek*. I hope for her sake she was here to get those eyebrows waxed. I moved out of her way and hurried over to a white Pontiac GT parked on the corner. Mama let me borrow her car for the afternoon so I could run to the store before going to pick up Miasha.

I was on my way to Dominick's grocery store and was still thinking about Chauncey. I didn't need a college education to understand I liked everything I saw. It's a damn shame, but I was more interested in knowing about Chauncey than I was about my date tonight. For the life of me I couldn't even remember that dude's name.

The second I pulled into the parking lot, Tyree called. "What do you want, Tyree?" I barked.

"What you think I want? To see my daughter. To come by and break you off some money and maybe take y'all up to White Castle's for some burgers."

I huffed into the phone. "You know I can't stand that place. I always get me heartburn."

"Well, Mickey D's then . . . damn, whatever Miasha wants."

"What Miasha wants is a father who pays his child support on time. Who knows what responsibility is," I retorted, then made a left at the corner.

"Damn, get off these nuts! I'm trying to be a daddy . . . even make you wifey, if you'd let me."

"Not happening. I'm busy tonight. Come by tomorrow with some money. Miasha needs some new shoes." I hung up before he started asking a bunch of questions. I was so sick of Tyree. He'll do good for a while, coming around regularly to spend time with Miasha, but the second he realized me and him wasn't happening, he'd start playing the disappearing act.

At the next stop light, I glanced down at my toes and started thinking about Chauncey again. Immediately, I pushed that thought away. After Tyree there was no more room for thugs in my life. I needed a real man ready for responsibilities. Not some brotha who was probably sleeping with every female who tipped him properly for his services. You better believe, first thing tomorrow, I'm calling Tiffany and asking her Chauncey's last name and then I'm looking him up in the clinic's database. Someone that fine had to have contracted something at least once. Maybe then I'd stop thinking about him.

7

Noelle

My best friend and I had just spent the entire afternoon shopping at Orland Square Mall. Now I knew what the expression "shop 'til you drop" meant, because after nine hours, I was dead on my behind. Macy's, Carson Pirie Scott, Coach, you name it, we were there.

"Whitney, I'll grab my bags later."

She climbed out of my Acura TL, frowning. "When? After Grant's gone to bed?"

"Yep," I said, and giggled because she knew me too well. "Grant told me to shop for our trip, but I think I went a little overboard." I couldn't help it.

A perfectly arched eyebrow rose. "A little? Try a lot. You tried to buy out the whole damn mall."

This was our first vacation and I was actually look-ing forward to getting away and spending time together in Aruba. Grant thought it was because I was excited about us being alone, but the truth of the matter is, I was looking forward to the trip because it was a week of sex and I was hoping to get pregnant. I know I promised Grant I would forget about having a baby, but I couldn't help it. It was all I thought about. We were in a financial position now that I could spoil my child. Grant and I got married right after I graduated. We struggled for years. I did hair while Grant went to school to be a teacher. I even did braids at home, trying to make all the money I could for almost four years until he graduated and got a teacher position. However, living on a teacher's salary, we never had much money. There were lots of things we went without. But not this time. I owned the hottest beauty salon on the south side of Chicago, and Grant had gone back to school two years ago and got a master's in English. We were financially in such a good position that our baby girl wouldn't want for anything. Ballet. Gymnastics. I know I was getting ahead of myself. I had to get pregnant first, and Aruba was the perfect location. A week ago, I stopped taking my birth control pills. The rest was now up to nature and the sexy little bikini I bought on clearance this afternoon.

"Whitney, before you leave c'mon in and have a slice of coconut cake. I baked it this morning."

"Oooh! Yes, I will. You know I love your cake." I helped load the trunk of her Lexus with her packages, then signaled for her to follow me up the stairs. Whitney's hands were planted on her round belly and I felt so jealous. I couldn't help it. I didn't want to be jealous, but I was. Whitney wasn't even married. I was. She and her baby's daddy weren't even together. Not that she cared. She wanted a baby, not a man, or so she says, although Whitney could have any man she wanted. Only she was very insecure and never knew just how beautiful she was. Whitney was tall and thin, and wore a short razor cut that was made for her heart-shaped face. I couldn't stand women like her. She was five months' pregnant and was barely showing, where someone like me looked nine months' pregnant when I was barely five. But despite how fat I looked, I loved being pregnant.

"It's crazy that all I want to do is eat."

"A baby will do that to you." I was talking from experience. She wouldn't know anything about that. I moved up the stairs and stuck the key in the lock.

"Noelle, what's that?"

I glanced over in the direction Whitney was looking and paused. "I don't know." We have a long wrap-around porch. I walked over to what looked like an infant's car seat. "Somebody must have left . . ." That couldn't possibly be what I thought it was.

"Is that a baby?" Whitney took the words from my mouth.

I reached down and removed the blanket and my heart stilled. There laid a beautiful little girl, barely six weeks old, with a Post-it note stuck to the front of a frilly pink dress that read, *Sierra*. She was wide awake and staring right at me.

Whitney rushed to my side and gasped. "Where did she come from?"

I shook my head. "How the hell would I know?" Who in the world would leave their daughter on the front porch of a stranger's house in late May? I looked to my left and then my right, checking to see if anyone was watching, then reached for the handle and carried her inside. Whitney grabbed a yellow diaper bag and followed. I placed Sierra on the coffee table, then the two of us just stared at her. Sierra was chocolate with a head full of curly hair. Her eyes were so familiar my pulse started to race. I had this weird feeling we had met before.

"She sure is a cute little thing."

"Yes, she is." I reached inside her diaper bag, looking for something that would tell me whom she belonged to. At the bottom of her diaper bag I found an envelope. Whitney got all up in my face, being nosy. What I saw scribbled on the front made my heart stop.

Gordon.

It was my last name. I opened the flap and removed the card inside. *What done in the dark...* was in big bold letters. My eyes snapped to meet Whitney's, and I could see the look of surprise on her face as she tried to find the right words.

"I hate to say this ... but, Noelle ... that little girl looks just like Grant. Especially those green eyes."

If there was ever a time I wanted to slap her, it was now. How could she even think such a thing? It was okay for me to think it, but for Whitney to suggest it was totally uncalled for. "Whitney, puhleeze! If that baby belongs to anyone, it's Scott."

She rubbed her belly like it was no big deal. "Oh ... yeah. I guess that is a possibility."

I rolled my eyes at her for even hinting that Grant had been messing around with another woman. My husband would never do such a thing. He had no reason to. I picked up the baby and held her in my arms.

"Well, she's definitely a beautiful baby," Whitney commented. She knew I was pissed and was trying to diffuse the situation. She never did like making me mad.

I couldn't stop looking at Sierra. She looked so much like my son. "Yes ... she is." She had the Gordon family's eyes and round nose. At that moment, I just knew this baby belonged to me. *I'm a grand-mother.* For some reason, having a grandchild felt almost as exciting as having a child of my own. "I've got to see her feet."

"Her feet?" Whitney repeated and laughed.

"You'll understand when you have a child of your own." I slipped off her little white bootee and smiled when I saw her flat feet and the burgundy birthmark at her left heel. Just like Grant. Just like Scott. I started laughing.

"What's so funny?"

"This is Scott's baby! I'd know those feet anywhere." I kissed her little cheek, then lifted her in my arms and held her close again. "This is my grandbaby."

"Good thing your old ass didn't try and have another baby. Your baby would have been younger than your grandchild." She started cackling like a hyena.

Okay, it was time for Whitney's ass to go. I needed time to digest the whole idea. "Don't you have something better to do?"

"No, actually, I came in for a piece of coconut cake, remember?" I watched as she moved into the kitchen and helped herself. "So which one of them chicks you think dropped that baby off on your porch?" Whitney called from the other room.

"There's no telling," I mumbled as I cradled my granddaughter in my arm.

Scott had a way with women. He was undeniably charming, just like his father. It started when he was a child and carried him through his teens. Girls flocked to him. By the time my son got to high school, I realized he was nothing but a ho. He would come home with a new shirt, pants, even Air Jordans the second they hit the street. Girls loved him and were willing to do whatever it took to get his attention. It was crazy. The house phone used to ring so much I had to change my number and made him get a job to pay for his own cell phone. Only he never kept a job because the women took care of him. Now, I'll admit my son is handsome, but he ain't all that. It's just he had a way of talking to women. Scott had a creamy brown complexion. I always admired how smooth his skin looked for a man, and long lashes that any woman would give her right arm to have. He was tall and built like a brick house, a running back who received a full athletic scholarship to the University of Wisconsin. He drove out Chicago in a brand-new Dodge Avenger. Scott said he bought it, but I didn't believe him. I knew better. Some girl was responsible.

"There were so many, there is no telling which one is trying to get her claws in my son."

Stepping into the living room, Whitney took a bite of her cake, then frowned. "You're right. There are too many. I told you before that boy was going to get someone knocked up."

"You're supposed to be his godmother. How can you talk about him?"

"Because I love him I can talk about him. And your son is a ho and you know it. My baby and I are hungry and tired. I'll call you later."

She turned to leave and I didn't stop her. I carried my grandbaby over to the table. Sierra smiled at me.

"You know your grandmother when you see her, don't you?"

When Grant finally got home from the baseball game, I was sitting in the kitchen giving Sierra a bottle. He dropped his keys on the table, moved over, and planted a kiss to my cheek. Ever since I prepared that

romantic dinner things had gotten somewhat better between us. Grant was spending less time hanging out
with his boys and more time at home with me. I still
felt like something was missing, but whatever it was I
was certain our trip to Aruba would solve the problem.

"Hey, whose baby is that?"

"Yours."

My husband looked like he was about to bolt out the
room. "What?"

I laughed, although I was somewhat disturbed by his
behavior. "She's your granddaughter."

Grant tried to laugh off his reaction. "I was going to
say, if I have a baby, then someone robbed my sperm
while I was sleeping."

Good answer. For a second there I thought maybe
there was something he and I needed to talk about.

Grant moved to the refrigerator and started to grab a
beer, then swung around. I guess when the light bulb
came on inside the refrigerator so did the one in his
head. "Wait a minute . . . did you just say that's my
granddaughter?"

"I sure did." I nodded and held Sierra up so he could
get a closer look. "Look at her. She's got your nose and
eyes. She looks just like Scott when he was a baby."

My husband stared at her for a long moment, then
that scared look returned to his face. "How do you
know she's Scott's?"

I quickly told him about coming home and finding
the baby on the porch; then I showed him the note and
Grant started rubbing the back of his neck. Something
about his behavior made me feel uneasy. "What's
going through your mind?"

"What did Scott have to say?" he asked.

"I tried calling him, but he didn't answer his phone.

I left a message and told him he needed to call home ASAP."

He raised an eyebrow. "In the meantime you need to call the police and report the child."

"Why do I need to report her? She's my grandchild. I can look at her and tell she belongs to us."

Grant stepped back, folding his arms, and released an impatient breath. "No . . . she belongs to someone else. You don't know if that's Scott's child for sure, and until we do, we have to report her to family services."

"Fine, I'll call Tina," I replied with a little attitude. Tina was a case manager at the Division of Children and Family Services. We had built a relationship after working together for almost ten years. "I don't care what you think, but this little girl is mine and I plan on keeping her . . . at least until I have a chance to talk to her mother and find out why she left her baby."

Grant cut his eyes in my direction and frowned. "Listen . . . I already told you I don't want to raise any more kids. I'm forty and ready to start enjoying my life. We're supposed to leave for Aruba in two weeks."

I couldn't believe his attitude. I put Sierra over my shoulder to burp her and followed Grant to our bedroom. "We're not talking about just any kid. We're talking about our grandchild. How can you turn your back on your own flesh and blood?"

Grant pulled off his jeans and reached for an old pair of shorts. He was getting comfortable, a good sign he was in for the night. His hanging out at the bar on Saturday nights was starting to wear on my nerves.

"I'm not turning my back. Grandparents are supposed to enjoy their grandchildren, then send them back home with their parents."

"Yes, but Scott's too young to raise a child. And the

girl who left Sierra obviously doesn't want to be a mother; otherwise, she wouldn't have abandoned her child. What kind of mother does that?"

He glared at me for a full five seconds before replying, "The kind that doesn't want the responsibility because she's too busy spreading her legs and hanging out in the street."

My jaw dropped. "That's not fair."

His eyes blazed in my direction. "Oh, yes, it is. You forget I work with these kids every day and all they care about is sex. I had at least three students this year that were pregnant. They have no idea how to take care of themselves, let alone another child."

"Which is why they need their parents' help." I carried Sierra over and laid her on a receiving blanket at the center of my bed. She was such a good baby. "I'd rather help my son and his baby's mama while they get their education; otherwise, they will end up struggling the rest of their lives. This way they'll at least have something to offer their child."

Sighing, Grant turned in my direction. The evil look in his eyes said he was dangerously close to losing it. "Listen . . . let's first find out if the baby belongs to Scott before we plan the rest of our lives."

I tried to remain calm because I didn't want any problems. "Fine, I'll call Tina, but let me tell you one thing . . . this baby is going to stay with us until we figure out what's going on."

My comment was met by a slam of the bathroom door.

8

Chauncey

"Yo, dawg, check out the ass on that female over near the door."

We all swung around on our seat to see what had Cecil's attention. I'll admit, the dark-haired chick had an ass like Kim Kardashian.

Dirk shook his head. "Yo, she got a helluva badonkadonk."

"Hell yeah, and she's waiting for a brotha like me to ride it."

I watched Cecil make a fool of himself as he imitated riding on the saddle of a horse. He bucked and sneered and I chuckled along with the fellas. Cecil was a fool, to say the least.

Tonight was boys' night out and we were hanging at Emperor's, a new spot on the west side. The club was so packed a brotha was lucky to have even found an available table left in the corner. But that's because we got here early.

"Dayumn, it's some fine hos up in here!"

I frowned. I hated when Dirk referred to all females as hos. I'll admit that there are a few I might have called the same thing, but there were several women I had mad respect for. I stood by and watched them two fools clown for the next hour. Dirk was one of those light-skinned, pretty muthafuckas who think every woman wants him. He's been married less than a year and already regrets giving up his player's card. Cecil is short and stocky, and actually acted like he had sense when he wasn't hanging with Dirk.

A pretty sistah sashayed her hips over near our table and struck a pose, sticking her big DDs out for the world to see. She had on a red catsuit that was hugging every curve. In fact, it was so tight you could see the dimples in her booty. "Which one of y'all wanna buy me a drink?"

Dirk gave her the once-over and smirked. "Drink? I was about to ask you the same thing."

She turned up her nose. "Be for real. I haven't bought a drink all night."

"Then you need to go back to where you came from because nothing over here is free unless you planning to give up some ass." Dirk had Cecil laughing and the two were like the peanut gallery. My boys can be so ignorant at times.

"I'll buy you a drink. What you want?" I reached inside my pocket for a twenty.

"I'm glad someone knows how to treat a lady."

Dirk called after her. "I do, too, if there was a lady around."

That chick got ready to tear him a new asshole when I placed a hand to the small of her back and signaled for her to follow me. I had planned on ordering a round of beers for the table before she had arrived, but now that I was buying her a drink, them fools could buy their own beer.

"Thanks," she replied over the beat of the music.

I nodded. "No problem."

She leaned her voluptuous hip against the bar and looked at me in a way I was used to getting from women. "You new around here?" she asked.

"You could say that." We ordered and shot the shit while we waited for the bartender to return with our drinks. I saw the appreciative gleam in her eyes. Don't get me wrong; Brandy was cute. She had a pretty smile, but it only took me five minutes to decide she was a little too ghetto for my taste. Not that I was looking for anything. Nevertheless, I loved making love to a woman just like the next man. Brandy had potential, but she didn't seem like the type to take no for an answer. With Tameka still clinging to my pants leg, there was no way I was traveling down that road again.

Brandy was talking about going back to school to get her GED when I spotted Tiffany stepping into the club with that fine-ass, Hispanic-looking friend of hers—Candace. They were both wearing slamming dresses, but Candace stood in a class of her own. The gold dress hugged her hips and plunged low in the front. I loved a woman with a small waist, big breasts, and a round ass, and Candace definitely fit the bill. Her hair was short and cute with gold highlights that showcased her golden brown skin. Ever since she rolled up in the salon earlier this week, I'd been thinking about her. With those succulent hips of hers, I couldn't help but wonder if she was good in bed. Hey, that's what men do. Even now I thought about wrapping her legs around my waist and sliding deep inside her. Damn!

Just thinking about it made my dick hard, and that was the last thing I needed right now.

She moved across the room with this smile that seemed to light up the entire club. Bet you every brotha in the club turned his head when they stepped inside. I wasn't having it. If Candace was going to get cozy on the dance floor with anyone, it was going to be me. I didn't even say good-bye to Brandy. I just walked off and caught the two lovely ladies as they were heading my way.

"Whassup, Tiffany?" I said, although my eyes were on Candace.

She stopped, struck a pose, and grinned. "Hey, Chauncey. You remember my girl, Candy?"

"Yes, I do." Damn! Up close and personal, she was prettier than I remembered. Just like a lollipop, she looked good enough to suck. "How are you?"

Candace glanced around the room and looked unimpressed as she spoke. "Fine. Tiffany, it's too packed in here. Let's go somewhere else 'cause I'm not going to be standing all night."

This was my chance. "Hey, me and my boys, we got plenty of room at our table. Y'all are more than welcome to join us."

Candace frowned at my suggestion, but thank goodness Tiffany was all over it. "That's whassup! Show us to your table."

I signaled for them to follow me over to where Dirk and Cecil were sitting and laughing like a bunch of hyenas. As soon as they saw me coming back with two beautiful women, their mouths dropped. "Yo, this here is Tiffany and Candace."

Everyone exchanged hellos. Candace was moving

to the chair beside Cecil. There was no way in hell I
was having that. I jumped in and offered mine. "Here,
sit here so your back isn't to the dance floor." Cecil
didn't look at all pleased. In fact, by the expression on
his face, I could tell he thought I was hating. Nah. I
was just protecting what was going to be mine. I was
preparing to take the seat beside her when I felt a tap at
the shoulder. I swung around. Damn! I had forgotten
about Brandy.

"Boo-boo, you forgot your beer," she purred.

"Uh . . . thanks."

I took the bottle and turned my back to her. You
would have thought she would have gotten the hint and
left, seeing that there were two females sitting at the
table who weren't there before. But, no, instead she
continued to stand there beside me like I was about to
finish where we left off. The fact that I left both her and
the drink behind should have been enough of a hint.

I took my seat beside Candace and Brandy sat in
the only other chair, which happened to be beside me. I
frowned at her presumptuous behavior. She just didn't
get it. Damn. It was my fault for offering to buy her a
drink. And my boys, especially Cecil, weren't even trying to bail me out. Instead, they left me hanging.

Dirk leaned across the table and zeroed in on
Tiffany. "What your man doing letting you out on a
Saturday night?"

"He don't own me. I'm a grown woman."

"Yes, you are," he replied as he looked down at her
breasts.

I was laughing under my breath because I give
Tiffany three more minutes before she cusses him out
and I was going to enjoy the show. The waitress came

by and I ordered drinks for the ladies and don't you know Brandy had the nerve to order another? Cecil and Dirk, too. I was feeling too good to complain and reached into my wallet and pulled out enough to cover a round for everyone. Thank goodness tips at the salon had been good this week.

For the next hour we all sat there drinking. I watched Candace as she laughed and talked with everyone at the table. The chick got sexier by the minute. When the music slowed down, I saw it as my opportunity to finally get some time alone with Candace. "Come. Dance with me."

She looked from me to Brandy all cockeyed like she was my girl or something. I guess she must have noticed Brandy reaching under the table trying to cop a feel. First thing I planned to do when I got her alone was straighten that shit out.

"Candy, go on," Tiffany encouraged. "You know that's your song."

She gave Tiffany an I'm-gonna-get-you-later look.

"Chauncey, I'll dance with you," Brandy replied, then had the nerve to rise from her chair and grab my arm.

I glared in her direction. "I'm talking to this sexy lady here."

She had the nerve to have attitude and was seconds away from saying something before Cecil cut her off. "Come on, little mama. Let's dance." He didn't even give her a chance to say no before he grabbed Brandy's arm and dragged her out onto the floor.

I returned my attention to Candace. "You don't wanna miss your song, do you?" I gave her my irresistible grin, then stood up and pulled out her chair. For a moment I thought Candace was going to say no before she got up and followed me out to the dance floor. I didn't waste any time wrapping my arms around her and pulling her sexy ass close.

Candace pushed against my chest trying to keep a little distance. "I don't have time for your chick to be tripping with me."

I pulled back so she could see me as I spoke. "That's not my girl. Just someone who asked me to buy her a drink."

"Yeah, whatever," she mumbled.

"Do you really think I would disrespect my woman like that?" I didn't wait for her to answer. "My mother raised me that if I can't be anything, the least I can be is respectful." I was through pleading my case. I held her close again as we swayed to Robin Thicke's new baby-making music. Candace rested her head on my chest and she felt good in my arms. I don't know what type of perfume she was wearing, but it was definitely meant for her. I glanced over at Brandy and Cecil, lip-locking and feeling each other up. That chick was no longer my problem. The way they were dancing, I was certain the second the club closed the two of them were heading to the nearest motel.

"You're a pretty good dancer."

"Hey, got to be if I want an excuse to hold a sexy female in my arms," I added with a grin that I hoped she found irresistible.

Candace pulled back and raised an eyebrow. "Obviously you have an answer for everything."

"Nah, I just know what I want and am willing to do whatever it takes to get it."

I could tell she was trying to keep a straight face. "I guess I need to add cocky to that list as well."

"I'd rather call myself confident." I chuckled and decided to leave well enough alone for now. I didn't want to lay it on too thick before I had a chance to get to know her. We danced one more song; then I took her hand and led her back to our seats.

The rest of the night I caught her looking at me when she didn't think I noticed. She was feeling a brotha. That much was a given, even if she was trying to play hard. But I liked that in a woman; nothing turned me off more than a female who threw herself at me. I like a challenge, and Candace came across as a strong possibility. In fact, I was feeling her so much, when she got up to leave, I couldn't come up with an excuse to keep the evening from ending.

"Night, Chauncey," she said, never breaking her sexy stroll toward the door. Her sultry purr vibrated through me. Cecil and Brandy had plans. Dirk was saying something about stopping through at some new strip club, but I wasn't listening. If he wanted to spend the night fantasizing about some hands-off pussy, then that's on him. I had my sights on getting the real thing. I pushed through the crowd and hurried out the door. It took me a second before I spotted Candace and Tiffany, heading to the parking lot across the street.

"Yo, Candace, hold up!"

She glanced over her shoulder, gave me a smile, but didn't stop. I caught up with her just as she reached Tiffany's car.

"Chauncey, what you want?" Tiffany was trying her best not to grin. She knew I was feeling her girl.

"I wanna holla at Candy for a second." I moved in front of Candace and smiled. I was sure I was showing all my teeth.

Tiffany stuck her finger in her mouth and pretended to gag. "Y'all gonna have to talk over there in front of *her* car. I got something my man's waiting on."

"I know it ain't no coochie, 'cause everybody knows yo ass ain't fucking!" Candace called over her shoulder.

Tiffany stuck up her middle finger and laughed. "Good night and don't do anything I wouldn't do!"

"Damn, a girl's gotta have some fun!"

The way they joked with one another, I knew they had to be close. Any other chick would have been ready to throw down in the middle of the street.

Candace signaled for me to follow her over to a cute white Pontiac GT. She hit the button on her alarm before she turned around and leaned against the car, poking her big breasts out. Even with a bra on, I could tell her nipples were hard and erect. I didn't waste any time. "I had a good time with you tonight."

She gave me a look that said she wasn't all that impressed. "You rushed out here to tell me that?"

"Who rushed?"

She laughed. "You. You're breathing all hard and shit."

Damn. I tried to slow my breathing and she started laughing. Tiffany pulled off and we both waved. "I'm trying to understand as fine as you are why you don't have a man."

She sighed, adding dramatic effect. "Too much drama."

I looked her in the eyes. "Not all of us."

"Maybe not, but I've had quite a few in my lifetime that I realized it ain't worth the drama."

"Men are just like a barrel of apples. There are always a few bad ones, but if you look through the barrel long enough, you're bound to find one that is close to perfect."

She gave a playful pout. "Perfect, huh?"

"Close to. Yo . . . nobody's perfect. All we can do is try to be the best that we can. Trust me. There are still a few good men out there."

"There is?" Candace glanced around the parking lot. "Where they at?" she asked.

"I see you got jokes."

She gave me a girlish grin, showing off white teeth. "What's your tattoos say?"

I held out my arms so she could see the words that started on the front of my left arm and finished on the right. "Hated by many . . . loved by few."

"Is that true?"

"What can I say? The world is full of haters. We can count on one hand the number of people that truly love us."

Candace smiled at the thought. "That's true."

I shrugged. "This was something I did when I was young and trying to prove that I was no longer a kid."

"I guess you think you're a man now, huh?" she added with a playful punch to my chest.

I licked my lips shamelessly before answering, "One hundred percent man."

She laughed and I joined in with her. Candace took a seat on the hood and we sat out in the parking lot, talking long after everyone had climbed in their cars and left. Candace was easy to talk to. She was staring down in my mouth and I was staring directly in her eyes. She was sexy as hell and I was captivated by her looks, her low sultry voice, and her personality. She knew how to have fun and I liked that about her. I listened while she told me about her daughter's deadbeat daddy and how she fell on her head with that one. She talked about a few more jokesters she'd encountered, and I have to admit I understand why the sistah had a wall up. However, I was determined to change her mind.

The manager was locking up the club when Candace finally flicked her wrist and glanced down at her watch. "It was nice talking to you, but I gotta get home."

"How can I see you again?" We sat there talking all that time and there was no way I was letting her walk out my life. I was feeling her. She was sexy and beautiful. Something about the way she carried herself said she was fire in the bedroom; but more than that, she seemed to have her head together. She was going to college, trying to make something of herself and raising her daughter on her own. I have to say . . . I likes that in her.

She was silent and gave me a look like she wasn't sure if giving me her number was a good idea. No wasn't an option. "Listen, Candace, I know you were feeling me tonight just like I'm feeling you. Let me have your number so I can call you. I'd like to take you to dinner or something."

"Uh . . . I don't know."

I didn't want to sound like I was begging, but I had to get her to see what she had right in front of her face. "How about I give you my number and if you're interested, then you holla at yo boy?"

She laughed. "I guess."

"You guess? Don't try to act like you don't wanna see me again."

"I didn't say that."

"Then what? You a virgin like yo girl?"

Candace huffed and laughed at the same time. "Nah, I likes to get mine." She licked her lips and made my dick throb.

"You do?" I teased coyly.

"Yep. It's just when I get mines, I make sure I'm careful not to get something else that takes a shot in my ass to get rid of."

I was nodding and laughing at the same time. "True that."

She pulled out her phone and I rattled off my number. I thought she simply was just going to save it and call me when she got good and ready. Instead, she hit Send and dialed my phone. I looked down and spotted a new number and nodded. The ball was back in my corner.

"Use it," she said.

"Most definitely." There was no way in hell I was passing up an opportunity to see her again. I helped Candace into her car, then leaned over into the window, staring down at her. She looked up at me and for the longest time we just stared. "I'll call you," I finally said.

Candace nodded and before I could kiss her, she pulled off.

9

Candace

"Hooker, quit stalling! I want to know what you think about Chauncey."

I sipped my margarita and tried to play it as cool as I could, but inside I was ready to burst. "I really like him. We stood in the parking lot talking forever. When I finally left, he called to make sure I made it home safely."

"That was nice."

I nodded because I never had a dude do anything like that for me before. Mainly because they were too busy trying to get inside my panties, and when I shot them down they moved on to the next suspect. "We stayed on the phone until almost four in the morning, talking."

Tiffany leaned back on the couch and smiled. "Damn, girl! I'm glad that the two of you hit it off."

"So am I. I would have never guessed that we would have had so much in common. After Tyree, I was through with thugs; but I must say with Chauncey I realized you can't judge a man by what's on the outside."

"Girl, puhleeze! It's what's on the outside that attracted you to him in the first place. Chauncey is fine," she said, rolling her neck as she spoke.

"Yes, he is." It had been a couple of days since we met and I looked forward to his calls. I felt like Miasha acted when I took her to Toys "R" Us. It was crazy and new and I know I was just caught up in the moment, but somehow I felt that things were different this time. Not once had Chauncey talked about getting him some. We talked about work, our dreams, and for once a man listened.

"You better keep him if you want him because there are dozens of them hoochies at the salon who would do anything to be you right about now," Tiffany warned, then shook her head. "Chauncey has already made a name for himself. His calendar is booked weeks in advance."

I jealously listened to her piece of advice. I don't know why, but I already felt like he was mine and definitely didn't want anyone else getting her claws in him.

"I can see why. He is definitely something to look at, especially with those long pretty locks, and the way he handled my feet with his gentle hands, guuurrrrl, I was about to come in my panties."

"You nasty," she giggled.

I was laughing and trying to keep a straight face at the same time. "I'm serious! It's the way he looks at me with those sexy eyes of his while he licks them juicy lips. Tiffany, girl, I am truly feeling his ass!" And I was certain he was feeling me, too.

Sex was going to be hard to resist with a man that

damn handsome, especially when his voice over the phone had the power to make the space between my thighs moist. All day I'd been dying to call and hear his voice, but I wanted him to do the chasing, no matter how tempted I was.

"I'm happy for you. When y'all getting together again?"

I shrugged my shoulders like it was no big deal. "He asked, but I told him I'd think about it."

Tiffany looked at me like I had lost my mind. "What? Think about it? What is there to think about?"

How quickly Tiffany forgets. "I'm going out with Deon tonight, remember?"

She sucked her teeth and rolled her eyes in my direction. "You better than me, because after he stood me up once, I would have called it a wrap."

Tiffany talks a lot of shit for someone who doesn't know shit about relationships. "He had to work."

"And he didn't find that out until he had you waiting one . . . two hours? Yeah . . . right," she said between sips.

"He apologized for that. He was delivering a baby and it took longer than he imagined. What was he going to do, tell her to quit pushing long enough for him to call me?"

Tiffany started laughing and I joined in. "I guess you do have a point, but I thought you just said you were really feeling Chauncey?"

"I am and that's why I wanna take it slow with him. I refuse to set myself up for another failure. I just can't deal with that. If it's meant to be, it will be. In the meantime, I'll see what ol' boy is talking about. There's nothing wrong with having options."

I spent so much time getting to know Chauncey and

so far I liked him. I liked him so much that I decided to take things slow with him. In the past, there were several times I found myself so caught up in the sex, I couldn't see how wrong the dude was until I found myself wondering how the hell I ended up with another fool. Nevertheless, it wasn't gonna be easy; not as fine as Chauncey was. But I was determined to hold out until I was certain that everything I was feeling about him was real. Tiffany smiled, but I could tell something was heavy on her mind.

"What's with the long face? In a month you'll be getting married to the man of your dreams."

"My wedding can't get here fast enough."

I could tell by the tone of her voice something was bothering her. "What's wrong?"

Instead of telling me, Tiffany stared at the wall behind my head and had this faraway look in her big brown eyes. If I hadn't known better, I would have sworn she was trying not to cry. "Kimbel is tired of me telling him no. A week and a half ago, things got a little out of hand and he stormed out the house and didn't come back until three in the morning."

"What do you mean by 'out of hand'?" I replied, digging for answers. I ain't ashamed to admit it, but inquiring minds wanted to know.

Our eyes met for a brief second; then she turned away and blushed. "We ended up on the couch with him going down on me."

My mouth hung open. I couldn't believe what I was hearing. My girl had finally had her coochie ate out. "Hold up. You lying?"

Tiffany sadly pushed her shoulder-length hair away from her face. "No, I'm not. I couldn't have stopped that man if I had wanted to. I don't understand it, but my body wanted something that my brain just couldn't control."

"Hell naw! You liked it, didn't you?" She tried to play it off, but I knew her ass too well. "Tif . . . don't even try to lie to me!"

She was looking at the wall again. "Okay . . . I'm not going to lie. Damn! It was unbelievable. I . . . I have never felt like that before in my life."

She rambled on about what happened and how far she let him go, and I sat there shaking my head, taking it all in. My girl had finally had her first orgasm. Hell naw!

"For the first time in my life I understand why some women can't go without sex. I could have Kimbel licking my kitty every night. Uhhh . . . of course I'm talking about after we're married."

That was guilt talking. She liked the feel of his tongue and needed to stop trying to front. I don't know why my girl is always trying to act like the Virgin Mary or some doggone body.

"If he was licking on your stuff, then why did he get mad?"

"Uhhhh . . ." Tiffany paused and took a long breath. I waited for her to continue, but I could tell by the way she was playing with her drink she was uncomfortable. "I . . . uh . . ."—she looked around as if someone might hear our conversation—"he got mad because I . . . I wouldn't do him."

"Oh, hell naw!" I started laughing. I know I shouldn't have, but I couldn't help it. I pictured him standing there with his dick in his hand, begging her to give him some head, and Tiffany looking like a kid who was scared of the dark. "I don't mean to laugh at you, but this is some funny shit. No offense, Tiffany, but I see why Kimbel was mad." I was laughing again, but I stopped when I noticed the embarrassed look on her face. Tiffany was so naïve. "Girl, you got that man all excited. You got yours, but you didn't let him get his. That's why he was mad. I'm surprised he didn't just take the coochie."

"Take it?" She looked like she was ready to slap me. "Candace, puhleeze. Kimbel would never do that. Instead, he left."

She brought her glass to her lips; then she had that stupid faraway look in her eyes again. After a while, her eyes pooled with tears and I felt bad for her.

"I'm afraid he's running out of patience with me. Ever since that night he's been distant and withdrawn, and we barely speak to each other."

"If he truly loves you, he'll respect your wishes and wait." I was getting mad now. Just like a man to try and pressure a female into giving him some. I thought Kimbel was different. I guess I was wrong. "He waited this long, hell . . . what's a few more weeks?"

"I know. That's what I was thinking, but ever since that night he's been acting funny. I mean really weird, like he doesn't want me around. Since it is *his* house, I decided to stay at Mama's the other night just to see if he said anything. The bastard didn't even call looking for me. That shit hurt."

I sat back on the couch, stunned. "Damn, girl. That's bad."

"I know." She looked like she was on the verge of tears. "Anyway, the girls were talking in the salon last week about men having needs and if I wasn't taking care of him, I better believe that someone else was.

When Kimbel stormed out the house the first thing that came to my mind was that he went to see someone who was willing to give him what I wouldn't."

I wouldn't put it past a man, but that wasn't what she needed to hear. "You can't be thinking like that. If he loves you, he'll wait."

"Yeah, but we're talking about a *man*. Come on, Candace. You know they think . . . with their dicks." She gave me a serious look.

I crossed my arms in front of me and shook my head. "Yes, but you have to stay true to yourself. You said you were holding on to your virginity for your husband, then that's what you do. Hell, I wish I had waited for the right man. Nothing worse than giving a man some and hating his ass later." Speaking of men . . . I hadn't heard from Tyree in almost a week.

"I don't know. I love him so much. I'm willing to do whatever it takes to keep my man."

"Does that mean you're thinking about giving him some?"

Tiffany looked around as if someone might hear our conversation. "Yes, and then I pray about it and re-mind myself to stay strong and wait."

"Then do that. I wish I had your strength. If I could do things over, I might have done things differently. Don't get me wrong; I love Miasha and I wouldn't trade her for the world, but it would have been nice to have gotten married first before I had a baby." I stared at her cocoa brown face and hated that she looked so sad. "You've waited this long, I think you can wait four more weeks. Kimbel's just frustrated, but he'll be fine. Trust me." I was trying to encourage her to be strong, but Tiffany didn't look convinced.

"I hope so. I'm just not sure anymore. I love that man and part of me feels that it's all right to go ahead and do it since I am planning to spend the rest of my life with him, anyway."

"Tiffany, don't say that too loud. Your mother might be listening."

I swore she flinched. "Yeah, that's the problem, every time I think about going ahead with it, I hear her voice in my head screaming at me to wait."

I would never say it to Tiffany, but her mother was a fruitcake. "Tiffany, you are a grown-ass woman with grown-up needs and desires. We all have weak moments. Don't let nobody dictate your life for you. Stay true to you; but if you can't, then do what you feel like you gotta do."

She smiled. "Thanks, Candace. I knew you would know what to do."

"Nah, 'cause a chick like me would have been riding that dick a long time ago."

Tiffany laughed and I gave her a hug. "Everything is gonna work itself out. Four more weeks and you can freak yo man all you want!"

After she left, I showered and dressed in this slamming blue jean halter jumpsuit that hugged my child-bearing hips and showcased my breasts. I was looking too cute. That med student didn't stand a chance. Shortly after seven, the door bell rang and I looked at the clock. He was right on time. I looked through the peephole, wanting a glance at him up close and personal, and what I saw caused the pulse at my temple to pound. Damn! I swung the door open and had straight attitude. "What do you want?"

"Is that any way to greet your baby's daddy?"

Tyree didn't even wait for an invitation. He walked in and headed straight to my kitchen and took a beer out the refrigerator.

"Excuse me . . . but this is my house."

"I'm thirsty." He popped the tab and gulped down half the can in one swig. I had bought those beers just in case my date wanted to come in later for a nightcap.

"What do you want?" I asked, looking impatiently at my watch. Deon was due any minute now.

"I came to see my daughter."

"She's at Mama's."

I guess Tyree finally noticed what I was wearing, because his eyes traveled all the way down to my stiletto heels back up to my chest. The hungry look actually made me feel naked. "Damn, baby, you wearing the hell outta that outfit! Where you think you going dressed like that?"

"None of your business. Now get the hell outta here." I needed to get him out fast. The last thing I needed was for that crazy fool to know I was seeing someone else, because there was no telling how he was going to act. I wasn't afraid of Tyree, but the last thing I needed was a scene.

Tyree moved into the living room and took a seat on my couch. "We need to talk."

"About what?" I glanced over at the clock on the end table. Tyree did, too, like he already knew what I was up to.

"I told you before, I want to talk about us."

"There is no us. Now go." Just in case he didn't believe I was serious, I moved to the front door and held it open. It was at that exact moment I spotted my date coming up the steps. "Oh shit!" I mumbled. I glanced from left to right. This was not at all how to start a first date.

Deon took one look at me and smiled. "Wow! You must be Candace."

He moved to the door looking every bit as fine as his picture. Not as good-looking as Chauncey, but gorgeous in a classier kinda way.

"And you must be Deon." I smiled at him, but it was short-lived. Tyree picked that moment to jump off the couch and move to the door like he was ready to start something. "This is my daughter's father and he was just leaving." I tried to push Tyree out into the hall, but he wouldn't budge. He just stood there inside the door mean-mugging my date.

"What's he doing here?" Tyree hissed, and moved beside me like we were a couple and this was our place together. I stepped away from him.

"Not that it's any of your business, but we're going out tonight." I smiled over at Deon and pulled him inside my apartment. "You need to leave." I was practically pleading with my eyes for him to get the hell out, but Tyree wasn't paying me any attention. He was too busy staring at Deon. I'll give it to med student, he was holding his own and didn't look like he was about to run off with his tail between his legs, like some of them other punks I had dated. "Tyree, I'll talk to you later."

"I ain't going nowhere." He took a step forward like he was about to get in Deon's face. I stepped between them, then pushed Tyree hard against the chest.

"I said get out! Don't make me call the police." As soon as he heard me mention the po-po he came to his senses and stepped out the door.

"Candy, we're gonna talk about this later."

I rolled my eyes at him, then slammed the door in his face. Immediately, I put a smile on and swung around to face my date. "Sorry about that." I spent the next minute trying to apologize. Deon yawned like he was suddenly bored and then had the nerve to scroll through his BlackBerry. *No, he ain't ignoring me.*

"You accept my apology?" I asked, then struck a sexy pose, sticking my twins out so he wouldn't miss the cleavage. Unfortunately, he didn't look at all interested.

"Listen . . . I'm sorry, but this isn't going to work."

Ewww! Was that his breath? I sure in the hell hoped not. "Why's that? I told you I was sorry about my baby daddy's behavior."

Deon gave an amused laugh. Damn! That *was* his breath. "See, that's the problem. I can't do the baby daddy thing. That's just too much drama for me. I also noticed that disconnection notice sitting there on your coffee table. I'm a struggling medical student, so I need someone to help me pay my bills and it's obvious that you can't even pay your own."

No the fuck he didn't.

"Thanks for wasting my time." Then Deon shook his head the way Papa did when he was disappointed in me.

I was tempted to pick up my phone and tell Tyree to come back and beat his ass; instead, I brought my hand over my nose. "Actually, Deon, you saved me from wasting my evening with some fool with stank breath." When he first came to the door, I thought that smell was Ms. Bridges across the hall, cooking a pot of chitlins, but now that he was standing in my apartment, I knew for a fact that was the dude's breath. "What you need to do is invest in some Altoids, because with breath like that, ain't no woman going to be interested in taking care of your narrow ass no matter how much money you have the potential to make." He opened his mouth, prepared to say something, but I held up a hand, cutting him off. "Trust and believe, if you were worth anything, your aunt wouldn't be wasting time trying to hook someone up with you and your tart breath. Now, get the hell outta my house so I can go grab a can of Lysol because you funked up my place."

As soon as I slammed the door, I went into the kitchen and reached under the sink for the can and sprayed the whole apartment. I was so pissed because instead of wasting my time with halitosis, I could have spent the evening with Chauncey.

I went to my room, changed out of my clothes, then put my pride aside and reached for the phone.

10

Noelle

"Hey Mom. What's up?"

What's up is that it took a week for Scott to return my call. Here I've been pulling out my hair, and had even pissed Grant off a few times.

After Grant's weird behavior about the baby, he had me thinking, and I couldn't help it, but I started acting suspicious. Smelling his underwear. Checking the incoming calls on his cell phone while he was asleep. I even went online and logged in to his cellular phone account and scrolled through his bills for the last six months, looking for any numbers that looked out of the ordinary. I was particularly looking for one that would have come from the hospital on the labor and delivery floor, on or about two months ago. Unfortunately, Grant just so happened to walk in and caught me, and I had to justify my actions by lying and telling him I was checking his telephone bill averages to see if maybe it was time for us to switch to another wireless company. Naturally, he wasn't buying it. Well, I had no choice but to start an argument about him not trusting me, and with the way he'd been behaving lately, if anyone should be suspicious it should be me. You better believe I reminded him that I wasn't the one hanging out at the bars and too tired for sex. I then stormed off and slammed the door. He had sense enough to come find me lying on the couch and apologize.

"What the hell took you so long to call me back?" I barked in the phone. "I've been calling you all week leaving messages. For all you knew, someone could have died!" Like his father, for instance, if I found out he had been messing around on me.

"I thought you were just calling to check up on me. Mom, I've told you before if you need to talk to me right away just send me a text message."

I don't know what it is with kids and the need to text all damn day. Whatever happened to two people having a phone conversation?

"How's Dad?"

That depends on how you answer my question. "He's fine. Everyone's fine. Can't a mother just call and see how her son is doing at college?" It was his first year away from home, and it was hard not having my baby around. "By the way . . . I was in the grocery store the other day and ran into Alissa's mother. Whatever happened to you and Alissa?" They had dated for almost a year. I hadn't really run into her mother, but it was the best I could come up with.

"She broke up with me for some nerd," he replied with a rude snort in the phone.

"Hmmm . . . I thought that was the reason you broke up with Teresa?"

"No, we didn't have anything in common. I stopped dating her and started seeing Clarice, remember?"

Clarice. How could I have forgotten about her? Quickly, I checked my memory bank. That relationship would have been about . . . thirteen months ago. "How's she doing?"

"I don't know. I haven't talked to her since I left for school. Look, Mom, several of us are getting ready to go to this coffee shop so I'll—"

I cut him off with a huff. "Before you hang up, answer one question for me. Do you have a child I know nothing about?" There, I said it.

Scott sputtered with laughter. "What did you just say?"

Did I stutter? "You heard me. Did you get one of those chicks pregnant?"

"Hey . . . I'm sure anything is possible," he replied.

"This isn't funny!" I snapped. I hated raising my voice to my son, always have; but he was testing me and today was not the day.

He was laughing now. "Mom, if I had a baby, I don't know anything about it. Why you ask?"

"Because someone dropped a baby off on my doorstep."

He was quiet. "Uhhhh . . . if that chick Aisha says her baby's mine, she's lying."

"Aisha? Who's Aisha?" There were so many I couldn't keep up.

"Uh . . . this chick I was banging my senior year."

I hated the way he talked to me like I was one of his friends. Reminding Scott how I felt was a waste of time. I know what the problem was. I spoiled him too much. Always tried to make sure my son never went without. Never made his rotten ass work for nothing, and now I was paying for it. Nobody's fault but my own. I couldn't even blame Grant, because every time he tried to pull off his belt to discipline Scott, I had come to his defense. After a while Scott knew whenever he wanted his way, all he had to do was run to me for help, which was why I couldn't understand why he hadn't bothered to tell me he had gotten some girl in trouble. We've always talked about everything, including the first time he had sex.

"Did Aisha have a baby?"

"Well . . . yeah, but it ain't mine. It's some other dude's," he said defensively. He sounded like a kid who had gotten caught bringing a copy of *Playboy* to school.

"Some other dude's?" I'm sad to say this, but it sounded like Scott had no intention of taking responsibility for his actions. "Did you use a condom?"

"Uhhhh . . . well, no."

Dummy. How many times did I hear his father talk to him about strapping up and protecting himself? "Scott . . . it only takes one time to make a baby."

"I know, but that baby don't look nothing like me!" he said on the defense.

"Well, guess what? I think the baby looks a whole helluva lot like you."

"That's not my baby."

"Scott, a mother knows her children and I know who that baby belongs to, and that's you." He was quiet. "Aren't you going to say something?"

"No, because you're not going to believe anything I say anyway, so what's the point." He blew out a long breath. I hated when he pouted. "So what she do, bring the baby over and tell you it's mine?"

"Of course not, that would have been too easy. She did exactly what I said she did, she *left* the baby sitting in a car seat on the doorstep." It still upset me every time I thought about that little girl sitting out on that porch waiting in the hot sun for someone to find her. What if we hadn't come home that night?

"I'm not surprised. Some women just ain't meant to be parents."

"That same rule applies to men. You and her are too young and immature. I just wish you had talked to your father and I and saved me all that unnecessary stress. I've been a basket case all week." Snooping around in Grant's car, and did I mention I sniffed his draws? I even checked his credit card receipts. I had been so paranoid this week, it was a wonder he was still talking to me.

"So what are you planning to do with the baby?" Scott asked, breaking in to my thoughts.

I shook my head. "Right now the baby is with me, but I really don't know what I'm going to do, considering your dad is pissed off about the whole thing." I sighed and forced myself to remain calm before I got myself all upset again. As much as I have grown to love Sierra in just a few days, her presence in my household was causing a strain on my marriage. Especially after I told Grant we needed to postpone our vacation until the mess was straightened out. He literally hit the roof. "I think the three of us should sit down and talk. In the meantime, tell me where this girl lives so I can go by and talk to her mother."

Scott hesitated. I was a second away from snapping on him when he finally spoke. "She lives in the Altgeld Gardens."

Altgeld Gardens? What the hell was he doing in the projects messing with some low-income chick? I busted my ass so my son would have a good life, a college education, then meet a nice woman and settle down. Instead, he headed straight to the neighborhood I ran away from and found him a chick who apparently had no plans of raising her own child.

"You need to come home next weekend."

"Okay," he replied, although it was apparent he wasn't happy about the idea. Well, too damn bad. I should have followed my first mind and made him spend the first part of the summer at home until football camp started, but no, I let him beg me into allowing him to take English over the summer so he could go ahead and move on campus early. Now I know it was just an excuse to run away from his problems, mainly, Sierra.

"Your butt better be here next weekend, or else . . ." I hung up, too angry to say anything further. Grant had been right all along. I babied that kid and to think I almost jeopardized my marriage, treating Grant like he was guilty of something my son had done. Sierra was my granddaughter, not my husband's love child. I mumbled under my breath, cussing out Whitney for even thinking that Grant would ever do anything like that to me.

I looked down at my watch and realized it was time for me to go and pick up Sierra from Ms. Santiago's home daycare. Thank goodness I was able to find someone at such short notice, but even still, daycare was expensive. Here I was spending a hundred dollars a week for child care, when Sierra's mother was probably at home laid out on the couch watching soap operas while collecting a check. I also know she had to be getting food stamps. She wanted the money, but not the responsibility. *Well, you got the wrong one, baby.* Daycare isn't cheap and neither is formula.

After I picked up Sierra, I headed toward the Bishop Ford Freeway to the address Scott gave me. Altgeld

Gardens. Block 5. The same street where my grand-mother lived until she passed away. After she was gone I had no reason to return to a poverty-stricken housing development that was far away from everything. We used to have to walk almost two miles just to go to the convenience store. It was a life that I'd rather forget. Thanks to Scott, I was back.

As I drew near 130th Street and Michigan Avenue, the main entrance into the development, I started to think that maybe I should have waited until Scott got home and we went over together. This was definitely not a place I wanted to be after dark. Besides, it was his child. He should be tracking down Sierra's mother, not me. But then again, he was too self-centered to do the right thing. He probably would make things worse and she'll be trying to take his narrow behind to court for child support. Nope. I was doing the right thing, going alone. Me and Sierra's mama was going to have a long talk. Don't get me wrong; I don't have a problem being a grandma and helping to raise my granddaughter, but Sierra's mother needed to learn something about re-sponsibilities that her own mother obviously hadn't bothered to teach her. Based on the environment where she lived, she and the mother both were too busy hang-ing in the streets to take the time to raise a child.

That place was like a damn maze. I passed the hous-ing unit twice before I realized I had the right address. It was a little misleading with that brand-new BMW parked out front. Luckily, I was able to park close to the door. Since I had no intention of going inside, I lowered the rear windows. Sierra was in her car seat sound asleep. I made sure the sun wasn't in her eyes, then moved up to the front door of the unit and knocked.

"Someone answer the got damn door!" I heard someone on the other side of the door scream. Goodness, was this the type of environment my granddaughter had to live in? I was tempted to just leave and pretend I didn't know where Sierra had come from, instead of returning her to this ghetto mess. Just thinking about her, I glanced over at the car making sure she was okay. I could see Sierra from where I was standing and she was fine.

I heard a lock turn and then the door swung open. There stood a big woman, wearing a pink rag tied around her head and beat-up house slippers on her feet. She turned up her nose and looked me up and down. "Can I help you?" From the look on her face, what she really wanted to say was, "What the hell you want?"

I painted on a fake smile. "Hello, I'm Noelle Gordon. Are you Aisha's mother?" I hoped like hell she said no.

"It depends. What she do now?" she said with attitude.

She looked like she was ready for me to say one wrong word so she could dust the front stoop with my ass. I've never backed down from a fight, but this chick was big like an Amazon and a rhino combined. She had broad shoulders, titties for days, and wide hips. I might be a big girl, but this chick had me beat. "I think my son is the father of Aisha's baby."

She pushed the screen door open so fast I jumped out the way. "Oh yeah? So your son's the little muthafucka who got her pregnant, then left for college?"

She better check herself. Like I said, I'm not scared, but I didn't come here for that. I came to talk. One parent with another. "Let's not start pointing the blame because it does take two to make a baby."

She gave me a nasty look. "The only thing my daughter is guilty of is trusting your son. Aisha told 'im she was knocked up and he refused to claim my grandbaby." Her hands were at her hips and her head was bobbing around on her thick neck.

"Listen, I didn't come here to argue."

She folded her arms. "Then why did you come?"

"To talk to your daughter about my grandchild," I said as calmly as possible.

She glanced over at my car. "Why isn't your son here?"

"Because he's away at school, but I already told him he better have his behind home next weekend. I'm hoping we can work out some kind of arrangement between us."

She grinned. "Hey, we'll take whatever help we can get. Pampers are expensive." Goodness, she was homely with a big-ass forehead! I guess Sierra got her looks from my side of the family.

"Yes, they are expensive." I smiled, feeling like we were finally getting somewhere. I glanced over at the car, then back at her. "Is your daughter here?"

"No, she's at school," she stated with a frown. "Even though she dropped out of school when she found out she was pregnant with my grandson, I made her go back to get her GED."

Did she just say her daughter hadn't graduated from high school? Goodness. Wait until I . . . hold up a moment. "A son? She had a girl."

"I think I would know what my daughter had," she said, rolling her neck. She then turned and moved inside the house, leaving me standing there.

Okay, something felt seriously wrong about all this.

And it only got worse when she came back out onto the porch holding a baby in her arms.

"This is my *grandson*. If I need to take off his diaper so you can see what he's working with, I will."

I shook my head. "That won't be necessary." Anyone could look at that boy and tell he was related to her.

She sucked her teeth. "What's your son's name again?"

"Scott Gordon."

"Gordon? This boy's a Miller. Anyone can look at his big bunion head and tell who his daddy is." With that she stepped inside and slammed the door in my face.

I left her place relieved, but no closer to finding Sierra's mother. Scott said Aisha's baby wasn't his. I should have believed him. He also said he didn't get anyone pregnant. I was starting to wonder if I should believe that as well. Once again I was wondering which of the men in my life was Sierra's father. I shook my head trying to get rid of that thought. Grant wouldn't do something like that to me. Or would he?

11

Tiffany

Ever since I refused to give Kimbel a blow job, things had been tense between us. I had even stayed two nights with Mama, hoping he would call and ask where the hell I was, only he didn't even seem to notice that I wasn't there lying in the bed beside him. Unfortunately, Mama was suspicious and wanted to know why I was back at home. No matter what I said, she swore up and down the reason I was home was because I had given him my virginity.

"You should have kept your legs closed!" she screamed while holding a Bible over my head. After the second night, I couldn't take it anymore and returned to Kimbel's house. He had been in Tennessee the last two days trying to recruit a senior to come and play basketball for Northwestern. His plane was scheduled to land at six thirty. I left the salon determined to make things right with my man. As soon as I stepped into the house, I reached for my cell phone and sent a text message.

Meet me at home. I got a surprise for you.

I hit Send, then rushed into the shower. I was shaking and excited at the same time. I couldn't believe what I was about to do, but if I wanted to save my relationship, I didn't have a choice. I climbed out, dried off, and went into my room to put on the outfit I had bought yesterday at Frederick's of Hollywood. Kimbel would be arriving shortly and I didn't want him to get home before I was ready. Hopefully he was coming straight home, but after our last night together, I wasn't sure about anything anymore.

Monday night I decided not to stay at Mama's and had come home, but I might as well have not been there because Kimbel moved to his side of the bed and acted like I wasn't there. When I rolled over and started kissing on him, he told me to quit trying to start something that I couldn't finish.

Well, tonight things were going to be different.

I rubbed mango-scented lotion and bath splash all over my body, then reached inside the bag and removed a short white silk gown. The only things holding it together were two ties on each side. Quickly, I slipped it over my head and pulled it down my curves. The sales clerk had suggested I buy it a size smaller for a perfect fit. I slipped into a pair of white high-heel slippers with the fur, then moved over to the full-length mirror and stared at the woman in front of me. Sexy. I not only looked naughty, but I felt that way as well. I couldn't believe it. I liked it. I would never be considered skinny. Not with my thick hips and thighs, but my beautiful C-cups and small waist made me the perfect package. I strutted around the room pretending I was on the runway shaking my butt and popping my hips as

I moved. I was looking too damn cute. "Baby, it's on. You hear me. It's on."

Riiiinnng! Riiinnng!

The phone scared me to death. I leaned across the bed and reached for the cordless phone. I assumed it was Kimbel calling to let me know he was on his way. I almost choked when I heard my mother's voice.

"Why are you out of breath?"

"No reason, Mama."

"No reason? You better not be over there doing the nasty," she hissed. "I already told you that man will have more respect for you if you make him wait."

I looked down at the negligee I was wearing and suddenly felt so dirty. "I know, Mama."

"Are you coming home tonight?"

"I . . . I decided to stay."

"Why? I thought he was angry at you because you wouldn't have sex with him?"

I don't know why I even told Mama except that I had been so hurt by his behavior that I needed someone to talk to me who would understand. I should have known she would throw it back in my face.

"He's my fiancé, Mama, and I came back where I belong."

"That man isn't going to be happy until he gets what he wants."

"Mama—"

"What did I tell you about giving the milk away for free?"

I closed my eyes. Mama was right. I needed to hold on to my precious gift just a little longer. What in the world was I thinking? I slipped my feet out the heels and was about to take the sleazy costume off when I spotted a picture of Kimbel and me on the nightstand. We had taken it when we flew to Las Vegas for Valentine's Day. It was the same night he had proposed.

"You need to come home. I told you moving in with that man was going to be a big mistake."

Moving in with him was the first time in my life I had felt free from her controlling claws. It was also the only time I stood up to her. Kimbel had given me an ultimatum: either move in with him or it was over. I couldn't blame him. He was tired of my eleven-o'clock curfew and having to live by Ruby Dee's rules. I waited until Mama was at work and I had taken all the things I needed, then left her a note that I had moved out. She didn't speak to me for almost a month.

"Mama, I got to go."

"Are you coming home tonight?"

I heard the garage door opening. Kimbel was home! My heart was pounding loudly in my ears. I was so excited.

"Tiffany, you hear me talking to you? Are you coming home tonight or not?"

"No . . . Mama, I'm not. I'm sorry."

There was a pause. "I knew you were going to turn out to be a slut just like your sister Melanie."

I fought back tears at hearing my mother call me a slut. I wanted so badly to tell her the real reason why my sister had left home. It wasn't because Melanie wanted to live with her boyfriend. It was because she couldn't stand living in Mama's house another day. But I didn't say anything. I never do. Instead, I listened as my mother belittled my big sister.

I missed Melanie. She had a strength I never had. And no matter how often Mother beat her with an extension cord, she stayed true to herself and didn't change who she was. Me, on the other hand, I did whatever it took to make Mama happy. Melanie wanted to join the military and see the world. The day she graduated she joined the Air Force and never looked back. Last time we spoke, she had made Sergeant. So often she tried to get me to leave and come live with her. But I couldn't. I was too scared of what my mother would say and what she would do. Melanie wasn't allowed to call or write our house. The last time I mentioned Melanie's name, Mother punched me dead in the mouth. As far as she was concerned, her oldest daughter was dead to her. I eventually lost contact with Melanie altogether. I missed her so much. Often I wondered where she was and what she was doing with her life.

"I expect you to act like a lady and have your butt back in this house tonight," she demanded.

"Mama, I love you, but I've got to live my own life." She was going off when I hung up the phone. There would be hell to pay, but I would have to deal with that later. Mama had temporarily killed the mood, but I wasn't going to let that woman stand in the way of my happiness. The last thing I wanted was to die a bitter old woman like her. I lit the scented candle on the dresser, then turned on Anthony Hamilton's new CD. I needed him right now.

I heard Kimbel calling my name. "Tif, where you at?"

"Up here!"

I slipped my slippers back on my feet, then moved into the bathroom and waited until I heard him enter the bedroom before I sashayed into the room. I wanted to make an entrance. "Hey."

Kimbel stopped midstride and stared over at me. I

watched his eyes travel from my breasts to my toes. "Hey," he murmured. He didn't know what to say, which was good because neither did I.

"How was your day?" The question was stupid and not at all what I wanted to say, but right now I was at a loss.

"Pretty good. You said you had a surprise for me?" he clearly looked amused.

I nodded. "Yes, I do."

I moved over to him. My legs were shaking but I didn't want him to know how nervous I was. "I don't want to wait any longer." I wrapped my arms around his neck. "I want you to make love to me." I tried to kiss him, but he pulled back and stared at me. I watched his Adam's apple bobbing at his throat.

"I thought you wanted to wait until after we were married?"

"I did at first, but why wait? We're engaged . . . you love me . . . and that's . . . all . . . that . . . matters," I said between kisses.

Kimbel pulled me close to him, wrapping his arms around me, and deepened the kiss. My body started to relax and I tried to forget about Mother and what she had beaten into my thick skull all those years.

"You're so sexy," he said as he reached for the ties, loosened the negligee, and pulled it over my head. I stood there wearing nothing but the high-heeled slippers while his eyes perused my length.

"And so are you." I reached for his tie and loosened it, then started on the buttons of his shirt. My hands were shaking so hard, but I had to do this no matter how much it was against my values.

Kimbel carried me over to the bed and lay me gently at the center; then he reached for his belt buckle and removed his pants. The entire time he shed his clothes, his eyes never left me. As I watched him pull his belt from the loops, I thought about Mother taking the belt to my butt that time she had walked into my room and found me fondling myself. She beat me that night until I was raw because I had been curious about how it felt to be touched down there.

Kimbel lay on the bed beside me and pulled me in his arms, raining kisses across my face and neck. I closed my eyes and for once allowed myself to enjoy him. His lips traveled down to my breasts, where he captured my nipple in his mouth and sucked and teased until I was squirming on the bed. "Just relax, baby. Daddy's going to make you feel good."

He traveled even lower and touched me just the way he had two weeks ago. His tongue darting in and out that he next replaced with a finger, first one, then two.

"Tif, I'm going to take my time, baby, because I want your first time to be perfect."

I pushed back a sob. My man was so sweet and thoughtful to think about how I was feeling. He positioned himself between my thighs and the second I felt him push, I flinched.

"Sweetheart, I'm going to take it slow, but I'm not going to lie. It's going to hurt a little."

I drew in a shaky breath and nodded. "I know that, Kimbel. I trust you."

He lowered his lips to mine and pushed his tongue inside my mouth. I met his strokes and tried to forget about what he was doing. "Wrap your legs around me." I did and he kissed me as he pushed hard inside my body. A scream tore from my throat and he stopped. "Are you okay?"

I nodded.

He kissed me. "We can stop."

"No . . . don't stop. Please finish." And to make sure he knew I meant it, I pushed his butt so he slipped farther inside. I grit my teeth and bit back the pain.

"Oooh . . . baby, you're so tight." He started to move, rocking back and forth until he pushed all the way through. It hurt like hell, but I held on. Forget the hype. I was hurting so bad it took everything I had not to cry. Kimbel kept kissing me and moving slowly at first, then his breathing got heavy and he started moving faster. "Baby, I'm sorry. It just feels too good. I can't wait any longer." He started pumping like a wild man. "Uuuughhh!" he cried; then he exploded. I opened my eyes in time to see his eyes close and the smile on his lips. He was happy, and that's all that really mattered, right?

Kimbel collapsed on top of me and I lay there glad it was over. "Baby, I'm sorry. Next time will be better for you. I promise." He pulled me into his arms and showered me with kisses. I waited until he had drifted off to sleep before I started crying my ass off. Mother was right. I should have waited. I had saved my relationship, but now I lost the one thing I had managed to hold on to for twenty-seven years. Now that my virginity was gone, I felt so empty inside.

12

Candace

As Jennifer Hudson blared from the speakers of my CD player, I danced around my apartment in a red satin bra that barely contained my 36Ds and matching low-rise bikinis. I moved over to the mirror to make sure my makeup was perfect. Earlier, my girl Tiffany hooked up my hair so it was looking short, sleek, and simply fabulous.

I was nervous about my date. I'd learned long ago not to expect a lot from a man, yet there was just something about Chauncey that had me thinking about him and smiling for no particular reason at all. I tried to remind myself it was only a date, dinner and a movie; yet my armpits were sweating again and I wasn't having that. I moved over to the fan in the corner, raised my arms, and allowed them to air-dry. Chauncey would be here in the next thirty minutes and Tyree still hadn't been by to pick up his daughter. I wanted him long gone before my date arrived. Chances were he wasn't coming, which was nothing new. I hadn't seen him around since he screwed up my date with Deon. I would just have to drop Miasha by my parents' house on the way, and that was probably for the best. The last thing I needed was a repeat of Monday evening.

I still couldn't believe I had almost passed up a chance with Chauncey for that funky-breath negro. To think I wasted time on that mess. I cussed Brenda every which way when I got to work the following day.

I moved to the full-length mirror and smiled. I liked what I saw. Thursday, I had gone shopping and found the perfect outfit. It was a short black dress with buttons straight down the front that molded my curves like a glove. I found a pair of red come-fuck-me heels and a matching belt to complement the look. Chauncey was in for a surprise. By the time I had Miasha's overnight bag packed, I heard a knock. I went to the door and was relieved to see it wasn't Tyree.

Chauncey grinned. "Damn, don't you look good."

I spun around, making sure he saw the view from the back as well, then returned Chauncey's smile. "You don't look bad yourself." He was wearing the hell out of Sean John jeans, white sneakers, and a T-shirt that hugged every muscle on his chest and arms. His locks hung free around his shoulders and he looked good enough to eat. As soon as I stepped aside and invited him in, Miasha came running down the hall.

He scooped her up in his arms. "Who do we have here?"

"Miasha," she said shyly, looking from me to him.

"What a pretty name for a beautiful little girl. Here, I brought you something." He reached inside his pocket and pulled out a large red lollipop. Her eyes lit up. It didn't take much to make my daughter happy.

"Can I have it?" she asked Chauncey.

"Sure, it's yours."

Miasha looked at me for approval. I nodded and she took it. "Thank you," she said, and ran down the hall to her room with her ponytail bouncing. I couldn't help but smile at how quickly Chauncey had won her over. Things were definitely looking up and the evening hadn't even started yet.

"You enjoying yourself?" Chauncey asked, taking my hand and squeezing it.

I glanced up at him and smiled. "Absolutely."

Tonight was probably the best night of my entire life. Chauncey first took me to my parents' house to drop off Miasha. Papa was at the church, but I invited him inside and Mama was falling all over herself, impressed by his charm and good manners. I wasn't surprised since she never cared for Tyree. I had to practically drag Chauncey out the house just to get away from Mama when she started twenty questions. Some of the things she was asking were questions that I had yet to ask him myself because I figured there would be plenty of time for that later.

When Chauncey suggested Italian, I thought he was going to take me to Leona's on Stoney Island or one of these neighborhood restaurants I'd been patronizing for years. Instead, he took me to this place downtown called Little Italy, and let me say that was the best Italian food I had ever had. As soon as I stepped in, I knew this place was a far cry from Olive Garden. I felt like I had stepped into Italy with the lovely décor and the guitarist in the corner playing Italian ballads. When the waiter came up to us dressed in all white and the chef came out of the kitchen to personally introduce himself, I was floored. It was nothing like the restaurants I went where Bubba or some other cat who had just gotten out of the penitentiary stepped out the kitchen wearing a hairnet on his way out back to smoke a cigarette. There was soft lighting and a candle at the center of the table, and we both had a glass of wine, something I never ordered when I had dinner only because I could get it cheaper at the liquor store on the corner. We had appetizers and fresh baked bread, and the seafood Alfredo was to die for. The food was truly authentic Italian food. No two for one or $19.99 specials. I stuffed myself trying to get every bit of my plate cleared off. Afterward, we had tiramisu, which was a coffee flavored cake and a premium blend cup of coffee. The entire meal, we talked about life just trying to get to know one another. I kept staring into Chauncey's gray eyes wondering what is wrong with this man that he is single. Chauncey was hood and I liked it in him, but he knew how to treat a woman.

Afterward, we headed down to Navy Pier and rode on the Ferris wheel, then decided to take a stroll up and down the pier waiting for the fireworks display to begin at ten.

"I'm glad you decided to give a brotha a chance."

"I'm glad I did as well." I stared up at the starlit sky. "This night has been one I will never forget."

Chauncey stopped walking and pulled me close to him, then pressed his forehead against mine. "Baby, this is only the beginning." At that moment, he did what I had been waiting all evening for him to do. He locked his lips with mine, and when he pushed with his tongue I parted my lips and let him in. He moved with such skill and confidence, Chauncey had me curious about what else he was good at.

As soon as we pulled apart, fireworks lit up the sky and Chauncey came up from behind and wrapped his arms around me as we watched the show together. The fireworks were just like the ones going on inside my head right now. My body was on fire. I don't remember the last time I had ever been this happy. *Only the beginning?* The beginning of what, I wondered? I was hoping he was implying that he wanted to keep seeing me because I would just die if he didn't. "I'm having such a good time tonight." I paused and found I was having trouble expressing myself. "I wish we could just stop time and this evening would never end."

"So do I, baby girl." He nuzzled my neck and planted kisses along my face. "I am truly feeling you, Candy."

I smiled. He had used my nickname. No one called me that but Papa and Tiffany, and Tyree when he was trying to get some. But hearing it coming from Chauncey made it sound just as sweet as the word. I closed my eyes and savored the close contact and felt myself leaned back against him. If this was just the beginning, I couldn't wait to see what happened next.

As soon as the show was over, Chauncey took my hand. "Come on, let's go."

"Where're we going?"

He gave me a puzzled look. "Sweetheart, I'm taking you to get Miasha, then we're going back to your place."

We picked up a sleepy Miasha and we were relatively quiet most of the ride. When Chauncey pulled up in front of my building, he put the car in Park and turned off the engine. Before I could find the guts to invite him inside, he reached in back and scooped Miasha in his arms and carried her into the building. Once inside my apartment, I took her from his arms and carried her into the room and lay her in the bed. Mama had already bathed her and she had on pajamas, so all I had to do was slip her under a *The Princess and the Frog* comforter. When I returned to the living room, I expected to find Chauncey lounging across the couch with his shoes off, but instead he was standing near to the door.

"Would you like something to drink?" I asked, and couldn't believe how nervous I sounded.

I was floored when he shook his head. "No, I'm fine, but thanks. I had a good time tonight."

Of course, I was disappointed that the evening was about to end. The fact that he wasn't trying to get me in bed and get some kind of return for all the money he forked out tonight had me stunned. Trust and believe, I would have clowned his ass if he had even thought about asking for some, but now that he was leaving, it had me thinking that maybe he didn't have as good a time as I had.

Chauncey lowered his head and gave me one of those kisses that made my panties moist; then he released me and moved to the door. "I'll call you tomorrow."

"Are you serious?"

He swung around and looked confused. "What?"

"You really leaving?"

He had the nerve to laugh like something was funny. "Yes, I'm leaving. Why? You want me to stay?"

"Uh . . . no." I wasn't sure what I wanted at this moment except that I wasn't ready yet for him to leave. Usually at this particular moment my date was trying to get him some before I shut him down and told him it was time for him to leave. I wasn't used to someone wanting to leave before I was ready for him to go. I guess I should have felt relieved. Except I saw Chauncey leaving as a sign he wasn't really interested. I walked over to him, wrapped my arms around his waist, and kissed him deeply; and when he cradled me in his arms, I felt evidence of his erection against my stomach. *At least he isn't gay.* And he had to be at least a little bit attracted to me for his dick to get hard.

Chauncey was the first to end the kiss. "Yo, I better go." He winked, then released me. "I'll holla at you tomorrow."

I saw the way he was looking down at his watch and suddenly it hit me. The reason why Chauncey was leaving was because he had a woman at home. "Yeah, whatever," I mumbled under my breath.

His brow rose and he moved toward me, then stroked the side of my face. "What's running through your head?"

I moved away from his touch and crossed my arms. "I'm just wondering why you're in such a rush?"

"A rush? Baby girl, if I had my way, I would spend the rest of the night making love to you, but I don't want to rush things between us."

"Why? 'Cause you got some female at home waiting for you?" Damn, I can't believe I blurted out and said that. The last thing I wanted was for Chauncey to think I was sweating him.

"Not at all." He shook his head, sending his dreadlocks swinging across his shoulders. It was hard to stay angry at someone who looked that sexy. "I know we didn't talk about it tonight, but I'm not seeing anyone. I hope your situation hasn't changed."

"It hasn't."

Chauncey reached for me and brought me close against him. "I like you, Candy. I am truly feeling you, so I don't wanna rush things between us. Yeah, I could have tried to get some tonight, but I'm not 'cause I got mad respect for you."

Was he for real?

"We can take this thing slow. All I ask is . . . will you keep it real wit your boy?"

I stared up into his beautiful eyes thinking I must be the luckiest woman in all of Chicago right now. "Absolutely. As long as you promise to do the same."

"No doubt."

We sealed the end of our evening with another long kiss.

13

Chauncey

I'd had dates before, plenty of them, but none had ever compared to my evening with Candace. That female was smart and intelligent and had a wonderful sense of humor. I liked that she had a good head on her shoulders, and even though I hadn't spent a great deal of time with her and Miasha, I already had a feeling she was also a good mother. All in all, Candace was the total package.

Once I told her I respected her enough to take things slow, we sat in her living room and talked about things such as sports and cars. She was not like other girls I dated who had nothing to discuss other than hair, nails, or their baby's daddy. I had such a good time, I hated to see the night end and couldn't wait to see Candace again on Thursday. I was taking her down to the pool hall to shoot a few. My life was looking up. I could feel it. One day at a time and everything would start to fall in place. For so many years, I had been in an environment that was designed for me to fail. I was determined to prove them all wrong.

I found a parking spot two blocks away from the YMCA. I got out and headed toward the building, grinning like a damn fool, and was moving up the sidewalk when I heard someone calling my name.

"Chauncey! You hear me talking to you!"

Oh, hell naw! I swung around and spotted Tameka running toward me. "Where the hell you been all night?" she spat.

I turned to my left and then my right. "You must be talking to someone else 'cause I know you ain't talking to me."

"There isn't anybody else out here. I'm talking to you and I want to know where you been. It's one o'clock!"

"Tameka, go home."

"Not until you answer my question." She had the nerve to cross her arms and act like she was my wife.

I ignored her and headed up the sidewalk. "You need to go home."

"I'm not going anywhere!" She ran and stood in front of me and looked mad enough to hit me. I wouldn't put it past her. Tameka was crazy. It wasn't until after I quit fooling with her that I learned she had stabbed her sister in the leg over a pack of cigarettes.

My eyes traveled the length of her and I'm not gonna lie. She looked sexy as hell with her petite self, standing there in low-ride jeans that showed off her beautiful abs. A skintight midriff shirt emphasized her large breasts that were like two succulent melons. But underneath all that beauty was a crazy-ass female who didn't know when to leave well enough alone.

"I've been sitting out here all night waiting to talk to you," she had the nerve to say with attitude.

I had to take a step back. "I don't remember inviting you to come by." One thing I hated was for a female to know where I lived. The only reason why Tameka knew my address was because she met me coming out the building.

"I need to talk to you."

"About what?" Now I had attitude. I had a wonderful evening and now she was trying to mess that up for me.

"Us."

I couldn't help it, but I laughed in her face. "There is no us. We were together and you messed that shit up acting all psycho."

"That's because you don't know how to act. I don't know how many times I gotta tell you, if you going to be my man, you need to come correct. I don't have time for you trying to be with me and the next bitch and then dodging my calls," she added with a bite to her tone.

"That's why we're not even together anymore."

"But we can be. That's why I'm here, so we can work it out." She rubbed on her breasts trying to intimidate a man. She moved forward, swinging her hips and licking her lips, reminding me how good they had felt wrapped around my dick. "You know you're not ready to let this go," she replied, then moved close enough for her breasts to rub up against my chest.

I stepped back, trying to put some distance between us. The whole time I was shaking my head in amazement at how persistent she was. Tameka knew damn well it was over between us, so I don't know why she was wasting her time trying to convince me otherwise.

"Sweetheart, you want something that I can't give you."

"That's where you're wrong. No woman will ever make you feel like I can," she smirked.

That's where she was wrong. I had spent the evening with a woman who made me feel like anything was possible. She was beautiful and independent. I like Candace a lot. We hadn't talked about a commitment, but I had a good feeling about the two of us. I wanted to get to know her better, and in order to do that, I didn't need any drama coming our way.

"Yo, Tameka. Take your ass home." I waved good-bye and started up the stairs. Don't you know that crazy chick tossed her purse at me? And I'm not talking about a small clutch purse. I'm talking about one of those big-ass purses women carried around with every damn thing in it like it's a suitcase. "What the fuck!"

She raised her voice. "Don't turn your back on me. We aren't finished until I say we're finished!"

I was still rubbing the back of my head when my cell phone rang. I looked down at the number then hit Talk. "Hey, whassup?"

"Hey, you. Where you at?" said a voice on the other end that made me smile. I guess Tameka noticed because she moved all up in my face.

"Who the fuck you talking to?"

I ignored Tameka's outburst and moved across the grass. "Hey, Linda. What's up wit ya?"

"I need to talk to you," she replied quickly over the phone. "Where you at?"

"I'm just getting back to the Y," I said, turning away from the evil look on Tameka's face.

"Meet me around the block in five minutes."

I glanced down at my watch. "All right. I'm on my way."

"On your way where?" Tameka demanded to know the second I ended the call. "I asked you a question. Don't make me break my foot off in your ass," she warned.

Can you believe the audacity of this chick? I glared in her direction. Tameka had her hands on her hips looking at me like she was seconds away from kicking my ass. That's one of the reasons why I couldn't stand her. Straight drama. The other reason was she was too damn ghetto. "I'm gonna go mind my business just like you need to do." I brushed past her and headed down the street.

Of course, she screamed after me. "Chauncey! It ain't over until I say it's over. You forget . . . I know everything about you."

The comment made me pause and look over my shoulder. Tameka was right. She knew more about me than I wish she knew. But she had been the first person I been with since my release from prison who hadn't seemed to mind that I had been locked up. Some women had a problem with that. I should have known Tameka would try and throw that back in my face.

"What would your date think if she knew what I knew?" She then had the nerve to smirk. Did that chick really think she had my balls in her hands?

"The best thing for you to do is keep that information to yourself." There was silence for a while. I thought that maybe I had finally gotten to her. But I should have known better.

"Keep playing with my emotions and watch and see what I do," she warned.

I flicked her off, then walked away, ignoring her

screaming at the top of her lungs. This was one of those times when I didn't mind calling a female a bitch. The chick was straight gutter and there was no telling what she would do. One thing for sure, I didn't want Candace to find out about my past before I had a chance to tell her myself.

I glanced over my shoulder a couple of times to make sure Tameka wasn't following me. Thank goodness she wasn't. By the time I stepped inside Charlie's, a small soul food restaurant with the best barbecue in town, even in the wee hours of the morning, Linda was already sitting at a booth. I moved toward the twenty-two-year-old, voluptuous woman with dark chocolate skin. She was a beautiful big-boned woman with long dark hair, big eyes and full lips, all evidence of her Nigerian background.

"Hey, you," I said with a smile and flopped down on the bench across from her.

"How you been, big brother?" Linda rose and leaned over the table and kissed my cheek. She looked so much like the small picture I kept in my top drawer of my father. He was the same man my mother put out when I was barely four. The way my uncle Jeff told it, Linda's mother appeared on our doorstep with baby Linda on her hip, demanding to speak to my father. It seemed he had been shacking up with her only a couple of blocks away. My mother put him out on his ass and never forgave him for messing around with Linda's mama. The tripped out part about it was, I hadn't even known I had a sister until I was locked up and received a letter from her. Linda told me her daddy handed her the newspaper, pointed to my picture, and said, "That's your brother," then walked out the room. That evening, she wrote me a letter and soon we became pen pals.

Linda even kept money on my books. Something no one else bothered to do for me. Not even my own mama.

I try not to go there, but every time I let myself, it pissed me off. The day I was convicted, Mama turned her back on me and never once looked back. When I was released, I was sent to a halfway house and I tried calling Mama, but the second she realized it was me, she slammed the phone down.

"You all dressed up. Where you been?" Linda asked, snapping my mind from the past. I couldn't do anything but grin.

"You're nosy, aren't you?"

Nodding, she pushed a strand of hair from her face. "I'm your little sister. We're supposed to be nosy."

I laughed because I often wondered what it would have been like if we'd had the chance to grow up together. "I had a date."

Linda sat back with a look of disgust. "A date? I hope it wasn't another one of them chicken heads you seem to be attracted to."

I shook my head. "Nah, this girl is different."

My sister must have read something in my eyes because she suddenly sat up on the chair. "Different . . . how?"

I smiled proudly. It felt good having someone in my life I could honestly talk about. "Linda, this chick ain't about what she can get or what I can do for her. She works, goes to school at night, and when she's not doing that, she is trying to raise her three-year-old daughter."

Linda looked impressed. "I like her already."

I sighed. "So do I. I can already tell she's going to be really special."

One of her eyebrows flew up. "Ooh! Big brother, this sounds serious."

I shrugged and took a moment because I didn't want to get ahead of myself. "I wouldn't say all that. However, I'm not counting out that possibility."

"Well, that's a lot better than your bed hopping."

Linda assumed I slept with every female I've gone out with. I know one thing for sure. I never slept with her best friend, Trina. She was sexy as all get out, but the second that chick slipped off her panties, I caught a whiff of her funky coochie and my dick refused to get hard. A woman had to have good hygiene to be with me. I guess her girl was too embarrassed to tell Linda the truth.

She leaned in closer to the table. "So when do I get to meet her?"

I laughed. My sister can be so persistent. "When the time comes, you'll be the first to meet her."

"I guess I can settle for that for now." The waitress arrived and we both ordered strawberry soda pop and rib tips. As soon as she moved to the next table, Linda cleared her throat and looked down at her acrylic fingernails. I instantly knew something was up. "I need to ask you a favor."

"Sure, what?" I had a feeling I wasn't going to like what she had to say.

Linda reached across the table and took my hand. "Next month is our family reunion and I would like for you to come."

I hesitated. "And what does dear old Dad have to say about that?"

She gave me a devilish grin. "I was planning to surprise him."

"No thanks. I'll pass." My father hadn't made an attempt to be in my life since I was 6 years old, so why the fuck should I? Back then he used to come by Ms. Hattie's house. She was the old lady who kept me until she passed away. Dad used to come by after work and spend time with me playing in the yard or just sitting and talking in the living room. But after Ms. Hattie died, all that stopped and I never saw him again. When I asked my mother why, she said he was too busy with his other family to have time for me.

"Come on. I think it's time you and Daddy talked," she pleaded with her eyes.

"Daddy knew where I was for five years and never once did he bother to send me a letter." I didn't mean to snap, but it was what it was.

"No, maybe he didn't; but he told me about you and knew we were writing each other," she quickly said in his defense, and pulled her hand back. "Come on. It would really mean the world to your little sister."

"You had to throw in the little sister part."

"Whatever it takes." She was grinning from ear to ear. "You can even bring your new girlfriend and her daughter." Her eyes were locked on me waiting for an answer.

"I'll think about it."

Apparently my answer wasn't good enough. She folded her arms, locking her eyes with mine. "Well, think hard. I really need you there." I could hear the desperation in her voice.

"Need me? Why?"

She reached down for a roll and avoided eye contact. "I met someone myself."

I groaned. I knew her sneaky behind was up to something. "I don't know if I want to hear this."

Linda started screaming and laughing at the same time. "Chauncey, you've got to listen to me!"

I couldn't help but laugh. "All right. Just save all the explicit details."

"Okay . . ." she paused long enough to take a deep breath. "I'm in love."

"In love? Woah! Back up a second." I sat back in the chair. "I thought you just said you met someone?"

"I did . . . four months ago." She looked happy. Unfortunately, it was hard for me to think of my sister with some dude who had the same needs that I did. The difference was he was doing it with my sister. "His name is Tommy and he's a medical student. I met him while he was doing clinical rotations on the surgery wing. He's from Detroit and comes from a big family, and he's sweet and kind and—"

Raising a hand in the air, I cut her off right there. "Slow down. You're wearing me out," I said. I was jealous at the thought of having to share my sister, especially since I hadn't known I had one for so long. Since I had been paroled, we spent the last eighteen months hanging out and getting to really know each other, and I realized despite our growing up in two different worlds we had so much in common.

"I'm just glad I can finally get this off my chest and talk to someone about it," Linda replied with a sigh of relief.

I just wished she was sharing her love life with someone other than me. Like I said, it's hard for a brother to think of some man banging his sister. "What about your mom or your girl Trina?"

She turned up her nose. "Mama would tell Daddy, and Trina is too miserable right now to be happy for me. Besides, that's why I have my big brother."

It was hard, but I forced a smile. I wanted to be happy for my sister; really, I did, especially since she was happy about me and Candace. "So when do I get to meet this cat?"

Leaning back against her chair, she smiled. "How about we go to dinner next week? My treat. That way we can talk about the reunion and come up with a plan as to how I'm going to introduce Tommy to Daddy."

"I can't wait," I mumbled under my breath. There was nothing I wouldn't do for my little sister. I just hope this wasn't one time I later regretted.

14

Noelle

"Ooh, Noelle, you are the bomb! My hair looks so good, Michael might suggest we forget about the class reunion and stay home in bed instead."

"Girlfriend, puhleeze, you better tell that man there's plenty of time for that later. What he needs to be doing is buying you a new dress and shoes to go with your new look." I spent the last two hours trying to get the weave out her head that someone glued to what little hair she had. Then I washed, dried, and gave her a short cut that was so flattering to her face you would have thought I had created the look. "And another thing . . . next time you let someone glue that mess in your hair, don't bring your behind to me. I don't know what y'all be thinking," I mumbled under my breath. It was enough my feelings were hurt that she had gone to someone other than me to do her hair just to save a few dollars. "You see where being cheap got you."

"Don't worry, Noelle," she reassured. "For now on,

won't no one else be touching my head but you. Trust and believe."

"You better not," I warned, and couldn't help but smile when she handed me a twenty-dollar tip, then headed out the door, strutting like she was on someone's runway. That's one of the reasons why I loved doing hair. I was an artist who got to be creative and afterward could see the finished product. Today, I was grinning and watching the girls on the couch, staring and admiring Christy's hair. I loved making my clients look good. You might have walked in looking like Chewbacca, but I guarantee you'd leave looking as sexy as Beyoncé.

I straightened up my area, then stepped across my pink and white checkered floor. Situations was a full-service salon. There were six stylists, three nail technicians, and Chauncey, who only did pedicures, and I even had someone in the back room, hooking up eyebrows and any other area of the body you needed waxed. Last year I decided to stop giving my money away to the Vietnamese and opened a shop in the front where we sold weave as well as hair care products, earrings, sunglasses, you name it. I believed in one-stop shopping and made sure my customers felt right at home the second they stepped inside my salon. That's why I had three couches for their lounging pleasure situated in front of a fifty-inch LCD television with every channel you could think of. Right now, the women in the front were watching *All My Children*.

"Tiffany, I'm going to my office," I said as I moved toward the back. She nodded, then continued yapping on her cell phone while she flatironed her client's head. I said it I don't know how many times for my stylists to show good customer service when in my salon, and that meant saving the personal calls for breaks. At the end of the day she and I were going to have a little talk. It was bad enough Chauncey had those hoochies coming in here disrespecting my salon. As a matter of fact, I planned to schedule a staff meeting an hour before the salon opened on Thursday just to remind my staff who's boss. If only I could say the same about my home. I had absolutely no control. On Friday, Scott had called with some excuse as to why he couldn't come home over the weekend, something about the coach ordering a mandatory meeting with the entire team. What was even worse was Grant was still hanging out way too much with his boys.

I grabbed a pop out the break room, then moved into my office. As soon as I took a seat, I slipped off my shoes and reached for the phone. "Hello? Ms. Santiago? Hi . . . this is Noelle . . . just checking to see how my grandbaby is doing."

"She's doing just fine. I just fed her and she's in her swing about to fall asleep." Her words brought a smile to my face.

That little girl had wiggled her way into my heart. I guess because she reminded me so much of Scott when he was a baby, or maybe because through her I finally had a little girl to spoil. "Good. Glad to hear it. Has she been crying a lot?"

"No, she is adjusting just fine. Relax, I got this under control."

"I know you do." I was so glad Tiffany had a good friend whose mother had a home daycare center. She limited her daycare to five children under five. Mrs. Santiago's husband was a minister, which made the deal even sweeter. The second I stepped into their home, I felt welcomed and knew they would take good care of Sierra.

We chatted a few seconds longer, then I got off the phone and logged in to my e-mail. As soon as I checked my incoming mail, I got mad. Grant used to send me a long romantic e-mail every morning, but lately he barely sent me three words. Ever since DCFS agreed to let me keep Sierra, the e-mails had stopped. I don't know why he was so against us keeping our grandchild. He always loved children, yet he wanted almost nothing to do with his own flesh and blood. I couldn't understand what had gotten in to him. Grant told me over the weekend he felt like we were getting in the middle of something that should be between Scott and his baby's mama. But I disagreed. Right now, we didn't even know who her mother was, and it wasn't like I asked her to abandon Sierra on our doorstep. What did he expect me to do? Just turn her over to the foster care system? I felt it was our duty as grandparents to provide for our grandchild. The old Grant would have agreed. This new person who was sleeping beside me every night, I had no idea where he came from, but wherever it was, I wished he'd take his ass back there and send my husband home. Grant had been hanging out almost three nights a week. Coming up with every excuse he could not to be around. I couldn't understand it. Lately, all we did was argue.

"Hey, Noelle. You wanna go to lunch?" I looked up to find Whitney standing in the doorway looking fabulous in a peach seersucker dress that showed off her small round stomach.

"Yeah, in just a minute." I typed a quick e-mail to Grant, letting him know I was cooking meatloaf for dinner. That was his favorite. I knew if anything could get him home early, that would.

Whitney stepped into my office and reached for a new no-lye hair relaxer called Attitudes a sales representative had sent to me to try in my store. "How's it going with the baby? Did you get a chance to speak to Scott?"

"Sierra's fine. She's a good baby. I couldn't ask for a better granddaughter. She's sleeping through the night and is eating good. I even found a wonderful home daycare that you might wanna use when your baby's born. If she has any openings." I glanced over at the computer screen checking to see if Grant had e-mailed me back yet and was disappointed when I saw he hadn't.

"Definitely give me your babysitter's number. So . . . did you talk to Scott?"

Damn, she sure doesn't know how to let anything go. "Yes, I've talked to him. Scott denies the baby is his, but what else is new? Most men refuse to admit they screw up. He claims if some female had a baby, she damn sure didn't tell him anything about it. I told him to bring his ass home next weekend so we can figure out who Sierra belongs to."

Whitney gave me a funny look. "Noelle . . . I know you don't wanna hear this, but . . . maybe she isn't his."

I cut my eyes at her. "Whitney, puhleeze! She looks just like him."

"I didn't say she doesn't look like him. Just because she looks like him doesn't mean she's his."

I sat back in my seat stunned. I couldn't believe she was trying to go there again. "Who else is she gonna belong to?" I asked, daring her to say it again.

She gave me a nervous look, then glanced down at the floor. "What's Grant say about the baby?"

"He doesn't want another baby in the house," I said calmly.

"I'm mean . . . did you ask him if the baby . . . could be his?"

"Hell no!" I glared across the desk at what was supposed to have been my best friend. How could she even think such a thing about my husband? I took that moment to glance over at my screen and my pulse jumped. I had a message from Grant! I reached for my mouse and opened it.

"Why not? I mean there has to be a reason why he doesn't want her there."

I ignored Whitney's question long enough to read his message:

The boys and I are going bowling after work.

Since when did my husband start liking bowling? I felt like grabbing my keys and heading straight over to the high school and give him a piece of my mind. Unfortunately, the last time I barged in his office, I found him whispering in the corner of his room with a beautiful woman. It wasn't until I cussed them both out that I found out she was the new school counselor. There was no way I was about to make a fool of myself two weeks in a row. Tears flooded my eyes. I just couldn't imagine my husband not wanting to spend time with me.

"What's wrong?" Whitney closed my office door, then came around and took a seat beside my desk. "You look like you just found out your best friend passed away, and I know that's not the case because I'm standing right here. Come on . . . tell me what's running through your mind?"

I covered my face with my hands, trying to hold

back my anger and frustration. My marriage was falling apart and I wanted to scream and cry at the same time.

"Everything. Grant's been acting so strange. It started before Sierra arrived, but since she got here, it has gotten worse. He won't hold her or play with her. It's like he doesn't want to have anything to do with her."

"Maybe he's scared."

I gave her a weird look. "You think so?" I asked.

"It's a possibility. Your daughter was stillborn and every little girl you have tried to adopt, someone has come and snatched away. Maybe he's scared of falling in love with Sierra and then her mother coming back to get her."

"Maybe you're right," I said, eager to accept the explanation and avoid the possibility that Sierra might be Grant's. It was possible. After I lost Rachel, I had been so devastated. It was then that Grant agreed to be a foster parent with the hopes of finding another daughter of our own. But each and every time we had one we adored, her unfit mother would call herself getting her life together and DCFS would give her the child back. Don't get me wrong; I believe in keeping families together, but none of them homes came even close to what Grant and I could offer. Now that I think back on it, I could have sworn he had been more devastated over Rachel's death than I was.

I shook my head. As much as I wanted to believe that was the reason, I couldn't. Grant had been acting strange long before Sierra had come into our lives.

"No, I think it's more going on than just that. He's never home, hanging out with his boys all the time. He even started working out again. I think . . . I think

Grant is having an affair." Whitney tried to look away but not before I had a chance to see the look in her eyes. "You're thinking the same thing. Aren't you?"

Her eyes finally met mine; then she shrugged. "I hate to say this, but that's how Landon was acting before I found out he was seeing someone else." I hated the look of pity in her eyes. Whitney had been with Landon for four years before she discovered he was cheating on her with a female he worked with. It took her almost a year to get over him.

"What should I do?"

"Noelle, I know you ain't asking me that. Aren't you the one who put a stripper pole in her bedroom so your husband didn't have a reason to go to those topless bars with his boys anymore?" she said with a smirk.

"Yes, I guess that was me." I hadn't used that pole in months.

"Make your husband pay attention to you. I know you still got a trunkful of those skanky costumes you used to love to buy."

I wiped the tears from my eyes and smiled. "You know I do."

"Good, then dust off the cobwebs on one; or better yet, instead of lunch, let's go down to that new adult store on State Street."

Maybe she was right. I hadn't done anything sexy and spontaneous since Sierra arrived at the house. Most evenings by the time Grant got home, I was already smelling like throw up and baby powder. There was nothing sexy about that.

"In fact, I'll be more than happy to watch Sierra for you for a couple of hours so the two of you could have some time alone together," she offered.

That's why I loved Whitney, she always had my back. I didn't have many women I could call a true friend except for her. "Thanks, Whitney." I reached for my purse and rose. "Let's go!"

Tonight I was going to fix whatever was wrong with my marriage.

"Where the hell you been all night?"

Grant didn't even look in my direction as he spoke. "A few of us went out to dinner and drinks after we got done bowling."

"Some of you like who?" He better not say that new guidance counselor Ms. Peachtree. She was cute. I'd give her that, but I've seen the way she looked at my husband, and I had no problem snatching those kinky twists from her head if I had to.

"Just a few of us. Damn! Why the twenty questions?"

"Because you should have called to let me know you weren't coming home so I wouldn't have bothered cooking." There was no way in hell I was letting him know I had sat there until ten o'clock dressed in a waitress's outfit ready to take his order. He could have had whatever he wanted on the menu, preferably me. By ten-thirty I had changed clothes and was heading to Hyde Park to pick up Sierra when I decided to drive past Ms. Peachtree's house. The reason how I knew where she lived was because last Thursday, I waited in the parking lot for her to leave the school and followed her home. It was a good thing I hadn't found Grant's car parked out there tonight, but that wasn't saying much. Her mini Cooper wasn't there either. I glanced over to the clock on the wall. It was now a quarter to twelve.

"Cooked? I'm surprised. You haven't cooked once since Sierra came into this house," he replied with a rude snort.

I folded my arms and raised my eyebrows. "It's hard juggling an infant and preparing a meal. If you would help me sometime with the baby, maybe cooking for you wouldn't be a problem."

"I already told you I didn't want a baby in the house, yet you went behind my back and did it anyway."

The look on his face told me he had reached his boiling point. Too bad. So had I.

"As far as I'm concerned, she is your grandchild. And as soon as I figure out who her mother is, then we can get her to take care of her responsibilities." I tried once more to explain my actions.

"What if she doesn't want the baby? Then what? Who's going to raise Sierra?"

I hesitated, because I knew Grant wasn't going to like my answer. "Well . . . I guess we will, at least until Scott graduates from college and gets a job so he can provide for his daughter himself."

"It sounds to me like you got it all figured out and you didn't even bother to ask me what I thought about the situation."

His angry tone put me on the defense. "I already know what you think. You don't want another baby in the house; but I'm sorry, I can't turn my back on my granddaughter."

"We don't even know if that child is Scott's!" he snapped.

"If she isn't, then I've definitely been fooled. I think

you're too blind to notice she has the same hazel eyes as you and Scott, and even that small, pudgy nose. If she doesn't belong to Scott, then the only other person who could be her father is you."

He gave me a look that said, *Don't even go there.* "Until we find out if she's Scott's, let DCFS take the child. Seriously, Noelle . . . I hate to see you get attached to this baby only to get your heart broken again."

I shook my head. "I can't do that. If she is, and I know she is, my grandchild, I would never be able to forgive myself for putting her in foster care."

He reached for a beer in the refrigerator, then moved to the family room and took a seat on the couch. For the longest time he sat there staring at the television screen, saying nothing.

I stood in the doorway with my arms crossed. "Are you planning to ignore me all night?"

"No, I plan on drinking this beer; then I'm going to go jogging, shower, and get ready for bed."

I don't know how we had gotten to this point. I'll admit ever since the baby came, Grant has only tried making love to me once. He was seconds away from going down on me when Sierra started crying from the other room, letting me know her diaper was wet. I don't think I'd ever seen Grant's dick get soft so quickly. I'll admit a baby can affect a man's libido; however, I don't care what he said, there was more going on than him not wanting a baby in the house.

Pushing away from the door, I went upstairs and checked on Sierra, who was sleeping like an angel in the bed. She was so precious. There was no way I could just turn my back on her no matter what my husband said. She was the innocent victim here. I went back down to the living room and the second I moved around the corner Grant slammed his flip phone shut.

"Who you talking to?" I asked.

"No one," he mumbled. "I was just checking my messages."

"Uh-huh." At this point, I didn't believe anything he said.

He rose and went to put the can in the trash. "I'm going to get dressed and go jog for a little while."

He pecked my cheek, then moved into the bedroom. Five minutes later he came out in sweats and a T-shirt and his MP3 player at his waist. I watched out the window as he jogged up the street, and as soon as he was out of sight, I hurried into the bedroom and rummaged through the clothes he had just taken off. I dug through every pocket looking for receipts or anything else that said where he had been all evening. When I didn't find anything, I reached for my key to his car and went out into the garage and started digging. I checked under the seat, between the seats, and the glove box. I was about to give up when I spotted a balled-up napkin on the floor mat. I smoothed it out. *Angelina's*. That was the name of the new restaurant people have been buzzing about over on the north side. He said they went to dinner. But tell me why they traveled to eat at an establishment that was more than forty-five minutes away from the school, especially when there were several good restaurants in the area?

I slammed the car door shut and went inside. Sierra started crying and I went up and changed her diaper and gave her another bottle. By the time Grant returned, she had been burped and was going back to sleep. I went into our bedroom and shut the door so we wouldn't disturb her.

"So where did you go to dinner tonight?" I asked, trying to remain as calm as I could.

"Applebee's." That was a damn lie. I could see it in his expression, because the fool couldn't even look me in the eyes.

"Oh really. What did you have?"

As he slipped off his running shoes, I saw him looking at me nervously out the corner of his eye. "I had the rib basket. Why?"

"I'm just curious. I heard there is a really nice restaurant on the north side called Angelina's. You ever been there before?"

Grant's golden gaze grew wide. "Ummm, let me think about that one a moment."

"Yeah, you think long and hard." I then held up the napkin so he could see I already knew where he had been for dinner.

"Okay, we went there tonight. So what?" he said, and shrugged like it was no big deal. If he was lying about dinner, what else was he being deceitful about?

"Why you lie?"

He pulled the sweaty T-shirt over his head, then sighed. "Because I didn't feel like explaining why I went to check out a new hot spot without you. You always act like your feelings are hurt if I try to do anything and don't include you."

"Probably because we rarely do anything together anymore."

I saw anger flash across his face. "That's your fault. I planned a vacation and you canceled it. Remember?"

For a moment, we both fell silent. Grant was right. I had postponed our vacation because I didn't want to leave Sierra alone, but there was no way he was going to make it my fault. We were having problems long before she came to live with us.

Before I could try to make things right, Grant moved into the bathroom and slammed the door behind him. I don't know what was wrong with our relationship, but I needed to find a way to fix things fast before it was too late.

15

Chauncey

"Why you like me?"

Candace turned up her nose and frowned. "What kind of question is that?"

"One that I hope you will answer." We were having lunch at Nikki's, a popular bar and grill at 97th and Western, eating Angus cheeseburgers and fries, and drinking cold draft beers served in frosted glasses. There were three pool tables to the far right, flat screens over near the bar to watch the game, and the smell of grilled steaks filled the air. Just the way I liked it. Tonight was probably our best date. We went and saw Denzel's new movie, then drove to Lincoln Park and walked along the beach, by ourselves, just talking and holding hands. At one time doing that would have sounded corny as hell, but I was at a different point in my life since I met her and had a deeper appreciation for the simpler things.

It had been a week since Candace and I had our first date, and each day things got better. Somehow that woman had managed to do something in a week that no woman had been capable of doing before—got me thinking about settling down. Never once had it crossed my mind we were spending too much time together, or that talking on the phone more than once a day was a bit much. Instead, it was the exact opposite. I just couldn't seem to get enough of her. We'd sit and talk for hours, or even just lie on the couch together and watch television. With most of the women I'd dated, after a little conversation and sex, there wasn't much else except to make plans for me to tap that ass again. But with Candace, it wasn't about the sex. She made me feel like anything was possible and that together we could do anything. She was great, and the truth of the matter is, I was crazy about her.

"Chauncey, that's a silly question," she replied with a soft laugh that always made me smile.

I leaned across the table. "Boo, I'm serious. I'm renting a room at the Y. I got a hoopty, and a GED. I see the way cats be checking you out. So I know you could have anyone you wanted, yet you're with me."

"Chauncey, like I told you before, I've dated the guys with money, education, and was bored to tears. There's just something about you that I find myself drawn to." She gave me her sexy sixty-watt smile.

"It must be my bad-boy image."

She stroked my arm on the table, running her fingers across the letters carved in my flesh. "It's not even that. Tyree's hood and I vowed I would never go out with anyone else like that." She paused long enough to frown. "I guess I like you because you keep it real. I'll be honest . . . in the beginning I was a little hesitant about getting involved with someone who looked like a thug."

Her comment made me laugh. "Nah . . . I had my days, but at some point we all have to grow up."

"I wish I could say the same about my baby's daddy, but Tyree maturing ain't gonna happen anytime soon." She didn't go into serious detail about her ex and I appreciated that. I just needed to know enough to know who my competition was, that's all. "I had enough little boys. At this point in my life, I need a man. Seriously . . . Chauncey, I love the way you take pride in your work. Women be sweating you and you just let it roll off your shoulders." She paused, sipped her beer, and laughed. "I never thought about a dude . . . a straight dude doing women's feet for a living, but you got the monopoly. Don't be surprised if other brothas try to follow in your footsteps. You know how they be hating."

I chuckled. "I'm already seeing it. One of my boys is talking about doing pedicures in his barbershop. With all those female clients . . . he said that would be reason enough for brothas to start flocking to his shop."

"See! What I tell you?" She screamed and started laughing again; then she got all serious and stared me dead in the eye. "So tell me what it is you like about me."

"What's there not to like? You're sexy as hell. Smart with a good head on your shoulders. I like a woman with enough class to have on my arm, who can also shoot pool and slug down a couple bottles of beer. A brotha would be a fool not to want to push up on you." Take tonight, for instance, Candace was wearing a pair of tight jeans and a gold blouse with matching stiletto heels. She didn't look like the hoochies at the table next to us. One had her ass cheeks hanging out her shorts and the other one needed a bra on because her breasts were practically sagging down to her waist.

"Now that you with me, all them other brothas can hang that up."

"Why is that?" she asked with a hint of amusement in her voice. I loved the way her beautiful eyes crinkled.

"Because I like what I got too much to want to share with anyone else." I leaned in close. "That's unless you got a problem with it."

She stared at me and grinned. "No . . . I kinda like the sound of it."

I lowered my head and kissed her. It wasn't a quick peck either. I lingered long enough to taste beer on her tongue and make her moan. Damn, I was horny! Our relationship wasn't about sex, because as of yet, I still hadn't gotten none. However, I'd be lying if I didn't say I couldn't wait to get between her thighs. The suspense was killing a brotha.

I ordered another round of drinks and we laughed and talked some more. I leaned back in my chair, enjoying her company and sexy smile. We were debating who was going to win the NBA Finals when my cell phone chirped, indicating I had a message. I pulled it out my pocket and glanced down at the text message on my screen.

She ain't even cute.

It was Tameka. I sat up on my seat and glanced to my left and right, looking to see if that crazy-ass chick was somewhere in the restaurant. If she was, I couldn't find her.

Candace gave me a weird look. "Is everything okay?"

"Yeah." I took one last sweep of the room, then

reached for my drink. I don't even know why I was worried about Tameka, not when I had this fine woman sitting across from me. Yet, I had enough history with Tameka to know there was no telling what that chick was capable of doing. "Candy? I wanna know if you'd go with me to my family reunion at the end of the month?" I don't even know why I was going to spend time with my father and his family, except to say I was curious.

"You're asking me to meet your family?" I nodded. "Sure, I would love to." I could see the look of surprise on her face that I was ready to introduce her to my relatives. "Being around family is a good way to find out about someone," she said.

"Well, to be totally honest with you . . . I don't know much about my father. He hasn't been in my life since I was six years old." I sighed. "It's a long story, but the gist of it is, he messed around on my mom with another woman and the two of them ended up getting a divorce."

"Are you saying he stopped being a father to you?"

Reaching for my beer, I nodded and couldn't believe it, but I started getting angry all over again. I don't even know why I brought him up and was allowing that man to spoil a perfect evening. "I never heard from him again until my eighth-grade graduation. He had married the other woman and they had my sister, Linda."

Candace gave me a curious look. "Now, if your father wasn't in your life, how did you know you had a sister?"

"She started writing me while I was—" I stopped when I suddenly remembered I still hadn't told her anything about being incarcerated. Damn. My cell phone rang and I was so glad for the interruption, I didn't even bother to check the caller ID first. "Hello?"

"You might wanna order the key lime pie. It's to die for," Tameka purred on the other end. I looked over my shoulder. She had to be somewhere in the restaurant, watching me.

"Whassup?" I replied, and tried to act like I was talking to one of my boys while I glanced around so Candace wouldn't become suspicious.

"What's going on is that you've taken someone else to *our* favorite restaurant and my feelings are hurt," she replied with a pout.

"Yo, shit happens."

There was a long pause. "You're so right. Shit does happen, so I advise you to watch your back." With that, the phone went dead. I felt a chill at the back of my neck and looked over my shoulder again.

"Is something wrong?" Candace asked. The frown on her face said she was smart enough to know something wasn't right.

I gave a nervous laugh. I didn't know what was worse, Candace asking about my past or Tameka stalking me. "Everything's fine. I just feel like someone is watching me."

"It's probably that woman sitting over near the bar. She's been staring you down since we got here." She tilted her head in the direction of the pool tables.

I swung to my left, and there sitting on a stool at the end of the bar was Tameka. As soon as she saw me staring, she raised her glass in my direction. That psycho was determined to make my life hell.

"Do you know her?" Candace asked.

I picked up my beer, draining half the bottle with one gulp before answering, "She's someone I used to know. Now . . . the only female I'm worried about is you." I leaned across the table and brought my lips down on hers. I was making sure it was clear to Tameka that what she and I had was over.

"Excuse me."

Startled, I looked up to find Tameka standing in front of our table, grinning like a damn fool. She was definitely up to something. "Whassup, Tameka," I replied, trying to sound like it was no big deal.

"Chauncey? I thought that was you! How you doing?" she added with theatrical effect. "I just had to come over and say hello to you and your . . . uhhhh . . ."

"This is Candace," I replied, hoping she would just get the hell away.

Tameka tossed her a fake smile. "Candace, huh? Well, it's nice to meet you. Chauncey and I go way, way back. In fact, we used to date. So I'll warn you, he doesn't stay in relationships long because he's afraid of commitment."

"Really? Well, Tameka, I'm here to tell you . . . that may have been the way things were when the two of you were together, but my man has eyes for just me. Isn't that right, baby?" Candace cooed. I looked over at her in time to see her wink. She knew Tameka was a shit starter. I could have jumped across that table and kissed her.

"Absolutely, boo. Now, if you would excuse us, Tameka, me and my *girl* would like to get back to our meal."

She looked humiliated for a second before she cut her eyes at me. "You can have him. It ain't like he eats pussy."

"Really? That's funny because Chauncey can't seem to get enough of mine." She held up her bottle.

"Cheers." Candace tapped her beer against mine, dismissing her.

If looks could kill, Candace and I would have blown up in smoke. "Whatever," Tameka mumbled under her breath, then started toward the door and practically tripped on the heel of her shoe.

Candace and I both took one look at each other and tried to hold it together until she exited the restaurant.

"Sorry, I couldn't help myself," she laughed. "That chick rubbed me the wrong way."

I was laughing my ass off. It felt so good. "No, believe me. I appreciated your help. I've been trying to get rid of that chick for months."

"You must have been doing something right; otherwise, she wouldn't be acting like that." Candace leaned forward, revealing all that luscious cleavage spilling from the top of her blouse. "What could that be?"

"I'll let you in on a little secret . . . I've never had any complaints."

"Hmmm . . . apparently not." Candace gave me a long, thoughtful look like she was finally thinking about giving a brotha some. Maybe Tameka's popping up just might turn out to be a good thing. "The look on Tameka's face, I doubt she'll be bothering you again."

"One can only hope."

This moment would go down in the history book as priceless. Hopefully, Tameka had finally gotten the hint, I had moved on and it was over between us. However, I lived long enough to know that nothing is ever that easy.

16
Tiffany

"You wanna suck my clit?"

I flinched. "What?"

Mrs. King gave me a concerned look. "I asked if you wanted some more fish."

I forced a smile and shook my head. "No, thank you."

I think I'm starting to lose my mind. Ever since I slept with Kimbel I have felt dirty. It's bad enough I went by Mama's and she immediately sensed that something was different about me. According to her, she could smell the scent of sex on my breath. As soon as I saw her reach for the fly swatter, I ran out her house and haven't been back since. Kimbel, on the other hand, has enjoyed every moment of it. It's been a week and we've been making love almost every night since. I'm not going to lie. It hurt the first few times; but now, I just couldn't seem to get enough of him. So how come each time I'm left feeling like a sinner? We're having dinner at his parents' house and even now

Kimbel was staring across the table at me, making me moist between my legs and feeling so dirty.

"Kimbel, your father has an announcement to make," Mrs. King said, breaking into my guilty thoughts.

Kimbel looked from one to the other. His parents were obviously happy about something. "What is it, Pop?"

Mr. King used to be fine in his younger days. Even now he had a distinguished look that appealed even to a chick my age. He had wavy salt and pepper hair, a goatee, and light skin that was glowing right about now. "Next month, I will be opening another funeral home." His chest stuck out with pride. Kimbel walked around to shake his hand, and I softly clapped my hands and congratulated him.

King Funeral Homes was the largest black-owned memorial service in the city. The family-owned business currently had five locations and would now be opening a sixth. Mr. King's dream was that someday all three of his sons would join the funeral business. So far the oldest, Charles, managed two of the locations. Carlton was the youngest and was still away at college, but he had every intention of joining the family business. Kimbel was another story altogether.

Kimbel had gone to Northwestern and later to the NFL. Mr. King had hoped after his injury he would have returned home and joined the business. Instead, Kimbel had gotten a job as a recruiter. He knew his father was disappointed, which was why he worked most of his weekends at the funeral homes.

"That's wonderful!" I cried.

Mrs. King's eyes glistened with happy tears. "We are so excited. All we ever wanted was to provide for our sons and their families."

I smiled. Unlike most mothers-in-law, I loved mine. She was the mother I wished I had.

Mr. King rose. "This calls for a celebration." He left the dining room, then came back shortly, carrying a bottle of thirty-year-old wine. "I've been saving this for the right moment." Glasses were handed out and the bottle passed around. And we all raised our glasses. "Here's to another successful business venture and to young love. In two weeks, I will be getting not only another funeral home but a beautiful daughter as well."

I had tears in my eyes because they were all so good to me. I had a wonderful life ahead of me.

For the next couple of hours we sat and laughed and talked and started on a second bottle. I had never been much of a wine drinker, so I was beyond tipsy. When Mrs. King decided to pull out the baby pictures, I excused myself and went to the half bath down the hall.

"Ahhhhhh . . . that feels good." Nothing felt better than going to the bathroom after holding it way too long. I looked down inside the stool and, just as I thought, my period had started. Luckily, I had thought to carry a tampon in my pocket. I flushed, washed my hands, and stared at my reflection. I didn't like at all what I saw. I looked sad. Almost disappointed at myself. I guess it was because after all those years of my mother instilling values in me, I had thrown it all away. I was so tired of feeling guilty. Two more weeks, I told myself. Two more weeks and I would officially be Mrs. Kimbel King.

There was a knock at the door. I opened it and Kimbel stepped in. "Hey, baby. What took you so long? I was missing you." He wrapped his arms around me and leaned me back against the sink. When he pressed his lips to mine I opened my mouth and allowed his tongue entrance. "I'm ready to go home so I can make love to you."

Oh, how I wished that was possible. I pulled him closer, loving the way my man felt. Kimbel was everything a woman needed. He was a gentleman, charming, and in the time we'd been together, he had proved he was committed to me.

"Baby, I can't wait. I gotta have you now," he murmured.

"What! We can't. Your parents are down the hall. They will know."

"No, they won't." He unzipped his pants and whipped his dick out. "Come on, baby. Take your pants off."

"I can't. I'm on the rag."

He jumped back. Kimbel hated touching me when I was on my period. Said it made him feel dirty. Whenever it was my time of the month, he insisted that I wear a pair of shorts to bed. Just in case I had an accident, he didn't want it on his clothes or our sheets.

Kimbel was devastated by my news. "Dammit, now I gotta go back out there with a hard-on. Baby, you know this is all your fault, right? You shouldna been looking so good," he replied, trying to make light of the situation, but I could tell by his eyes he was disappointed. I gave him a sympathetic smile and felt sorry for him. He was holding his penis in his hands. Kimbel was right. He was so hard the veins were popping out around the head. "I don't think I'm going to be able to get this back in my pants." He looked worried, almost frightened. "Baby, please, you gotta . . ."

Hell no! I knew what he was asking. There was no way I could think about doing such a thing, yet he looked so miserable, and after all, it was partly my fault that my man found me irresistible.

"Tiffany, sweetheart, please. In two weeks you're going to be my wife, but I've gotta be honest . . . if you're not willing to please your husband in every way that he asks, then we're going to have problems. What happened to love, honor, and obey? I love eating you out, but my wife has to be willing to do the same."

I couldn't believe we were having this discussion at his parents' house. "Well . . . when I become your wife, we can talk about it then."

"I think you're full of shit. I truly don't believe you're ever going to be willing to satisfy me properly. I'm so sure that . . . look . . . my dick got soft. Fuck!" He fixed his pants, then gave me a look that was like a cloud had gone up around him. I had never seen him like that and I didn't want to start now. His parents would know something was wrong between us and I wasn't having that. I needed my world to be perfect. Already, I had gone against everything I believed in and gave him my virginity before our wedding. What difference did it make now? I might as well give my fiancé what he wanted in order to keep him happy and to keep him from suddenly having second thoughts about marrying me. My mother would beat the black off me if he did.

I was still contemplating what to do next when Kimbel reached for the door and turned the knob. "Wait! Okay . . . okay . . . I'll do it." I took a seat on the stool and urged him to come and stand in front of me. Smiling, he reached for the switch and turned on the exhaust fan, which was loud enough to muffle any noise coming from the room. I sure hoped so. The last thing

I needed was for his parents to think their son was marrying a slut. I waited nervously while Kimbel unzipped his pants again. The second it sprung free, I noticed he was hard again. Staring down at it, I licked my lips.

"Come on, baby, you can do it. Just wrap your lips around it," Kimbel urged, and placed his hand at the back of my head and pushed me forward. I parted my lips and he guided the tip inside my mouth. "Awww, baby. That's it," he groaned.

I tried to pretend I was sucking on a Popsicle while he rocked his hips and pushed deeper and deeper down my throat. I gagged a few times, then controlled how deep I wanted him to go. Kimbel started moving faster and after a while I started to feel a little more confident about what I was doing. Just knowing it was my lips that were making him grunt and groan gave me a feeling of empowerment. It wasn't long before Kimbel was pumping hard enough to make my jaw hurt.

"That's it, baby. Oh, that feels sooooooo good. Ooooh!" he howled. Then the next thing I knew, Kimbel exploded in my mouth. I held my breath and waited until he stopped moving. There was no way I was swallowing. As soon as he pulled out, I moved over to the sink, spit, and rinsed out my mouth. That was one thing I would never acquire a taste for.

"Come'ere." I turned around and Kimbel pressed his lips to mine. "Thank you. I now know there isn't anything you won't do for your man, and that means a lot to me." Kimbel gave me a long, passionate kiss. "I love you, Tiffany. I can't wait to walk down the aisle and make you my wife."

His words were exactly what I needed to hear, and for the first time all week I didn't feel dirty. I choked on a sob. "Thank you, baby. I needed to hear that."

Kimbel cupped my face with his hands and looked down at me with a stern look as he spoke. "I don't care what your mother says about premarital sex, there's nothing wrong with a woman pleasing the man she's planning to marry."

I simply nodded. If I kept telling myself that, then maybe before the night was over I just might start believing it.

17

Candace

"Thanks, Mama. I don't know what I would do without you."

"You know there isn't anything I won't do for my granddaughter."

Thank goodness I had Mama; otherwise, I don't know what I would do when I needed a babysitter. It was enough my mother watched Miasha for me during the day and while I took classes at Kennedy King College two evenings a week, but every now and then Sylvia wanted to flex her balls and make us work overtime.

Tonight, my supervisor waited until four o'clock to tell us she needed the support staff to stay after work to purge files. We had to box up all the patient records that were more than five years old so they could be sent to a national archives company for electronic processing. It wasn't our fault Sylvia waited until the last minute to get it done. Yet we had to bust our ass and stay late just because she wasn't doing her job. I hung up the phone, then slipped off my shoes and reached for the first box just as Gloria stepped into the room.

"You want me to order a pizza or something?"

I shrugged. She can be nice when she wants to be. "Sure, might as well if we gotta be here."

She picked up the phone and ordered a large pepperoni pizza, then took a seat beside me. "Okay, I wasn't paying attention when Madame Witch explained. What are we supposed to do?"

She didn't hear because she was too busy flirting with one of our physician assistants. I reached for the list on my desk. "Here are the items that need to be purged from the files of every patient who hasn't been seen in the last five years and shredded. After we do that, we need to box up the records. They're being sent to a contract company to be scanned for electronic recordkeeping."

Gloria gave a long sigh and already looked bored. "I guess this whole paperless processing is for the birds."

"Yeah, I agree. It would have helped if we had been doing this regularly instead of waiting five years to rush and do it before the medical board comes to visit our clinic at the end of the month." We each reached for a file and got busy. The sooner we got started, the sooner we could get out of here. We were almost done with A-C when I looked up to find Sylvia standing in the doorway. She had the nerve to have her purse on her arm and a briefcase in her hand.

"I'm getting out of here. Just remember we need those records ready to be shipped in the morning. Catch y'all later."

"Bitch," Gloria mumbled under her breath the sec-

ond the door slammed. We took one look at each other
and started laughing. "She making us do all the work
while her ass is going home. What's up with that!"

"I know that's right." Gloria could be cool when she
wanted to be as long as you weren't trying to step on
her toes. We worked on the files until they arrived with
the pizza, then decided to take a ten-minute break.

Brenda peeked her head around the corner. "Ooh, is
that pizza I smell?" she asked, like she didn't see the
box on the counter.

"Help yourself. Although I shouldn't let you have
anything after trying to hook me up with your cousin,"
I added with a playful roll of my eyes.

The LPN gave me an apologetic look. "I told you
I'm sorry about that." I'll give it to her. She'd been
telling me sorry ever since I recapped my experience
with him and his tart breath.

"Cousin? What cousin?" I should have known
Gloria's man-crazy ass wasn't going to miss the opportunity to meet someone.

"Brenda tried to hook me up with her cousin."

Her brow rose. "What's he look like?"

"Cute, single, and a medical student."

I saw the dollar signs in her eyes. "Can a sistah get
the hook up?"

"What happened to Pierre?" I asked between
chews.

She cut her eyes in my direction. "He lost his job
and I had to let that fool go. So can I have this dude's
number or what?"

I was about to warn her about Deon looking for a
woman to take care of him, not to mention his bad
breath, but thought better of it. "Brenda, I think he and
Gloria might be a match made in heaven."

"I agree. I'll give you his number before we leave." When she looked at me out the corner of her eyes, it took everything I had not to laugh. "I'm just about done getting patient records ready for clinic tomorrow. I don't mind staying after and helping you with the files," she offered between bites.

She'd been working late a lot lately. "Don't you have a man at home waiting on you?"

She took a long, deep breath, shifting her body on the chair with agitation before speaking. "Puhleeze, I had to get rid of him. Too needy. There is nothing worse than a needy man."

Gloria laughed. "I know that's right. I dated one for a while and all he talked about was I love you . . . I love you so much," she mocked.

As I listened, I realized one thing I could say about Chauncey, there was nothing needy about him. He was confident, and that was one thing about him that attracted me most.

"What you smiling about?" Gloria asked.

"Nothing?"

She wasn't buying it. "Yes, it is. What, you got a new man in your life?"

"Yeah, I do." I was grinning so hard my face hurt.

"Well, don't just sit there. Tell us all about him. Is he fine? Does he have a job?" Gloria had her skinny tail all up in my face, but for once I didn't mind. I had to tell someone. I gazed up at the ceiling thinking about the last forty-eight hours.

"He's all the above." I took a deep breath. "Girrrrl, remember Shemar Moore in that Tyler Perry movie, *Diary of a Mad Black Woman*?"

Gloria reached for a slice of pizza, then nodded. "Oh sure. When he had his hair braided?"

I nodded. "Well, that's how Chauncey looks, only better."

Brenda's eyes got really wide. "Ooh! His name even sounds sexy." Brenda was "oohing" and "aahing," but Gloria had gotten quiet and I could tell she was jealous.

She shucked pizza from between her teeth. "Shemar Moore ain't all that. I thought you were going to say Jamie Foxx or somebody." She was hating.

"Oh, but my man is. There ain't nothing soft and pretty about him. He's all man, and he knows how to work a sistah!"

Brenda sat there shaking her head. "Damn, you are so lucky. All I seem to find is someone else's leftovers."

I saw Gloria looking at me out the corner of her eyes before she got up to turn on the CD player. She hated that I had found someone. If she'd stop sleeping with every man she met on the first date, maybe they would respect her enough to call her again.

"What's Deon look like?" she asked, changing the subject.

I shrugged. "He's actually cute. He's a black Dr. McDreamy."

The smile returned to her lips. "Gorgeous and educated . . . I can't wait to meet him. Brenda, you really should call him for me and get that hooked up."

"Okay."

Gloria reached for her cell phone from her back pocket and dialed his number. The entire time she was talking to him, I couldn't help remembering how funky his breath was and lost my appetite.

I reached for another file and realized it had been misfiled in the E's. I started to stick it with the other K's when I noticed the name on the file folder and almost peed myself.

Kimbel King.

I quickly thumbed through the record, making sure it was the same Kimbel King who was engaged to my best friend, Tiffany. What I saw made me wanna dash to the phone and call her. Unfortunately, we had rules about privacy acts and patient confidentiality, and as much as I wanted to tell Tiffany, there was nothing I could do but toss his file in the box and reach for another. But as the evening progressed, I kept wondering if maybe she already knew and just hadn't told me. It really wasn't my business if he had. Maybe she loved him enough that it didn't matter. But at the same time, what if she didn't know? While Gloria worked on getting herself a date for the weekend, I finished the E's and tried to think of a way to ask Tiffany without her knowing that I already knew. She was my best friend, and there was no way I could just ignore something this vital. Tiffany was getting married in two weeks and could possibly be making the biggest mistake of her life.

18

Chauncey

I ran my hand down my girl's back, not stopping until I reached her apple bottom.

Candace pulled back and stared up at me. "Did you just touch my ass?"

"Naw . . . I touched *my* ass." I leaned in and pressed my lips to hers. The last couple of weeks had been unbelievable and like nothing I'd experienced with any other female. But now I was ready to take our relationship to the next level.

We were in her living room slow dancing to the sounds of Mariah Carey. Miasha was sound asleep in her bed. I closed my arms around Candace and held her against my chest while she ran her hands down my back.

"Thanks for dinner," I said, and pressed my lips against her hair.

"I just wanted to show my baby I got skills," she said, and looked pleased that I enjoyed her cooking dinner for me tonight. Smothered pork chops never tasted so good.

Candace ran her hands along my back. Her fingertips slipped under my shirt. "Now I wanna show you my other skills." I pressed my lips to hers. "I want you to make love to me." She looked at me and was so sexy with her eyelids sensuously low. My heart was pounding so hard. The day had come when I could finally make love to my woman.

I reached up and unfastened the top button of her shirt. Her lips parted slightly. I unbuttoned the next few buttons slowly until I reached the bottom. The shirt fell open. I slid it over her shoulders, then tossed it across the room, not caring where it ended up. Candace unhooked her bra and it fell to the floor. I stepped back and took it all in.

"Damn, you are fine as hell."

Her breasts were large and round, and her nipples were like dark Hershey kisses. I held one of them in my hand; the other hand I slipped down into the waistband of her jeans.

"Let me help you out." She purred and unsnapped the button and pulled down her zipper. I slid them down over her hips and allowed them to fall onto the carpet. All I could do was stare at her in silk pink panties that left nothing to my imagination.

"Turn around," I instructed, then watched my woman strut her stuff in front of me. "Damn, you are beautiful."

Candace smiled. "Thank you," she said, and licked her lips.

I couldn't wait to have those lips wrapped around my dick, but that would have to wait. I needed to be inside something warm and wet. I hadn't had any in almost six weeks. The longer it took, the more my dick throbbed with the need.

"Bend over," I said, and realized my voice cracked. "I want to see you from behind."

She kicked her panties away, then bent over the couch. Candace was wearing nothing but those sexy stilettos. Damn, she was a sight to see. I didn't think my dick could get any harder. I moved up behind her and ran my hands over the smooth cheeks of her caramel ass.

"You got a fat ass." My hands roamed over her skin and reached in front of her and fingered her nipples, and when I rolled them with my fingers, she pushed up against me.

"Come'ere girl." As soon as she turned around, I scooped Candace in my arms and carried her down the hall to her room. Once she was on the bed, I pressed a kiss to her cheek, then pushed her back against the pillow. Reaching down, I slid my finger along her slippery folds. She was wet and ready for me. I plunged a finger deep into her, loving the way she felt warm and wet. I drew out slow, then in again and added another finger. Candace whimpered and pushed against me. I teased her until she was rubbing her clit against my finger, gasping and crying out my name until she couldn't take it anymore. When she came, I pulled her by the hair and crushed my mouth to hers. "I want to be inside of you." I sucked her lower lips. "Tell me you want me inside you."

"Yes," she said. "I want you inside me."

I pulled off my jeans and boxers, then grabbed a condom from my wallet. I slipped it on, then spread her legs and moved inside. She wrapped her arms around me and thrust her hips forward and I slid in even deeper.

"Chauncey," she whispered as I moved inside her body.

"Baby, I'm right here." She pressed her warm and wet lips to my neck.

"Yesssss," she breathed. "Don't stop."

I stroked her long and deep. She was so wet and open that I knew I wouldn't last long. Not as good as she was feeling. I thrust harder and moved faster until she dug her fingernails into my butt.

"Yesssss, Chauncey . . . I'm coming!" she cried and rocked her hips, meeting my strokes with her own. I brought my lips to her and increased my speed until I cried out with the release I had been waiting weeks for. I wrapped her in my arms and dropped kisses along her face and neck.

"Chauncey, let me ask you a question."

"Baby, you can ask me anything." And I meant that. I didn't want to have any secrets between us, which was why in the next few days we needed to have a long talk. I hadn't told her yet about my incarceration or how I had gotten there. I knew I needed to tell her. The time just never seemed to be right. However, I knew if our relationship was going to continue, I was going to have to find a way to tell her. I just wish I felt confident about how she might handle it.

"What's on your mind?"

She hesitated, almost as if she was afraid to speak. "If you knew something that might change your best friend's life forever, would you tell him?"

I stroked her arm as I spoke. "I guess it depends on if it's something that he would wanna know or not."

"I think he would want to know this."

"Then I would tell him."

She raised up on her elbows and stared down at me. "Even if it means losing your job?"

"I can always find another job. True friends are hard to come by."

She blew out a long breath and looked so relieved for a second I thought she was about to cry. "Thank you, baby."

"You're welcome." I leaned over and kissed her cheek.

Candace drifted off to sleep in my arms and I lay there with my eyes closed, but I wasn't sleeping. I was thinking about my girl, because Candace was most definitely that. What she had said about knowing something about someone had me thinking. She could have easily been talking about us.

I was crazy about Candace. Our relationship had reached a level that I never expected to reach with a female. I didn't want to do anything to jeopardize what we had, and that's why I tried to keep it real with her. But I wasn't being completely honest with her and that ain't right. The problem is, I didn't know how to tell her about my past. Sometimes I felt maybe it was best to just leave the past in the past and focus on the future, and that's what I have been doing each and every day since Candace walked into my life.

My eyelids started to get heavy about the same time I heard a knock at the door. I tapped Candace on her shoulder. "Baby, someone's at the door."

She mumbled something I didn't understand, so I got up, slipped back on my boxers, and went to answer the door. I turned the lock and looked outside and some tall nigga was standing there. I looked him up and down. "Whassup?"

He got all in my face. "I should be asking you that. Who the fuck are you?" he asked, and balled his fist. Homeboy don't want none of this.

"I'm Candy's *man*," I replied, and waited for him to take a swing at me or something that would make me dust the floor with his ass. "Whassup?"

His nostrils flared. "I'm Miasha's daddy. Where's Candy?" he demanded.

I gave him a smirk. "She's asleep." I didn't have to say a word, but the look on his face said he knew the deal. His business was now my business.

He took a step forward like he was about to bum-rush a muthafucka, but I blocked the doorway. "I said she's asleep."

"Man . . . fuck you!" he growled.

"Naw, fuck you. This may be your daughter's house, but you're gonna show her and Candace some respect. Next time you wanna come by . . . you need to call first." With that I slammed the door in his face. He could take that shit up with Candace tomorrow; in the meantime, I went back to the room and climbed under the covers with my boo.

"Who was that?" Candace mumbled. I could tell she was half asleep.

"Nobody," I replied, then curled up close to her naked warm body. I was here to stay, and her baby daddy had no choice but to get used to the idea.

19

Tiffany

Candace asked me to meet her at T.G.I. Friday's for lunch, which was fine since I was scheduled to go to the bridal shop up the road this afternoon so I could try on my wedding gown. It was still hard to believe that in one week, I would finally be Mrs. Kimbel King.

The last couple of weeks had been so mind-boggling, I couldn't keep my secret to myself anymore and I had to let Candace know I had finally crossed over and gotten me some. Now I knew what all the girls had been going on and on about. Sex was wonderful! I couldn't get enough of Kimbel and, apparently, he couldn't get enough of me. I woke up this morning with him sliding deep inside of me. I wrapped my legs around his waist and allowed him to stroke me long and fast until he spilled his seed inside. It was amazing the way the two of us came together. After he was done, I took a long, hot shower and found myself thinking about our future together. It was going to be wonderful. I was ready to be a good wife and mother to our children. I had already made up my mind. While we're on our honeymoon, I planned to toss my birth control pills in the trash. I'd started taking them two weeks after Kimbel proposed so I would be prepared on our wedding night. As far as I was concerned, the sooner we started a family the better. I adored my goddaughter, Miasha, and couldn't wait to have a child of my own.

I spotted Candace moving into the restaurant looking fabulous in a jean mini and a midriff Baby Phat shirt that showed off her firm stomach. Dang, my girl was fierce! I hoped to look just as good after I gave birth to Kimbel Jr. "What's up, hooker?" I greeted her playfully the second she moved up to my booth.

"Hey, sorry I'm late," she said, and dropped down on the bench across from me. "We've been busting our butts in the office all morning, trying to get ready for a big inspection that could shut down the clinic if we don't pass."

"Not a problem. As soon as I leave here I have to meet with the seamstress at the bridal shop so she can work on the hem in my dress."

I noticed Candace frown. "Yeah, I, uh, need to go in and do my fitting as well."

"Yes, you do. You forget my wedding is Saturday! I still have so many last-minute things I need to get done. Good thing I took the week off."

She kept her eyes locked to mine like she was searching for the right words. "Uh, yeah, speaking of that . . . Tiffany, I need to talk to you about something."

Whatever it was she needed to say looked like it was important. However, there was no way she was telling me her news before I told her mine. "Okay, in a minute, but first I need to tell you something." I gave her a devilish grin.

"What is it?"

I waited until the waitress took our order and left. I ordered a diet drink and the fried green beans, and Candace ordered the spring rolls and iced tea.

"Tiffany, seriously, I really got something I need to tell you."

Damn. Candace looked so sad I guess I could wait a few more minutes. "Okay, so what you want to tell me?"

"Well . . ." she hesitated, avoiding eye contact. "I don't know where to begin."

I shifted on the seat. I was so excited I couldn't sit still and was seconds from bursting. Candace was taking too damn long to say whatever it was on her mind. So you know what, her news can wait. "Candace, I did it!"

"You did what?" She was watching me like a hawk.

Leaning in close, I whispered, "I had sex with Kimbel."

Her jaw dropped. "What!" She was far more stunned than I had ever expected.

"You heard me. I finally did it."

"B-But why? I thought you were waiting until after you were married?"

I would have sworn she looked pissed off, and that completely threw me for a loop. I'm almost sorry I disappointed her.

"How could you?" she asked in a strained voice. "What would your mother think?"

I shrugged a shoulder. "Who cares about my mother? I had to do what I had to do to keep my man happy."

Here I was telling her the most exciting news of my entire life, and all my best friend did was just sit there for the longest time. I swear her eyes looked shiny, like she was about to cry.

"How was it?" she finally asked.

"Oh, my goodness! Candace, it was wonderful. I would never have imagined feeling that type of connection with a man. He was so gentle and compassionate and I ain't gonna lie . . . he made me cry." I blurted out in one breath.

Candace gave me a tight-lipped smile and was real quiet while I talked. The way she was acting you would think she was jealous. I would have thought Chauncey was handling his own in the bedroom, but maybe he wasn't on his job. That's too bad because my fiancé was.

She looked frustrated. "I guess you changed your mind about oral sex as well, huh?"

"Girl, I slobbered all over them nuts!" I fell over on the bench laughing, then glanced at her hoping to see a smile; instead, her expression made it look as if she felt sorry for me. "What's wrong with you?"

"Tiffany, why didn't you wait?" she wailed.

Why was she tripping? The way she was acting you would think I messed around with her man. "Candy, what difference does it make?"

"It makes a lot of difference. I just knew you hadn't slept with him yet . . . that you were going to wait until after you were married."

"Like I said, what difference does it make?" I loved Candace like a sister, but she was starting to get on my last nerve. She's got some balls getting in my ass because I decided to give my fiancé some before our wedding. Hell, she has screwed dudes who hadn't even treated her to a bucket of chicken.

"We're getting married in a week. Quit tripping!" Why was she looking nervous? And then it dawned on me. "Oh shit! Candy . . . are you afraid Kimbel is going to change his mind now that he's gotten the goodies?" I had thought the same thing, but after last night's performance, I knew my man wasn't going anywhere. He loved me and I was even crazier about my boo.

"Oh no," Candace moaned, then balled up her fists and pressed them against her face. "This is such a mess. I should have said something to you as soon as I found out, but I just didn't know how."

"Say something to me about what?" I hadn't seen her look this worried since Miasha had pneumonia.

"Tiffany, what I'm about to tell you, you can't say anything, okay?" Candace leaned across the table.

"Have I ever told anybody anything you've ever told me?"

"Yes, you have," she replied.

"When?" I shot back.

"That time I told you I saw Desiree cheating on our math final."

"Girl, that's high-school shit! We're adults and nothing you say to me will go beyond this table."

"I'm serious. If you do, I'll lose my job." She was practically pleading, which meant whatever it was, it was definitely serious.

"You got my word."

Candace took a deep breath. "Okay . . . remember when I told you we've been working on boxing up old patient records for this big visit next week."

"Yeah," I said, wondering where the hell this conversation was going.

"Okay . . . well . . . I was purging files when I reached inside and . . . well . . . I found an old patient record of Kimbel's."

While trying to keep a straight face, I scrambled my brain trying to figure out why my man had gone to the clinic. "*Oh-kayyyy*, he came in to be checked," I shrugged. "So what? I'm sure there have been times when you thought you might have caught something from one of those thugs you've messed with."

"You can act like a bitch if you want to. For your information, what your man's got, penicillin can't cure," she informed me with a roll of her long neck.

"What he's got?" I couldn't miss the way she tightened her lips. "What are you talking about?"

"Tiffany, I hate to tell you this, but . . . Kimbel has herpes."

20

Noelle

"I've got something to talk to you about."

I put down the book I was reading and looked at my husband as he walked into our room. "What is it you want to talk about?"

As soon as Grant started clearing his throat, I should have known something was up. "I decided to go ahead and teach summer school."

"Is that all?" I said with a sigh of relief. I thought he was about to say some shit that was going to make me want to cut his dick off. "I figured as much since you're at the school practically every day even though school's been out for almost two weeks."

He started clearing his damn throat again.

"You need a cough drop?"

Grant gave me a strange look. "Why you ask me that?"

"Because you keep clearing your throat. Now quit stalling and tell me what you want to tell me." Grant knew damn well I wasn't one for games, and he's been playing a lot of them lately. For the last week he'd been coming in at all hours of the night, smelling like liquor. I had done the laundry just yesterday and found lipstick on his shirt collar.

"Well, it's about my summer job. You know how I am all about helping kids and trying to make a difference. Well . . . uh . . . the job I'm taking this summer is out of town."

"Outta what?"

He shifted his eyes and I could tell he was stalling. "Out of town. I'm going to be teaching at a school out of town."

"Out of town like what? In Missouri or Indianapolis?"

"No . . . farther than that."

"Down south?"

"Uh . . . a lot farther than that."

I sat up straight on the bed and crossed my arms against my chest. "Is the job in the United States?"

He coughed against his fist, then cleared his throat. "No . . . it's in Korea."

"Korea?" He had to be joking. However, the look on his face told me he wasn't.

"Hold up. Before you go off, just give me a few minutes to explain. It's a short-term teaching program. I'll get paid to live in Korea for four weeks teaching English to students. They'll pay me a salary, provide me temporary housing. I'll make more those four weeks than I could working around here all summer. Also, the kids over there will appreciate me a lot more than these spoiled-ass, don't-wanna-education kids we have here in the U.S., and you know it."

"All I know is my husband walked in the house and told me he was planning to spend the next month in Korea." My stomach clenched. Why did I feel like my husband was trying to get away from me? "Why so far away?"

"Noelle, it's a wonderful opportunity. I want to do this."

I wanted so badly to tell him hell no. He hardly spent any time with me anymore as it was. "I guess if that's what you want to do," I said, trying to be the supportive wife.

He breathed a sigh of relief, then smiled. "Thanks for understanding. I leave in two weeks."

"Wait a minute . . . you've already taken the job? I just thought you were thinking about it at this point."

"I thought about it and decided to go."

"So I guess what I think doesn't matter?" I asked pointedly and waited for an answer.

"It does matter. You've known for years I've wanted to teach overseas."

"Yeah, but I didn't think it would be this year." Okay, Grant was really starting to get on my nerves.

He heaved a heavy sigh. "It wasn't like I had planned it that way. What I had wanted was to spend the summer on vacation with my wife, but we're not doing that now, are we?"

I sucked my teeth all loud and ghetto. "Okay, so now I get it. This is your way of getting back at me for canceling our vacation."

Grant took a seat at the end of the bed, then turned and faced me. "Teaching overseas is not me trying to get back at you. You freed up the summer, not me. All the summer school assignments are already taken. I figure if we're not going on vacation, I might as well work. Why not get out the country at the same time?"

"Okay, then answer this . . . Are you no longer happy being married to me?" I was trying to act calm, but I was so scared of what he might say, or even worse, what he wouldn't say.

"Why you ask me that?" he said, avoiding the question.

"Because it sounds to me like you're trying to find any excuse to get away." I shot back.

He gave a loud, forced laugh. "Now you're being ridiculous."

"No, you are. What happened to us, Grant? We used to be happy, but ever since you turned forty you've changed."

He just shook his head, then replied, "Nothing's happened. I haven't changed. I've just realized that tomorrow isn't promised to any of us. I'm trying to enjoy life and you want us to sit around like a couple of old folks, playing with grandkids and sitting out on the porch in rocking chairs," he said, and rose from the bed. "Well, you're on your own. I'm getting ready to start enjoying life with or without you!"

I sat there staring at him trying not to start an argument, but as far as I was concerned, one had already started. My husband was leaving me and there was nothing I could do about it.

21

Tiffany

I was parked in front of Fantasy's on Cicero. Inside, the music was loud and people were chatting and having a good time. Among the partygoers were Kimbel and his boys. They had reserved a room in the back for their bachelor party. *Sneaky asshole.*

It had been four days since Candace dropped the bomb and ruined my life. Afterward, I went home and it took everything I had to hold it together when Kimbel walked into the house. When he tried to make love to me, I informed him he wasn't getting no more until we were married. He looked pissed, then shrugged and left it alone. I waited until he climbed under the covers before I tried to get to the problem at hand.

"Kimbel, in a couple of days we're going to be taking a big step in our lives."

"Yes, baby, we are." He pulled me tightly in his arms.

"And this is our chance to put everything out onto the table. No secrets."

"No secrets, baby," he repeated.

"Is there anything that you would like to tell me or think I should know?"

"Like what?"

"I don't know. Anything."

"Anything, huh?"

"Yes, anything. I don't want there to be any secrets between us."

Okay. Uuhh . . . a'ight. Well, there is something that I think you should know before we get married. It might change your mind about us."

"I doubt that. I love you for you, and it's gonna take a lot to change the way I feel," I said, even though I was nervous as hell what he was about to say.

"Okay, all right. Here goes. Listen closely." I held my breath and waited. "Tiffany . . . baby . . . I've got bad gas." He then released a long, loud fart. "Ha-ha!" Kimbel started laughing, then threw the covers over my head and pinned me to the bed. I screamed and thrashed around until he finally released me. His chuckles became kisses and the next thing I knew, we were making love until the wee hours of the night. That man knew how to manipulate me into doing anything he wanted, and I hated him for it.

The following night I couldn't sleep and didn't realize I was standing over Kimbel, watching him sleep until he sat upright on the bed.

"What the hell are you doing?" he asked.

"Nothing," I told him.

"Then why the hell you got that knife in your hand?"

I glanced down, and sure enough I was holding one big enough to carve a Thanksgiving turkey.

"Oh shit! I must be sleepwalking or something," I replied, then started laughing hysterically.

Kimbel packed my bag and decided that maybe we needed a few days away from each other until our wedding day. My leaving was actually a relief because there was no telling what I might have done if I'd stayed. Who knows, I might have tried to chop his dick off. Ever since, I've been staying with my mama. I lied and told her we wanted some time apart before our wedding. It was now the night before our big day and I needed Kimbel to tell me the truth.

My cell phone rang. I glanced down and saw it was Candace. I'd been avoiding her calls since I saw her on Monday. The only reason why I answered was because deep down I needed her to stop me from what I was about to do. I guess Candace was wondering why I wasn't at my own bachelorette party.

"Tif, where you at? Everybody is here at the restaurant but you." She was loud, and it was clear she was upset she had gone to all this trouble for me and I wasn't even there.

"I'm not coming."

It took her a second to find her voice. "What do you mean you're not coming?"

Candace can act so dumb at times. She just threw something heavy on me the other day, telling me some news that she'd been holding for almost a week. Six fucking days. If she had told me when she first found out, then I wouldn't have slobbered all over Kimbel's dick a second or third time. Instead, she waited until five days before my wedding to tell me the fool had herpes.

"Where the hell are you?" Her tone had softened and I could hear concern.

I looked up at the large neon sign flashing. "I'm sitting in my car outside Fantasy."

"Fantasy? Isn't that where Kimbel is having his bachelor party tonight?"

"Yep."

"So why are you there?"

Candace really doesn't get it, does she? I guess she's so into Chauncey she can no longer think straight. "I need to talk to him and find out why he didn't tell me."

"What? I thought you promised me you wouldn't say anything!" she screamed in my ear.

I snorted rudely in hers. "Are you kidding? You expect me to keep something like this to myself. I've got to ask him about it."

"Tiffany, I could lose my job," she pleaded.

"No, you won't. I won't even tell him how I found out, but I've got to ask him." Candace grew quiet. I knew she was pissed, but deep down I knew she understood and didn't blame me.

"Why haven't you said anything before now? Dammit, Tiffany, why you wait until the night before your wedding?"

I shrugged even though I knew she couldn't see me. "I guess I was trying to find the guts."

"Okay, so why don't you wait until in the morning to ask him."

"I can't do that. I need to know now." Candace was screaming and saying something, but I wasn't interested in hearing anymore and hung up. I couldn't let another minute pass without knowing the truth.

I stepped into the club and frowned at the twenty-dollar cover charge, but it was a small price for what I needed to do. What happened in the next few minutes would dictate my future. Tomorrow afternoon the church would be decorated and over five hundred of our family and friends would be in attendance to celebrate my union to the only man I've ever loved. All I needed to hear was he was sorry for not telling me; that he was afraid if I had known, I would have changed my mind about marrying him. I needed him to ask for my forgiveness. Marriage was all about standing by your mate through sickness and in health. I planned to do just that as long as I knew Kimbel loved me.

The joint was packed with couples on the dance floor, bumping and grinding. I weaved my way through the dark, crowded club toward the back where I knew Kimbel and his boys were at. His friend PJ was standing in front of the door. If he saw me, there was no way he was letting me in. I waited until some chick with a wide ass and dressed in spandex walked by and caught his attention. PJ moved over to the bar and was busy spitting game when I made my way to the door and slipped inside.

The large room was so dark it took my eyes a while to focus. When they did, I gasped. There had to be about a dozen strippers in there, dancing around the poles, giving lap dances. I stayed off in the cut and slowly worked my way around the room looking for Kimbel. There was a threesome going on in the corner and I practically broke my neck trying to see if my fiancé was part of it. Thank goodness, he wasn't; otherwise, I was going to have to clown his ass. I had walked around the entire room and was about to leave when I noticed a light coming from under a door in the corner. My heart started pounding, but nothing was going to stop me from turning the knob and looking inside. What I saw made my heart stop. Kimbel was screwing some chick from behind. He was so into it, it took a second for him to notice I was standing there. I heard a scream and realized it was me.

"What the hell? Oh, shit! Tiffany . . . what are you doing here?" Kimbel looked like he was about to pee on himself.

I was up all in his face. "Is that all you have to say? It's the night before our wedding!" The Hispanic girl had the nerve to roll her eyes and look insulted. "Get your flat booty ass away from my man!" I screamed, then grabbed her by her hair and pulled her up out of that closet. Kimbel had the nerve to come to her defense.

"Tiffany . . . why you tripping? Don't act like you don't know what goes on at these things." Kimbel was buckling his pants and talking at the same time. He must really think I'm stupid.

"You supposed to love me enough not to do something like that."

"Baby, I do love you. All I was doing was getting all my playing out the way before I become your husband." He had the nerve to try and justify his actions. "I had a buildup. If you hadn't made me wait so long, none of this would have happened. In actuality, it's really your fault."

"You know . . . you're so full of it." I noticed some of his boys standing around and watching, but I didn't care. "Tell me something, Kimbel . . . when were you planning to tell me you had herpes?" I stood there and watched him try to hold it together.

His eyes grew wide. "Excuse me?"

I walked over and pointed my finger all up in his face. "You heard me! The cat's out the bag. You got the package and you didn't even plan to tell me." I kid you not, it was like in the movies. Out of nowhere his fist flew through the air and came crashing down against my right cheek. Next thing I knew, I hit the floor.

"Fucking bitch!" he screamed. "If I got it, then I got that shit from you!" He started kicking me in my head and shoulder. All I could do was just lay there and cradle my head with my hands. Thank goodness his best man rushed over and pulled him off me. The music stopped and someone had turned on the lights. Everyone was watching and staring at me lying on the ground.

"Trifling bitch! No wonder you didn't want to give me any until we were married. You had no intentions of telling me, yet all this time you were trying to pass yourself off as a virgin. Good thing I found out when I had."

"What's going on?" I knew that voice. I looked over to find Candace racing into the room. The last thing I wanted was for her to find me like this on the ground. "What the—" She rushed over and dropped down beside me. "Tiffany, are you okay?"

"I'm fine," I mumbled, and let her help me to my feet.

"What the hell happened?" Candace screamed at Kimbel.

He was standing beside PJ, glaring at both of us. "Your friend here was trying to infect me with her germs."

Candace's hands went to her hip in a defensive position. My girl is not one to be messed with. "No, she wasn't. You forget where I work? The fucking free health clinic! I'm the one who read your file and told her you had herpes, you nasty fuck. If you have no respect for yourself, at least have some for her. Come on, let's go."

She helped me off the floor. I looked out the corner of my eyes at the smirk on his face as he told his boys we were lying. I couldn't help it. I ran up to Kimbel and hit him hard in his nuts.

"You bastard!" I screamed over and over again. I don't know how I made it back to Candace's mama's car. In fact, I don't remember my legs even moving, but the second Candace pulled away from the club, I started bawling my ass off. "I can't believe he treated me like I was some trick. Can you believe that shit?"

"No." I could tell she was trying to be as sympathetic as she could be. "He had no business putting his hands on you."

"You were right. I shouldn't have gone in there. I don't know what I was thinking, but then that's the problem. I wasn't thinking." I couldn't believe it. My entire future blew up in my face in a matter of minutes. Now I no longer had a fiancé and the only thing I possibly got out of the deal was herpes.

"It's a good thing you found out the type of person he is now instead of later."

"I guess so," I replied as I wiped my eyes with the back of my hand. "But now what am I going to do? I don't have a place to stay and I have a big wedding tomorrow that I need to cancel."

Candace reached across the seat and squeezed my hand. "Don't worry about nothing. I'll take care of everything."

Maybe so, but there was still my mother to deal with and the possibility that I might have contracted herpes. At the moment, I seriously didn't know which was worse.

22

Noelle

I was sitting on the couch in the living room when I heard bass thumping loudly from outside. As soon as a blue Dodge Avenger pulled into my driveway, I cringed. I don't know how many times I had to tell my son to quit driving through the neighborhood with his stereo on blast. We lived in a middle-class neighborhood and were the first black family on the block. Folks stereotyped us enough as it was. Next thing we know, my neighbors will start putting FOR SALE signs in their yards.

"You're daddy's home." I looked down at my grandbaby and smiled. Sierra was such a sweet baby. It was just a shame she had a couple of dummies for parents.

Scott turned the car off, then took the stairs two at a time and came plowing through the door. "Whassup, Mom?"

"What's up is that I told you to come home three weeks ago."

"I had things to do. Coach is serious about grades

and football camp." He shrugged like it was no big deal. Well, I'm here to tell him, I was holding the big deal.

He gave me that irresistible grin that while growing up made it hard for me to stay mad at him. Scott was a beautiful baby who grew into a handsome man. And I'm not just saying that because he's my son. Fine is fine. That's why I understood why the women loved him. Like his father, he had looks and a personality to match. A natural-born salesman, he had the gift of gab and used it to his advantage. Through high school my son never had a job, yet he always had money in his pockets thanks to the stupid females who believed everything that came out of his mouth. And as I said before, part of that was my fault. The second he hit junior high, I schooled him on women and the games we played so that he would never be a doormat to some female. Sometimes I think I trained him a little too well. He'd been breaking hearts ever since.

"What you need to be doing is trying to be a father to your daughter." I held her up for him to see. Scott leaned forward, took one look, then headed to the kitchen.

"I thought Aisha had a boy?"

"That's not your baby, but this one is."

He called from the other room "Mom, she's cute, but she ain't mine."

I rose and followed. "You barely looked at her, yet you know this isn't your child."

"Man, quit playing!"

"Man? How many times I got to tell you I ain't your man or anyone of them knuckleheads you hang with." You would think he was a bad kid instead of a B-student with a full athletic scholarship.

"Sorry, Mom, but she's not mine. Do you know how

many women would love to have my baby? Believe me, if it was mine, I would know."

"It's not an *it*, it's a her." Damn, now he had me saying it.

I heard him mumble "whatever" under his breath. So help me God, I was only seconds away from knocking him upside his head. "I don't know what's going on, but I do know my granddaughter when I see her. She's got the same thick curls and hazel eyes. Come and look at these feet." I held her up so he could take a closer look. "Those are Gordon feet."

Scott gave a strangled laugh. "Mama, those can be anybody's feet." Walking over to the refrigerator, he removed an orange soda, popped the tab, and brought it to his lips.

"So, you're saying you always used a condom? Because you said something different a couple of weeks ago."

He grew quiet. "I almost always strapped up."

I looked at the stupid expression on his face. "Almost isn't good enough. Is it, Sierra?" I cooed in a baby voice. She smiled up at me. "Look! Look at how she looks when she smiles." Scott looked, but he still wasn't convinced. "You know what, Scott Marquez Gordon? You better knock that smirk off your face and take this shit serious." I hated to curse around the baby, but I needed to make sure he knew I meant business. "This is serious. One of those chicks left this baby on the doorstep and I advise you to quit wasting my time and find out which one it is."

He blew out a long breath. "Fine. I'ma go turn a few corners and see what I find out."

"You do that."

"Do what?" Grant said as he stepped into the house. "Hey, Scott. When you get here?"

"About five minutes ago and Mom's all up in my face."

Grant gave me a look but remained quiet. Good choice. Grant knew better than to mess with me, especially after the stunt he pulled, waiting until he had already accepted a teaching position overseas to inform me. We'd hardly spoken two words since. "I sure was all up in his face. I told him he needed to figure out which one of them chicks he'd been sleeping with left this baby on my doorstep."

Grant shook his head, reached for a beer, and proceeded to leave the room. "I'm gonna leave the two of you alone to figure it out."

"Grant, he's *your* son. The least you can do is talk to him about taking care of his responsibilities, because if you had talked to him about using condoms, maybe we wouldn't be in this mess."

"If I'm not on *my job,* then by all means you handle your business. Like I said, I'm not getting in it."

That was always his answer when he felt like I was butting in someone else's business. Hey, if I didn't get involved, then what? If I stayed out of it, neither Scott nor his suspect baby mama would live up to their responsibilities. "Fine, go on in the other room. I always have to handle everything."

My husband gave me a look that said, *You're pushing your luck.* He was pissed again, although I doubt he ever stopped being mad at me. Grant could be so stubborn at times, Well, guess what? So can I. I watched him move into the other room. Scott started to follow.

"Uh-uh, I'm not finished with you yet. This little girl needs a father *and* a mother. Get your butt out there and find her!"

He strolled out the room, said a few words to his father, then I heard the loud thump of his music again. That boy better not come back until he's found Sierra's mama.

I went upstairs and put Sierra in her crib, then moved into the bedroom in time to catch Grant changing his clothes. "Where you going?"

His eyes darted around the room, making contact with everything but me. "Out for a minute."

"Out where?" I asked suspiciously. "You just got home."

"Damn, Noelle, get off my back!"

I winced. His outburst had struck a nerve. Even so, I wasn't about to let him walk out that door before he gave me a straight answer. "You still haven't answered my question."

He gave me this look like I had a lot of nerve questioning him, but I didn't care. Something was wrong with our marriage. I learned a lot in my thirty-eight years, and I was far from being a fool. We hadn't made love in weeks. Last night I reached over to him and he ignored my advances. I had a right to be nervous because Grant messed around on me before. It may have been nineteen years ago, but he messed around. He never admitted it, but I saw the signs. Even back then he was distant. Going out all hours of the night. We argued a lot and eventually, Grant moved out of our apartment and in with one of his college buddies. For three months I spent every second I wasn't doing hair trying to track his every move, but never discovered anything. We eventually got back together, and when I asked him if he'd been seeing anyone during our breakup, he swore to me he hadn't. I forced myself to believe he was telling me the truth. By then I was pregnant with Scott and all I cared about at that point was making my marriage work.

"I'm leaving in ten days and thought I'd go to the game with the boys tonight." He couldn't even look at me as he spoke.

I felt my stomach clench. My gut told me he was lying. "You're leaving the country in ten days. What about spending some time with your wife?"

He gave a sarcastic laugh. "For what? Half the time you don't even notice I'm here. You don't have time for me. When I asked you on Saturday if you wanted to go out, you said no. You're too busy with the baby. In eighteen years, ever since Scott was born, you never have any time because you're too busy raising kids."

I didn't answer because he was right. Sierra had become my life. Wednesday, Grant had asked me to go out to dinner and since I couldn't find a babysitter, I declined. But as far as I was concerned, neither of us was in a position to be selfish right now. We had a granddaughter who needed us.

"I bought that new Tyler Perry movie at Walmart today. How about we have a movie night?"

Grant looked like he was undecided, and that threw me for a loop. Any other time he would have jumped at the chance to curl up on the couch with me and watch a movie.

"And how long will that last before the baby starts crying and interrupts the movie?" Grant looked at me pointedly, waiting for my reply.

"If you're wanting some kind of guarantee that won't happen, then I'm sorry. I can't do that."

"Maybe tomorrow." He barely looked at me when he answered.

I moved over in front of him and took his hand. "Grant, what's happening to us? We don't spend any time together. We rarely talk. I'm not understanding what's going on."

He sighed, then just stood there staring at me. "I don't know what's happening."

I gave him an evil look. "Answer one question . . . Do you want this marriage?"

Grant flinched. "What the hell kinda question is that?"

He just didn't get it. "One that I want you to answer, because the way you've been behaving lately, I would say the answer is no."

"That's not true. I love you. Always have. I'm just having trouble adjusting to the fact that our lives are changing." Backing away from me, he regained his personal space. "There has never been just you and I; there has always been us plus two or three. When are we going to have our time? Just you and me. I planned a vacation, hoping to start our new life together and look what happened. We're now grandparents."

So that's what it was. Sierra. "I'm sorry that you're having a hard time accepting that you are now a grandfather, but life isn't always the way we want it to be."

"And that's the problem."

"So where do we go from here?" I asked, trying to blink back tears. I was scared.

"I'm not sure where we go from here. Maybe the distance will do us some good." He came over and wrapped his arms around me. "When I get back from Korea, we'll sit down and work on us . . . I promise." He kissed my forehead, then stepped away and moved inside the bathroom.

When he got back? I had a feeling if I waited that long to fix my marriage, it would be too late for us.

23

Tiffany

It had been five days since that fiasco at the club. After spending an evening crying my eyes out, I went to stay at Mama's while she and Candace went to church and announced the bad news. If I thought I was going to get sympathy from my own mother, I was badly mistaken. The second Mama got back from apologizing to our family and friends, she tore into me. I was lying on the couch curled up in a ball when she tossed a shoe at my head.

"I have never been so humiliated in my life!" she screamed.

"Mama, it's not my fault," I pleaded, but it was useless.

"Yes, it is, because I taught you better than that!" I thought by telling her the truth, she would have at least a little bit of sympathy. What a joke. "That's what you get for spreading your legs! If only you listened to me. Now nobody will want you!" By the time she was done, I was crying all over again. Mama was not at all moved. She made herself a gin and tonic, then called me every kind of slut she could come up with. The more I cried, the more she yelled at me. Hell, she might as well have spit on me because I was left feeling like crap.

The next day I packed my bag and decided to go on my honeymoon anyway. After all, it had already been bought and paid for. Why waste more money if I didn't have to? I had hoped spending five days in sunny Jamaica would brighten my spirits, but by day three, happiness was far away no matter how much rum punch I drank.

I made myself get out of bed, then slipped into a cute pink bikini and headed down toward the beach. I remember when I bought the outfit, I couldn't wait for Kimbel to see me in it. Well, because of me and my big mouth, that wasn't going to happen.

I followed the path to the white sand beach. It was beautiful. The grounds were filled with palm trees and other tropical plants. Reggae music was coming from the bar. Everybody was laughing and having a good time. *If only Kimbel was here with me, then this trip would be perfect.* I don't even know why I was wasting my time thinking about that asshole after the way he beat me upside my head with all his friends watching. Kimbel didn't have any respect for me or our relationship. I had simply been a joke to him. My love had meant nothing, and that hurt more than anything.

I found a lounge chair close to the water and took a seat, then reached for the book I brought with me. I hoped reading about someone else's drama would be a great escape from my own pathetic life.

"Good morning, ma'am. You're looking mighty

healthy. Would the pretty lady like another Long Island iced tea?"

I glanced over the top of my sunglasses at the dark-skinned Jamaican brother with a pair of sexy legs standing beside me. After three days at Sandals Montego Bay all-inclusive resort, he knew my drink of choice. "That would be wonderful." I figured the drunker I was, the less time I had to think. A few minutes later he returned, singing a happy little tune. "What are you so happy about?" I snapped, wanting everyone to feel as miserable as I did.

"Every ting is irie. What's there to be unhappy about?"

"A whole helluva lot, so take all that cheeriness somewhere else." I shooed him away from me like a pesky old fly. I wanted to wallow in self-pity, and his smiling and singing was making that impossible.

He laughed like I had just told him a joke, then had the nerve to hold out his hand. I thought he was waiting on a tip or something. "My name is Baughn, pronounced like James Bond. Can I ask you your name?" He then had the audacity to take a seat in the chair beside me. It was then with him sitting too close for comfort that I noticed just how attractive he really was. He was wearing shorts and a uniform polo, but even in that monkey suit he was gorgeous with smooth chocolate skin and large dark brown eyes. But what I couldn't miss were his pearly whites since he was grinning so hard you would have thought he was auditioning for a toothpaste commercial. He was just too damn happy for me.

I turned my nose up at him. "Uhhhh, excuse me, but aren't you supposed to be working?"

Baughn gave me a devilish grin. "Yes, mon. I'm taking a break. Now, answer my question."

It was obvious he wasn't leaving until I told him. "Tiffany, now go away." I dismissed him with a wave, but he totally ignored me.

"Tiffany, what I would like to know is why a woman as beautiful as you is so bitter?"

He actually looked like he was interested and not just being nosy. I don't know why, but I guess I needed someone to talk to who wasn't going to be biased. I told him about finding my fiancé screwing another woman the night before our wedding. I left out the part about him having herpes and me possibly contracting it. "This trip was supposed to be our honeymoon."

As soon as I was done talking, Baughn started shaking his head. "What a bumbaclot your man is. No worries. Be happy, because you deserve better. There is no way I would do tat to you. My mudda raised me to cherish a woman," he said with a heavy accent that the longer I listened to it the more I liked it.

Maybe that's the problem. Kimbel's dad was a womanizer. Had been for years. Everyone knew it, even his wife; but there was no way she was giving up the lifestyle she had grown accustomed to.

Baughn rose. "Well, I better get back to work. It was nice talking to you."

After he left, I thought about what he said. Yeah, I didn't deserve the way he treated me, but that didn't stop me from sitting there thinking about him and that Shakira wannabe stripper he had bent over, touching her toes. As I thought about how Kimbel had made me look like such a fool, I watched Baughn move around the beach, smiling and serving guests. What a carefree life.

I was getting ready to go back to my room when he returned. "Hey," he began, then looked around like he was making sure no one was listening. "I was wondering if you would like to have dinner with me tonight?"

That was the last thing I had expected to hear out of him. "Isn't there some rule about you dating the guests?"

"Yes, but I won't tell if you don't." He was cocky, and I liked that in him. He was willing to risk his job to go out with me. Baughn gave me a beautiful smile that caused me to give him one of my own. His joyfulness was starting to be contagious.

"I'm sorry, but I wouldn't be good company."

"Why don't you let me be the judge of tat. Come wit me and I will take your mind off your problem."

Sure, might as well. I guess anything was better than sitting in my room feeling sorry for myself. "I guess so."

"No, you either want to go or not."

"I said . . ."

"Pretty lady . . . yes or no? It's that simple . . . Tiffany."

I felt a tingle in my tummy. I liked the way my name sounds with his Jamaican accent. He was standing there looking all sexy and shit, who could resist. "Okay."

Baughn looked pleased with my answer. "Good. I'll meet you near the gate at eight PM."

"I'll be there."

I turned on my heels and headed back to my room with a little pep in my step and a smile. This would be the first time in almost eight months that I went out with someone other than Kimbel. *Get used to it, because it definitely won't be the last.*

* * *

"That shit was hilarious!" I was laughing so hard my side hurt. Baughn had taken me to Frank's, a jerk chicken restaurant on the beach. I ain't gonna lie; I had a fabulous time talking to him and listening to him talk about his country with calypso music playing in the background. We had just finished our dinner when this woman came in and walked over to this table in the corner where this dude was snuggled up with this female. Next thing you know she was screaming and going off. You didn't have to be a genius to know that was her man and he was stepping out with another female. Before the hostess could tell them to keep it down, the old girl grabbed the chick's wig and flung it across the room. It landed on the next table in this dude's soup.

"Yes, mon. I do not know which to feel more sorry for. It was pretty funny."

I didn't mind when Baughn reached down and took my hand and we swung our arms back and forth as we moved to his Toyota Corolla.

"What would you like to do now?" he asked.

"This is your world, not mine," I said with a shrug of my left shoulder.

Baughn swung me around in his arms. "What I would like to do is make love to you." He pressed his lips to mine. The kiss was nice. Really nice.

I looked into Baughn's eyes and saw the desire burning there. "Then lead the way." The old Tiffany wouldn't even dream of going off and being alone with a man she just met, but that person no longer existed. The new me was going to be spontaneous and daring.

Baughn took me to a smaller hotel in the heart of Montego Bay. "I live wit my mudda," he said by way of an explanation. I didn't believe him. Men were liars as far as I was concerned, but it didn't matter. Obviously he already had the evening planned, because he didn't even stop at the desk. He took my hand and led me up to the room. He was confident, that was a given. And I'd have to admit that I liked it in him. As soon as the door was shut, he pulled me close to him and I pressed my lips to his and kissed him like a starving woman. His lips were soft and gentle, and his kisses were wet and deep.

"For an American, you are an excellent kisser," he murmured.

"For an American?" I laughed, then leaned back and gazed up at his face. "I guess that's supposed to be some kind of compliment?"

"Absolutely, pretty lady." He swooped down and captured my mouth again. I closed my eyes and gave in to what I was feeling. I tried to block Kimbel from my mind, yet he kept popping up in my head. I pretended it was him I was kissing. That it was him who was gently removing my clothes and had carried me to bed. But when Baughn reached inside his pocket and removed a condom, I couldn't pretend any longer because Kimbel and I never used condoms. I didn't make him because I didn't think he had to. I had planned to spend the rest of my life with him. I had trusted him with all my heart. Baughn parted my thighs and slid inside, and the tears started to fall. This was not at all how I was supposed to remember Jamaica.

"Hey, you all right?" He stopped and stared down at me. I nodded, not at all trusting myself to speak. Baughn started kissing one cheek, then my eyes and all my tears away. "It's going to be irie. Time heals all wounds," he murmured close to my ear. I wanted so desperately to believe that everything was going to be all right. But right now I couldn't see past the hurt or the pain. He continued to shower kisses along my face and when he brought his lips back to mine, I wrapped my arms around him. This time when he moved, I rocked my hips with him, matching his rhythm. Eventually, his strokes became longer and deeper.

"Oh, yes," I cried out. He felt wonderful inside of me. For the next few minutes, I couldn't think of anything except how good he was making me feel.

"You like, mon?"

"Yes, I like, mon."

It was different. It wasn't at all the way it had felt with Kimbel. Baughn's strokes were smooth and controlled, like he had all the time in the world. He had skills and the sex was great, but what was missing was the emotional attachment that Kimbel and I had. Without my heart being involved, it was just sex. At least it was good sex.

"That's it. Just relax . . . be happy. Yes . . . all I want is to make you feel good."

He was definitely doing that. Despite how wrong it was, he felt wonderful. It wasn't long before I was crying out his name, and it was like he waited until he was certain I was satisfied before he came. I laid there in his arms thinking maybe having someone like Baughn in my life might make getting over Kimbel easier.

24

Chauncey

"I don't know if I can do this."

Candace took my hand. "Yes, you can. Just go in there with your head up high and show your father what he missed not being a part of your life."

That was easy for her to say, her parents were still together, and she and her father had the type of relationship I would do anything to have. She also didn't have to live with the fact she had done time in jail. It was a talk we still hadn't had, but I was going to have to make the time. I was planning a romantic weekend for two in Wisconsin. I figured we'd see the sites after I told her about my past. I was hoping that it was a long enough drive that by the time we made it back to Chicago, she would have found it in her heart to forgive me for not being honest with her.

I turned off the ignition. "A'ight. Let's do this."

I saw my sister's red Camry coming up the road. I waited until she parked at the end of the block before we climbed out. While Candace got Miasha out her car seat, I reached on the back seat for the cheesecake that Candace had made. I wouldn't have brought anything if it hadn't been for her. My mind had been consumed with thoughts about how this day would go down. I looked over at the two-story brick house located in Oak Park, Illinois. After working more than thirty years for the CTA, my father had done well.

I closed the car door just as Linda and her date got out. As soon as I saw him rise from the passenger's side, my mouth dropped. "Are you for real?" No wonder she wanted me to come with her. Dude was white.

Candace moved beside me and looked equally surprised. "You didn't tell me her boyfriend was white," she murmured.

"That's because she didn't tell me." I was certain my little sis purposely left out that piece of information. We had planned on getting together before the family reunion so she could meet my girl, but we could never work out a good time. But a white boy? I pictured her being open to all things, but this wasn't one of them. The way they were holding hands and grinning at each other, it was obvious she was really feeling the dude.

"Hey, big brother," she called, as she moved across the street to where we were standing.

"Whassup." I met Linda halfway and immediately noticed she was avoiding eye contact. That's okay, because the first chance I get her alone we were going to have a talk.

Linda leaned in close to the dude. "Well, this is the guy I've been telling you about." She got this dreamy look in her eyes for a second, then said, "Tommy, this is my brother Chauncey."

"It's a pleasure meeting you," he said by way of a greeting followed by a handshake.

"Same here." For a white boy he wasn't bad looking. He wasn't one of those trying to fit in by acting black. He was a true all-American Caucasian kid with blond hair and blue eyes, exactly what one would picture as a doctor.

I introduced them to Candace; then we all headed up the sidewalk. Linda came around beside me and squeezed my hand. I glanced down at her pleading eyes. She knew how to get to me every time. "I'm so glad you came, Chauncey. This means a lot to me."

"Anything for you."

Miasha was holding her mother's hand and I walked in front of them. Two men were standing in front of the house talking.

"Uncle Carl. You remember Chauncey?" Linda said, after giving one of them a big hug.

The tall man rose slowly and removed his hat. "Well, I'll be damned," he said, smiling yet tearful. "I haven't seen you since you were but *that* tall." He lowered his hand to his knee.

"Yeah, it's been a long, long time," I replied, embracing him. I never forgot all the shiny quarters he used to give me.

"Welcome home, son." He made me feel at home and I got all misty eyed. I pulled it together before he released me.

I introduced him to my girls; then we followed Linda through the side gate and entered the backyard. There was music playing. Ribs could be smelled, cooking on the grill, and people were laughing, playing cards and having a good time. Linda led us around, introducing us to everyone, and I didn't miss the look on everyone's face at the mention that I was Fred's son, especially since some had never seen me before. What blew my mind was that instead of people saying, "I didn't know Fred had a son," I heard, "I heard a lot about you."

"It's good to see you again."

"It's about time you came back home."

My two aunts smothered me with kisses, then took the liberty of introducing me to dozens of cousins. I smiled, shook hands, and within minutes felt right at home, almost like I belonged, but I wasn't trying to fool myself into believing that. This life had been taken away from me when I was too young to understand why. No matter how good they made me feel, I was still a stranger looking in.

It wasn't until we reached the corner of the yard that a tall, butter brown man moved toward us. That face, although older, had been stuck in my head since I was a kid. For a moment it felt like time had stopped. It was like our entire life together flashed before my eyes. I saw him smiling down at me, pushing my swing, teaching me how to hold a bat. Those were the memories I had tried to hold on to for so long before Mama told me the truth about my father.

"Son, I'm glad you came."

It was his home, yet he looked more out of place than I felt. I swore there were tears in his eyes, yet I simply nodded when what I wanted to do was punch him in his mouth and demand he tell me why he denied my existence all those years. I wanted to know why he turned his back on me and forgot he had a son when I so badly needed a father. Linda put her hand to my back. I knew she was trying to calm me down and some of my tension eased. Now was not the time. We had family and children around, along with my girl and Miasha. I took a deep breath and walked away, and didn't realize until I reached the other side of the yard that my hands were balled in tight fists. I didn't know if the anger would ever go away.

I'll have to say, for the rest of the afternoon, I had a ball hanging with my cousins, playing basketball and shooting the shit. It felt good knowing the same blood ran through all our veins. Mama's family was small and so spread out we rarely ever got together as a whole except for funerals. But the Colemans were a large group.

After I won the last game, I moved up behind Candace, who was talking to my stepmother, and wrapped my arms around her waist. I loved the way she leaned back against me, making me feel like I was her man and as long as we had each other, nothing else mattered.

"Chauncey, you've got a great girl." Elaine smiled and looked so much like my sister, Linda. I liked her right away. When I looked at her beautiful face with her strong Nigerian features and friendly eyes, not once did I think of her as the female who stole my father away from me and my mama. I'm a true believer that all's fair in love and war. What I didn't excuse was any man who turned his back on his children. "Don't be a stranger. You're welcome to our house any time."

"Thanks, Elaine. Appreciate it."

We were chatting, the three of us, when my father moved up beside me and tapped me on the shoulder. I jerked away from his touch.

"Sorry, I, uh, would like a chance to talk to you . . . alone . . . please," he pleaded.

I was ready to tell him to go to hell, but the worried looks on Elaine's and Candace's faces made me think twice. There was no need for a scene.

"Be nice," Candace warned under her breath.

I followed him inside the house away from the others so they couldn't hear our conversation. Once he shut the sliding glass door, I swung around with my arms crossed. "What you wanna talk about?"

My father's eyebrows bunched like he couldn't believe I would ask such a thing. "Us. You're my son and I would like a chance to get to know you."

I gave him a look meant to squash any expectation of us ever having any type of relationship. "Why? You weren't interested all this time, so what's going to make now different?" I was pouting and knew it, especially since deep down I really wanted answers.

"Now that you're grown, your mother is no longer standing in the way of me being around my son."

"What?" I stepped to him, breathing fire now. There was no way I was going to let him talk bad about my mama. Maybe she and I didn't have the best relationship, but she had been there when I needed her most. "What's she gotta do with you turning your back on me?"

He tried to reach out to me, but I backed away, so instead, he put his hands in his front pockets. "Son, I'll admit I did your mama dirty," he began shamefully. "I was wrong for the way I treated her and I'll have to answer to God someday; but even though she and I were no longer together, I still tried to be a part of your life, but your mother wouldn't let me."

"You're lying!" There was no way he was going to get me to believe she was the reason why he had not been a part of my life.

"Son, it's true. She refused to let me see you. Luckily, Ms. Hattie was nice enough to let me sneak by and see you every day, but once she died . . . I had no way to see you. Your mama still refused to let me be in your life, and I didn't have the money to try and fight her in court. I would call her from time to time, drop by on your birthday and Christmas with gifts, and beg her to let me see you, but she refused."

I couldn't breathe. No way was this happening. "Quit lying!" I got all up in his face ready to punch him in his mouth for lying about my mama. Yet, I couldn't do it.

"Son, it's the truth." I studied his face and watched his bottom lip quiver. I didn't even know this man, but I couldn't deny what I saw right dead in front of me. He wasn't lying, but yet and still, I wasn't ready to believe it.

Tears glistened in his eyes and his expression struck a nerve. "That's why I came to you the day after you graduated eighth grade, hoping that I would finally have a chance to be a part of your life, but before I could explain, you stormed off."

I remembered that day. The second he walked up and told me how proud he was, I spit on the ground and walked away.

"Chauncey, you are my son and I've always loved you. I figured the only chance I ever had was by you getting to know your sister. She wrote the letters and I made sure you always had money on your books and magazines to read. I hoped that in time you would welcome me into your life again."

I kept shaking my head. I couldn't believe it had been him making sure I always had toiletries and reading materials. I never had to beg or want for anything. For five years, I had thought all that time it had been Linda sending me those things, yet it had been him.

"If you cared that much, why didn't you try to write me or come see me?"

"Would you have put me on the visitor's list? Would you have returned any of my letters?"

"No, I wouldn't."

My father tried to resist a smile and so did I. I guess he knew me better than I knew myself.

"Son, all I want to do is start over. All I ask for is a chance." He was pleading, and it was his own fault our relationship was the way it was.

I looked through the glass doors and spotted Elaine and Candace, making it no secret they were watching and waiting to see what would happen. I then looked over at all my aunts, uncles, and cousins, people I had never gotten a chance to know, and the little boy inside wanted so badly to feel part of something. Unfortunately, the man in me wasn't that easy to convince. "I'll think about it."

He nodded and looked pleased with my answer. "That's all I ask for."

I turned and walked away and signaled to Candace it was time to go. If I didn't get away from there, I was going to grab that man and cry like a baby. Deep down I was happy to have a father again.

25

Noelle

"Hello. Is this Rianna?"

"Yeah, who's this?"

"This is Scott Gordon's mother. I'm calling to see if you gave birth to a child and left her on my doorstep."

Click.

No, she didn't hang up on me. All I did was ask her a question. I dialed her phone back and she answered after three rings.

"I guess I should take that as a no."

"A baby? Are you for real? I couldn't even stand him kissing me. Scott liked to slob in my mouth." *Click.*

When she hung up, I didn't bother calling her back. Instead, I scratched her name off the list. This was ridiculous. If my son hadn't been sleeping with almost every girl at his high school, I wouldn't have to be working so hard. I spent the last week trying to track down every girl my son's been involved with and had yet to find one person who has had a baby or knows of a female who did. I turned the page of the yearbook. So far I had gone through all the graduating seniors in the book. Now it was time to start calling the former juniors. Someone knew something, and I was determined to find out what it was.

Regardless of what the outcome was, there was no denying I had fallen in love with my granddaughter. Every time she looked up at me I saw so much of my son. It was amazing how much they looked alike. Which was why I was determined to find out who the mother was so we could decide how to proceed. Scott didn't have any luck finding the girl he knocked up. However, he promised to be home after finals, then together we could find Sierra's mother. In the meantime, I was going to continue to look for her on my own.

I left the salon around three, picked up Sierra, and headed home. Grant was leaving in four days and the tension was still heavy between us. Every day was the same thing. We stepped around each other and barely spoke. Often I found him staring and watching, like he wanted to say something but nothing came out. I didn't know what was bothering him and what had caused our marriage to sour, but I was tired of worrying myself to death about the whole thing. I decided to just leave it in God's hands.

I stepped inside the house, carrying Sierra in her car seat. Grant was sitting on the couch in the living room.

"Hey," I said.

"Hey," he said, and didn't bother looking up from the television.

I went to our bedroom feeling frustrated as I asked myself, was this what my marriage had come to? My husband spent more time hanging out in the streets with his friends than he did with his wife. I knew in the past I had neglected my husband's needs and had put the salon first, but I thought our marriage was strong enough to survive anything. I guess that's what I get for thinking.

I fed Sierra, burped her, then rocked her to sleep. The second I lay her in her crib, I decided to take advantage of the opportunity and jump in the shower. Grant was still downstairs watching television. I was hoping that since we had only four days left together, he might feel like talking this evening.

I was in the shower for what felt like forever, thinking about my failed marriage and trying to decide what it was going to take to get it back on track after Grant got back. One thing was for sure. I could no longer go on like this. Either he was ready to seek marriage counseling or I was ready for him to find another place to live. I'm sure one of his drinking buddies would be more than happy to let him move in. Under the spray of water, I bowed my head and prayed to God to help me save my marriage.

By the time I stepped out the shower, I heard Sierra crying and groaned. There was no telling how long she had been awake, crying her eyes out. I quickly reached for a towel and wrapped it around my body. As I stepped out the bathroom, I suddenly halted. Sierra had stopped crying. I moved down the hall and when I heard Grant's voice, I froze.

"Little lady, what's all that noise for? You want someone to talk to?" He was speaking in a soothing voice that I hadn't heard him use in years.

"Hey? How's it going? Do you know I'm your grandpa?"

I stood outside the bedroom door and watched my husband sitting in the rocking chair, cradling his granddaughter gently in his arms. I was so choked up at the sight of the two of them, I didn't know what to say. Not once since she had moved into our house had he held her. Now he was holding her like she was the most precious thing and talking to her like they'd known each other for years.

I stood there for what felt like forever, with him rocking in the chair until she finally went back to sleep. Grant carried her over to the crib and lay her gently on her back. When he swung around our eyes met and I swore his were cloudy with tears.

"She looks just like Scott," he replied.

I nodded, not trusting myself to speak.

"Come're," he commanded, and I didn't waste any time moving into his outstretched arms. "I am so sorry. So very sorry." He kept saying it over and over as he held me tightly.

"For what?" I finally asked, because I needed to make sure he was apologizing for the right thing.

"For my behavior the last couple of months." I was just glad to have him holding me. He brought his lips to mine and I kissed him back, loving the way it felt just to be touched by my husband. "I've been so stupid." He backed me slowly out the room and down the hall to our bedroom, where we helped each other out of our clothes and I wasted no time getting under the covers. Not once did my eyes leave his body.

"Noelle," he said, and crawled on the bed beside me. I couldn't stop looking at him. My nipples hardened. Moisture gathered between my thighs. "Baby, I'm going to warn you. The first time's going to be quick. I promise the second one I will take my time." He put his hands between my thighs and rubbed his finger along my kitty. I arched my back anticipating

what he was about to do. I was breathless with antici-
pation.

Slowly, Grant slid inside. I sighed and lifted my
hips off the bed. It felt so good having him make love
to me again. I moaned as he rocked, and before long
his strokes became stronger. I wrapped my legs around
his waist and tried to control the rhythm, but he lowered my thighs back to the bed so he could move as
deep and hard as he wanted.

"Yes, baby," I moaned. Grant grabbed my hips,
holding me in place, and pumped wildly. My back
bowed as his thumb found my clit and pressed against
it. He rubbed while he stroked. "Yessss!" I screamed,
and he covered his mouth with mine, silencing me so I
wouldn't wake Sierra. I came hard. His breathing increased and then he came. I don't think we lay there
more than fifteen minutes before he was inside of me
again. It went on and on and I swore my husband
couldn't get enough of me. I lost count of my orgasms
and half lost my mind, crying and shaking for the next
two hours until he finally cried out and collapsed on
top of me. We lay there holding each other until our
hearts slowed; then Grant raised up in the bed and
stared down at me.

"Baby, there is no excuse for my behavior," he said
by way of an apology.

There was no way I was letting him off the hook
that easily. Not after everything he put me through.
"Why? Why were you acting that way?"

"I was scared."

I didn't have a clue what he was talking about.
"Scared of what?"

He bowed his head, then breathed, "Of getting
old."

"Getting old?" I totally didn't understand what the hell he was getting at.

Grant rolled onto his back with his hands behind his head, staring up at the ceiling as he spoke. "I guess I'm scared of getting old. I looked in the mirror one morning and realized I was forty. We spent years struggling to make ends meet and raising kids. Now that we're in a better position financially and can enjoy life a little, there's another baby in the house. Having a grandchild scared me, because it means that I'm getting old and time is running out." He sighed heavily. "I know now that sounds crazy, but I don't want to sit back one day and see that life has passed us by. We never got to do anything or go anywhere because all we ever did was raise kids and work hard. It wasn't until I held that little girl I realized that we are truly blessed enough that we can open up our home and offer her a good life. She's a Gordon. I can see it in her face and her eyes, and we Gordons stick together."

I felt like a heavy weight had been lifted from my chest. My husband was going through a midlife crisis and I hadn't seen it coming. "I'm so glad to hear that. I was so afraid, I didn't know what else to do."

"I'm sorry, baby. You forgive me?" he asked, turning on his side and facing me.

"Yes, I forgive you." I was just glad that we were talking again. I was confident that in time things would be back to normal.

"The whole teaching overseas was because it was something I had always wanted to do and I was afraid I might not get another chance. But if you don't want me to go, I understand." His mouth said one thing, but his eyes said another. The opportunity was important to him.

I would rather he stay here than be in another country for a month with other teachers from around the world. I guarantee there will be females. I bet the first chance one of them gets, they're gonna try and make a pass at my husband. But as much as I wanted to say no, I knew it wasn't fair of me. I needed to trust him. "No, you go. I know how much this experience means to you."

I watched his shoulders sag with relief and a smile curl his succulent lips. "I love you, baby," he replied with a kiss.

"And I love you."

I put in a movie and we cuddled under the covers until Sierra started screaming, then Grant went and got her and she joined us. I couldn't help but smile because this was the way it was supposed to be.

26

Candace

"What's that smell?" I stepped into the apartment to find Tiffany sitting on the couch and my apartment smelling like burnt paper. "Tiffany, did you hear what I said. What's that smell?"

She looked at me long enough to say, "Oh, I was burning Kimbel's pictures on the patio."

"What?" I hurried through the kitchen and out the sliding door to find my barbecue grill lit on my small patio. The blaze was roaring. Right beside it was a bag of charcoal and lighter fluid. Was that chick crazy or what?

The day after Tiffany got back from Jamaica, I made the mistake of inviting her to stay with me. Her mama can be a straight bitch, and I knew she was getting tired of hearing how she had made a big mistake by giving it up so soon, so I suggested she come and stay with me and Miasha while she got herself together and found another place to live. Ever since, she's been half going to work, canceling her hair appointments, and spending the day lying around the house, listening to sad love songs and crying over that infected fool. I honestly didn't know how much more I could take.

I went and grabbed the fire extinguisher from the pantry and put the fire out. "You've got to get yourself together," I replied when I stepped into the living room to find her staring at the television screen. She had no idea what she was watching. The local news was on and I knew she didn't watch the news. "You got to quit tripping over that dude. He ain't worth it."

"It's not that," she finally said, then trained sad eyes in my direction. "I'm now damaged goods. Nobody else is ever gonna want me."

"You don't even know if you have it yet. Why don't you wait until after you've been tested before you start jumping to conclusions?" She was acting like a CD on repeat. I've been hearing this same song all week and I had it up to here.

"I know I've got it. I have this gut feeling," Tiffany whined.

"You are starting to sound crazy."

She cut her eyes in my direction. "Okay, so what would you do in my situation?"

"I would go get tested instead of sitting around moping over that fool."

"That's easy for you to say; you're not in this situation. I'm just scared."

"Scared of what?"

"What I might find out."

"You act like you got AIDS or something. *That's* when you need to be tripping."

"Who knows? I go get tested and I might discover that herpes is the least of my worries. There ain't no telling what else that bastard might have." She hopped up from the couch and was pacing back and forth across the length of the room. "I don't know how I was ever in love with that grimy muthafucka." She looked like she was itching to punch someone.

"Love is blind. Trust me, I know."

"But this was supposed to be my one and only. He knew the rules from day one, and yet he manipulated my ass into giving him my most precious gift. This is so fucking unbelievable." She flopped back down on the couch and started crying again. I didn't know what to say at this point.

"Listen, Tiffany, everything is going to be all right." I took the seat beside her.

"I might have sores growing in my mouth at any moment. I can't believe I went down on him. I had his tainted penis in my mouth. Dammit! How could I be so stupid?"

"Girl, I'm sick of listening to you talking about this. Just bring your behind down to the clinic and get tested."

"Hell no! I'm not coming down to no freakin' free clinic. Every broke bitch in town goes there, and Thursday night is dirty dick night. I don't think so. I'll make an appointment and go see my own gynecologist."

"Good. As long as you take the test and get this mess over with, 'cause you're starting to get on my damn nerves. I already told you Chauncey said he could hook you up with one of his boys."

She rolled her eyes at me, then curled up in a ball on the couch again.

"No, thank you. I don't think I'm ready yet to start dating again."

I'd be damned before I sit around moping over some muthafucka. "Why don't you come to my company picnic with me and Chauncey?"

She shook her head. "I don't think so."

I was through trying to talk to her. Just as long as she didn't burn down my apartment, she could lie on my couch all day and mope if she wanted to. I went into the room and changed out of my work clothes and got ready for my afternoon, but I could hear her in the other room, crying again. I think it was time for me to find Tiffany another place to live. Even Chauncey was starting to get annoyed by her behavior. Whenever he came over, Tiffany wasn't even respectable enough to go in the spare bedroom; instead, she would sit out on the couch with us and want to talk about Kimbel. When she wasn't talking about him, she was crying. I had hoped five days in Jamaica would have made her feel better. I had even hoped she would have met some Mandingo who fucked her brains out; but if that happened she sure hadn't told me. All she talked about was that fool Kimbel. Whatever! I pushed my friend's problems aside and got ready for the afternoon.

"Park over there."

Chauncey pulled into the parking space at the end of the park and turned off the car. I took a deep breath and stared across the seat at his fine ass. I was still amazed how far we had come in such a short time. We had been seeing each other almost every evening I didn't have class, and the days that I did, after I got Miasha to bed Chauncey and I would talk on the phone until we both fell asleep. It was amazing how in such a short time

Chauncey had become such an important part of my life. So important that I had invited him to my company picnic.

The city annually gave us a day they called "giving thanks." It was being held this year at Jackson Park located behind the Museum of Science and Industry. There were amusement rides, food vendors, games, and live music.

I climbed out and helped Miasha from her seat. Together, the three of us moved through the park and it felt like we were a family. When Chauncey took my hand, I smiled up at his handsome face. This was definitely going to be a good day.

Miasha started jumping up and down. "Mommy! Mommy! Can I have a balloon?"

"Sure you can," Chauncey said before I had a chance to answer. I smiled over at him and took a moment to admire how good my man looked in stonewashed jean shorts, a Chicago Bears' jersey, and fresh white sneakers. I wasn't looking bad either. I was rocking a pink tennis dress with a short pleated skirt and crisscrossed pink sandals.

Chauncey scooped Miasha up in his arms and carried her over to buy a balloon. I took the opportunity to glance around, looking for whomever I knew. Everybody at the clinic was required to be there. Chauncey and Miasha returned and we strolled around the park eating cotton candy. I found my supervisor and made sure to walk up to her. Not necessarily so she could meet my man, but to make sure Sylvia knew I was here so I would get paid. She had made it clear, anyone who didn't show up was going to be charged four hours of annual leave.

"Well, well, who do we have here?"

I swung around and Gloria was all up in my face. Whoever did her weave needed to find another profession, because I could see the tracks at the front of her head.

"Hey, what's up, Gloria?" I said, then saw the way she was looking at Chauncey. Her eyes traveled over his body, pausing at his chest. I been around her long enough to know she liked everything she saw. That chick better check herself. "This is Chauncey and you already know Miasha."

"Of course I know Miasha." Her eyes were glued to my man. "Chauncey, huh?" she purred seductively. She then had the nerve to stick her flat chest out like she had something for him to look at. Her breasts were like two bumps in the road. "Hmmm . . . you look familiar."

Chauncey chuckled, then shook his head. "Sorry, but I've never seen you before."

She wasn't ready to let it go, but I was on to her. Gloria was just looking for an excuse to flirt with Chauncey. "No . . . I've seen you. I just can't seem to put my finger on it. A man as fine as yourself, I never forget a face."

Well, she needed to forget this face, because *it* and everything else belonged to me. He was my dream come true and I'd be damned before I let some chick steal my man.

"How did your date go with Deon?"

Frowning, she held her nose, then mumbled, "Oooh . . . puhleeze."

Laughing, I took Chauncey's hand. "We'll see you later." I dragged him over to the other side of the park. As far away from her as I could. I introduced him to all my coworkers and everyone adored him. We had a ball.

Chauncey competed in the potato sack race and even volunteered to go in the dunking booth after he found out the proceeds went to a local charity. On several occasions, I spotted Gloria staring at him from across the park.

"I think you have an admirer," I said to him as we were eating Chicago dogs.

"Oh yeah, who?"

I nodded my head in the direction of the kissing booth where Gloria was working. "She's waiting for you to come over." I teased between chews.

He frowned. "There ain't nothing that string bean can do for me." I couldn't help but grin at his comment. "I like my women with curves." He leaned down and pressed his lips to mine. I glanced over my shoulder at Gloria in time to see the jealous look on her face. I giggled and wrapped my arms around him. Chauncey was mine and nobody was going to change that.

27

Chauncey

While hugging Candace, I got mustard on the front of my jersey. I went into the men's room to try to get it out. Luckily, it took all of two minutes.

I was having a good time. With the three of us together, I couldn't help it, I felt like I finally had a family. Other than my sister, I didn't have anyone else. But I did now. I wasn't ready yet to think about my relationship with my father. I had already spent too many hours trying to sort out what he had told me and figure out how much of it was true and what part was a lie. Right now I needed to focus on what was important, and that was my new family. I had Candace and Miasha, and I planned to keep them. If things continued to go as well as they did, I planned to talk to her about taking our relationship to the next level—moving in together.

I was walking out the men's room when I spotted Gloria standing against the wall outside the door. The grin on her face told me she had purposely been waiting for me. I saw her watching me long before Candace had mentioned it. Gloria wasn't half bad. Kinda skinny with puppy dog eyes. Her best assets were a small, narrow waist and an ass that I could have balanced a glass of water on top. But I was a titty man and baby girl didn't have any.

"Hey," she said to me. Her tongue slid across her lips while she stared down at my crotch. I'll have to say it was the first time a woman looked at me and made me feel uncomfortable.

"Whassup . . . uhhh . . . Gloria, right?"

"Yep." She stepped forward. "I saw you go in there, so I thought I'd wait and see if you needed anything."

What I needed, she couldn't give me. "I'm good . . . really."

She moved closer until she was invading my space and pressed her hand against my chest. "You're sexy as hell, but you already knew that, didn't you?" she said, then laughed. "Why don't you call me some time." She took a piece of paper from her pocket and tried to put it in my hand.

"Nah, boo. No disrespect, but I'm good." I turned and walked away. I couldn't believe how scandalous she was, trying to holler at me when my girl wasn't looking.

"Chauncey!"

This girl was going to make me say something to her she wasn't going to like. I swung around and met her slick grin. I should have known she was going to be trouble.

"You know . . . I finally figured out where I know you from. You used to mess with my girl, Tameka. I've seen your picture on her phone."

It took everything I had to hold it together at the

mention of that stalker. She hadn't called me once since she saw me out with Candace. I shrugged. "Yeah, that's the past."

I watched her bring a hand to her waist and rest her weight to one hip. "I don't know, because the way Tameka talks, you still sliding up over there. Matter of fact, you were at her place last week when I called." She smirked to herself as if she'd just heard a private joke.

I laughed, then shook my head. "You got it wrong. Somebody may have been over there, but it wasn't me. I haven't messed with that girl in months."

"Really? Then I guess that's her loss." She licked her lips and I watched her eyes drop to my crotch again. "I heard you are packing, and the way my girl talks about you all the time, I can't blame her for still wanting some of that."

I glanced over my shoulder to make sure none of Candace's coworkers were around listening. "Listen . . . I've moved on. It's about time Tameka does the same."

Gloria giggled like she had a secret. "Wait until I tell her I saw you."

I walked away without even bothering to say good-bye. Damn, I had pretty much thought I had gotten rid of that crazy chick. Now there was no telling how she was going to react. Seeing us at a restaurant was one thing, but knowing I was out doing the family thing in front of one of her friends was another thing altogether. All I can say was, she better not try to mess with Candace; otherwise, she'll have hell to pay.

28

Tiffany

You ever hear about someone ripping your heart from your chest? Well, that's what I felt like. I can't breathe. I might as well die. Sure, Jamaica was fun; but that was just a way to bandage the wound that hadn't healed. Baughn was just a fling. I'll admit he was sexy as all get out and a very nice guy, but he lived in Jamaica and I'm here in the States. What kind of relationship could we really have? That's why I left the country without saying good-bye. I know it was wrong of me, but it is what it is. I didn't want him to get any wild ideas in his head of using me to get a green card. Besides, I still loved Kimbel with everything I had, and that kind of love just doesn't go away overnight. At least it doesn't for me. If only he felt the same way. Lord, was I ever gonna stop loving that man?

I came back to Chicago and found Kimbel had moved all my stuff out of his house and had it delivered to my mama's. Can you believe that? You know she had a fit. I just don't understand it. He didn't even wait for the dust to settle or for the two of us to talk and see if we could salvage our relationship. Instead, he just tossed me out like yesterday's trash. I don't understand it. What we had in eight months, it takes some people a lifetime to find.

During my time away, I did some serious thinking and had time to understand that part of our breakup was my fault. I shouldn't have confronted him like that in front of everyone. Stupid. Stupid. I should have talked about his little situation in private. Through sickness and in health, isn't that what marriage was all about? Kimbel was right. If I hadn't been holding out on him, he wouldn't have needed to go and bang some stripper. My fault. Mama was right. I was the one to blame for everything.

As I sat there staring at the television, feeling sorry for myself, I began to wonder what Kimbel was doing. I knew I shouldn't, but I couldn't help it. I had no willpower when it came to him. I picked up the phone and dialed his number, hoping he would answer this time. If not, then just to hear his voice. I was shocked when he picked up, because he'd been avoiding my phone calls all week.

"Hello?" Kimbel sounded shocked to hear from me.

"Hey." My heart was pounding so hard I didn't know what else to say.

"Tif, is that you? I was just sitting here, thinking about you."

My heart leaped. I knew it! I can't even begin to tell you how good that made me feel. "I was thinking about you, too." My feelings for him hadn't changed. After everything that happened, I still imagined spending the rest of my life with him.

"Listen . . . I'm sorry things went down the way they did. Can you forgive me for hitting you?"

"Yes." I choked on a sob. I was so relieved we were finally having this conversation. Even with everything he put me through, I still loved him. "I forgive you."

"Ummmm . . . anyway, I would like to get together tomorrow . . . if that's good with you?"

If that's good for me? Hell, right now would be even better. But I didn't want Kimbel to think I was anxious to see him. The fact he wanted to get together meant he still cared. "Sure. Where would you like to meet?" The nearest Holiday Inn would be fine with me.

"Actually . . . I can just drop by the salon on my way home from work tomorrow."

"Work?" Is he for real? A reunion like ours needed to be somewhere private. I glanced down at my watch. If I hurried, I could make a trip to Frederick's of Hollywood before they closed. "How about lunch?"

"I already have plans. Listen, Tif . . . I just need to meet long enough to get my ring back."

"Excuse me." I swore my heart stopped pumping. There was no way I had heard him right. "Did you just say you wanted to meet so you could get your ring back?"

Don't you know he had the nerve to chuckle. "C'mon, you didn't think I was going to let you keep it?"

"Yes, as a matter of fact, I did. I thought we'd sell it to help cover some of the wedding expenses."

Kimbel gave a rude snort. "Didn't you get the memo? The bride's family is supposed to pay for the wedding, not me."

Okay, he was pissing me off. "We had agreed to pay the bills together. You know damn well my mother can't afford it and neither can I."

"That's not my problem. You called off the wedding, not me."

"I wonder why the hell I did that!" I spat in the phone.

"Tiffany, I'll be by your job tomorrow."

"Come by if you want and I'll tell everyone you have herpes. Get this in your head . . . you ain't getting shit back!" I slammed the phone down.

29

Noelle

"How's your searching going?"

It was lunchtime. Whitney and I were sitting at Giordano's and had just ordered a stuffed pizza with everything. For the past couple of days, it had been a zoo at the salon. Everybody wanted their hair, nails, and toes done for the Taste of Chicago. Vendors and performers from all over the country had booths set up all along Lake Shore Drive for two whole weeks. I stopped going to the event years ago. I've gotten too old for concerts and I hated crowds. However, Stevie Wonder was scheduled to perform over the weekend, so I was almost tempted to go.

"Nope, still haven't found Sierra's mother. Scott said he checked with all his chicks—he could remember by name—and no one admits to having his baby."

Whitney gave me a sympathetic look. "Maybe she'll pop up."

"At this point, I don't care if she ever shows up. I love my granddaughter. I just want to know who she is and why she left her. After that she can take her stupid behind on back to doing whatever she was doing before," I began between sips. "It's the not knowing that scares me."

"Why's that?"

I forget I have to have patience with Whitney because she's about to be a mother. She's spoiled and has been selfish all her life. My girl has a lot to learn about loving a little person who's a part of you. My blood ran through Sierra's veins, and that made her as much a part of me as Scott was. "Because at any moment that woman can pop on my doorstep and try to take Sierra back. Now that my granddaughter is with me, I can't see her not being a part of my life."

"I didn't even think about that." She wouldn't. Whitney knew nothing about giving birth to a child and being willing to die for your own flesh and blood if you had to. "But at least Grant's being supportive."

At the mention of my husband's name, a smile curled my lips. By the time Grant had left for Korea, everything in our relationship was where it needed to be. We spent those last four days together, screwing like a couple of rabbits, and he also took the time getting to know his granddaughter. Whitney even babysat so we could have a night alone. Before he boarded that plane, Grant said he had no problem raising Sierra if we needed to.

"Yep, one thing I can say is I have a good man."

"Yes, you do," Whitney replied with a look of envy. I was starting to realize the whole deal about not wanting the man only the baby was a lie. Her baby's daddy, whoever he was, she wished he was willing to be a part of her and her baby's lives.

"I just wish Scott would take this situation seriously.

He thinks it's a big joke as he tries to remember the names of his girls from one week to the next."

"You're being hard on him. Maybe he really doesn't know whose baby it is."

I shook my head. "Then that's sad. He needs to stop sleeping around so much."

Whitney gave me a look like she wanted to say something, then thought better of it. She always said I babied her godson too much. This was one time I didn't need to hear, "I told you so." She had been right all along. Scott was a spoiled brat, and it was time for him to start growing up and taking care of his responsibilities. I didn't have a problem raising Sierra, but you better believe I was going to make him start helping financially.

I finished eating a slice of pizza, then cleared my throat. "The reason why I asked you to lunch was because last night I remembered something. It probably doesn't have anything to do with Scott, but remember that girl who asked him to the Sadie Hawkins dance. The one he went with on a dare?"

She nodded. Whitney had been there that day she had come by the house to pick Scott up for their date with her camera in hand. The teenager was real skinny and nerdy looking, and I was embarrassed to say, I remembered thinking, *How in the world had she convinced Scott to go with her.* Later, he admitted she agreed to tutor him in College Algebra for the rest of the year, which I translated as, she agreed to do his homework because I don't remember her ever coming over to study.

"Sure I remember her. Real plain and wore thick glasses."

"Right," I said, nodding my head and getting excited

as I spoke. "Well, I ran into her at the mall back in February and her stomach was sticking way out."

Whitney's eyes grew large. "You don't think . . ."

I shrugged. "Hey, I'm just saying she was pregnant. I don't know who the daddy is, but I'm definitely going to find out. I'm just surprised I hadn't thought about her before." I had added the dates in my head, and give or take a few weeks, I was right on the money.

Whitney frowned. "I seriously doubt Scott would have been interested in her."

"Maybe. Maybe not. Do you remember her name?"

She shook her head. "Nope." She said it so fast I had this feeling that Whitney was lying. But she wouldn't have any reason to, so I knew I was being overly paranoid about this whole thing.

"Well, trust and believe, I am definitely going to find out."

"One thing I had always envied about you is your determination." Whitney looked at me as if she was contemplating something, then suddenly held up her glass. "Here's to solving the mystery."

"Here, here." I tapped my glass against hers. I was going to find that girl one way or another. I just hope I could deal with the truth once it was staring me right in the face.

30

Tiffany

I headed over to the gym feeling like one vindictive bitch. I don't necessarily believe in all that eye for an eye crap, but after what Kimbel did to me, my reasons were justified. As soon as I pulled into the parking lot, I drove around until I spotted his Jaguar that he always parked on an angle so it took up two parking spaces. He was such a vain bastard. I was just too stupid at the time to realize it.

Before I climbed out, I slipped on a Cardinals base-ball cap and dark sunglasses, and grabbed my gym bag like I had every intention of hitting the elliptical machine. The college student at the desk was too busy sending a text message to notice me walking by his desk, which was good because I didn't want anyone to know I had been here. I walked down toward the weight room, peeked inside, and spotted Kimbel on the leg press machine. Good. That gave me plenty of time to put my plan in action. He always worked on his legs first, then moved to arms and abs. I frowned at his back. *Asshole.* Yesterday, the Allerton Hotel slapped me with an $8,000 bill for a wedding reception that never happened. When I contacted Kimbel and begged him to cover the debt, and in exchange I would return his ring, he had the nerve to laugh in my face and tell me he wasn't paying for shit. Yeah, okay . . . in a few minutes we'll see who's laughing.

In an oversize sweat suit and with my hair pushed under the cap, I walked down to the men's locker room, knocked twice, then stepped inside. Water was running, so someone was in the shower, which meant I needed to work fast. I scrambled toward the back and moved down through the rows of lockers until I spotted Kimbel's locker. I knew it was his because I had given him the blue combination lock. I had used it for years before buying another one and given him my old one. I gave it a twirl, remembering the combination by heart; I had it opened in no time. *Sucker.* Men can be so dumb. They're always trying to get over on someone, but forget that some women are just too smart for games. I reached inside his gym bag and removed his wallet, then snatched out both the Visa and Mastercard. Each had limits I could only imagine having. After a second of hesitation, I removed his debit card as well. Last month I was driving when Kimbel had me pull up to the ATM drive-thru and gave me his PIN number (4-5-8-1) because as he said, we were engaged and there were no secrets.

As I was returning the wallet, his cell phone vibrated. I couldn't help myself. I reached down deep in his bag and removed it. Tricia popped up on the screen. I stared down at it for a moment while I tried to calm my nerves, then stuck it in my pocket along with his credit cards. I was almost to the door when I heard

someone coming. The shower had stopped and whoever was in the locker room was about to discover me
if I didn't act fast. Quickly, I slid under a small table in
the corner.

My heart was pounding like crazy. The door opened
and a dude stepped in wrapped in a towel and moved to
the locker in front of me. Damn! Now I was trapped
until he dressed and left. When he dropped his towel, I
forgot all about being trapped under a table. Everything they ever said about white boys was a lie. This
one was hung and gorgeous. I watched him slap lotion
on his body, then slip into a pair of boxer briefs that
hugged his thighs. He was gorgeous and I was enjoying the show.

"What's happening, dude?"

I almost let out a scream when the door flung open
and Kimbel stepped in. "You got it."

"You playing ball with us this weekend?" he asked.

"Nah, man. I'm going to Georgia to do some re-
cruiting, and taking this honey with me."

White boy shook his head with envy written all over
his face. "Man, I want to be like you when I grow up."

"Yo, milk does a body good." They gave each other
dap, then shared a laugh.

He-he-hell . . . Kimbel thought his ass was funny. I
guess he was taking Tricia with him. There was no
telling how long he and the skank had been seeing each
other. I sat there thinking about how long he'd been
playing me until I was tempted to slide out from under
the table and scratch his eyes out. The sexy white boy
finished getting dressed, then swung his bag over his
shoulder and left. I waited until Kimbel grabbed his
towel and headed to the shower before I climbed out

from under the table. As soon as I heard water running and him singing off-key to Jodeci's "Forever My Lady," I hurried over to his locker and took his clothes—drawers and all—and stuffed them in my bag. Next, I switched his combination lock with the one in my bag. After taking a deep breath, I pulled my hat low over my eyes and headed toward the exit just as a lanky dude stepped through the doors. I jumped back in panic and waited to get busted. Thank goodness he was too busy wiping sweat from his eyes to notice.

"Hey, whassup."

I mumbled "what's up" under my breath and hurried out to my car. I had bought myself some time by changing the lock. By the time Kimbel figured out what was going on, the deed would be done.

The second I got to Candace's, I got on the phone and, in a deep voice, paid all the wedding bills with Kimbel's debit card. Wasn't too much he could say since the bills were in both his and my name. And as far as the hotel was concerned, Kimbel had called, not me. I was laughing my ass off when my duffel bag vibrated. It took me a second to remember I had his cell phone.

First thing I did was listen to his voice mails, including the one's he saved, and got pissed off all over again. I was right. He was planning to spend the weekend with Tricia. We would have been married two weeks and already he was planning to step out on me. It took me a second to think of a plan before I decided to send her a text.

Before we spend the weekend together I need to be honest with you. I have herpes.

I hit Send and was cracking up laughing. I finally felt like I was getting even. Five minutes later, she texted back:

> What the fuck???

Then Tricia started blowing up his phone. I let it go to voice mail. As soon as his phone indicated he had a new message, I couldn't resist listening: *You sorry muthafucka . . . Lose my number!* I was having so much fun I decided to share that important bit of information with everyone he had saved in his phone. He had a lot of numbers, so it took almost thirty minutes to reach everyone, especially since messages were coming in as fast as I was sending them. The comments were hilarious. After I was done, I pulled out his credit card, ordered six dozen roses, and sent them to Kimbel at his job. Then I ordered him some of those male enhancement pills and had them delivered to his job as well. I was having too much fun. After all, he was so self-centered, why shouldn't he spend his money on himself? I then went and filled my tank with gas, bought groceries, and stopped by his bank and withdrew $500 from the ATM. As far as I was concerned, it was for pain and suffering. I went to bed that night with a smile on my face.

The next morning, I was in the bathroom at the salon when Debra came banging on the door. "Tif, Kimbel's here!"

Oh shit! I almost peed on myself trying to hurry and get off the toilet. I washed my hands and made it out the room. The second Kimbel spotted me, he moved across the floor, practically foaming at the mouth.

"You stupid bitch! Why you do that shit?"

He was making a scene and had a large audience, but I acted like I hadn't noticed.

"Do what?" I tossed the paper towel in the trash and pretended I had no idea what he was talking about.

"Don't play dumb. You know what I'm talking about."

"No, I don't, so enlighten me. Enlighten all of us what your *problem* is." Might as well include the entire salon, because as loud as he was shouting, everyone was listening. "Or would you rather I tell everybody myself?"

Kimbel glanced nervously around the room. I dared him to mention his little problem to the crowd. "I didn't think so. I have no idea why you're here, so unless you're gonna tell me, I advise you to get the hell outta here. I've got work to do."

"Tiffany, you a'ight?" Chauncey asked, as he moved over to my station mean-mugging Kimbel.

I smirked and signaled for my next client to take a seat. "I'm fine, Chauncey. Kimbel was just leaving."

My ex-fiancé backed away toward the door. If looks could kill, I'd be one dead chick. "This isn't over," he warned.

Kimbel better believe it wasn't over. Not until I said it was.

31

Candace

I'm in love. Can you believe that shit? I said I wasn't going to let another man steal my heart, but by the time Monday rolled around, I knew there was no denying my feelings.

Chauncey pulled up in front of the free clinic. I was reluctant to get out of his car. He had taken me to Wisconsin Dells for the weekend. We stayed in a cabin, rode the water rides, and had a romantic dinner for two. The entire time we left our cell phones off because we didn't want any interruptions. The weekend was about me and him. Last night while he was making love to me, Chauncey whispered in my ear the words I have been waiting for. *I love you.* By the time I told him I loved him, too, tears were streaming down my face. I never felt like this about a man before. Not even with Tyree. With Chauncey, I had let my guard down and allowed myself to love and give love and that was so scary, but I knew it was the only way; otherwise, I would never know what true love was.

"Thanks for a wonderful weekend."

"You welcome, boo." He flashed the sexy smile of his. That man did things to me.

Glancing down at my watch, I frowned. It was almost eight o'clock. Time to clock in. "I hate having to go to work today."

"Don't go. Take the day off and spend it with me. Our weekend doesn't have to come to an end."

I stared up into his beautiful gray eyes. His words were so enticing. My Aunt Brittany had taken Miasha to Indianapolis, so I had the house to myself for the next two days. I would love to tell Chauncey to drive off and we spend the rest of the day and night at my apartment; but as much as I wanted to spend every moment with this dude, I knew that was the quickest way for a man to grow bored. The chase was important in a relationship and no matter how fine he was, I could not lose sight of that. Even though I had fallen in love with Chauncey, I wanted to be with him for longer than six months or a year. I knew deep in my heart I wanted to share my life with him, hopefully as his wife. And acting too eager and desperate for a man was the quickest way to run him away.

"Yeah . . . right. Sorry, but I need my job."

He shrugged. "Just a thought." I could tell he was disappointed, but I was glad he didn't push the issue. "Then, how about I take you to dinner tonight?"

"Dinner sounds wonderful." I leaned in and he pressed his lips to mine and kissed me like I might never see him again. There was no way I was letting that happen. Not now. Not after I had waited all my life to meet a man like him. I wrapped my arms around his neck and opened my mouth, and his tongue slid inside. I met every stroke, loving the way he felt and tasted.

This was my man and I wasn't letting anything mess up what we had. I was almost tempted to tell him, to hell with work, to put that sucker in Drive, and to go back to my place, but I had time. Plenty of time. We're taking it slow, I had to remind myself. I pulled back and stared down at him. What I saw startled me. I've never seen Chauncey look that serious before.

"Tonight I need to talk to you about some heavy stuff."

My heart fluttered. "Okay." I was going to go crazy the rest of the day. *Damn, at least give me a hint.*

"You have a good day," he said before I had a chance to pry. "I've got a schedule full of pedicures for the afternoon. I'll be by around seven."

I held my breath as I thought about all those women coming in to have my man play with their feet and felt a tinge of jealousy. Memories of him doing the same to me came burning to the forefront. "You make sure you get them heifers to back the hell up, because you're taken." I tried to say it like it was a joke, but I was dead serious.

Chauncey chuckled, then signaled for me to come closer and pressed his lips to mine again. "I will. Now get inside before I peel away from the curb and take your fine ass hostage."

I laughed, then reached for my purse and climbed out the car. As soon as I shut the door, I leaned inside. "Thanks, baby."

"I'll see you tonight."

I sighed and backed away as he pulled away from the curb. He had barely made it down the street and I was already missing him. "Candace, girl, you got it bad," I mumbled under my breath.

I moved inside the building and hurried into the bathroom. If I didn't go to the bathroom now, there was no telling when I would get another chance to go before lunch. I was coming out the stall when I ran into Coco. Damn. She's my girl and all, but she was going to want to ask a lot of questions about Chauncey and I was late enough as it was.

"Hey, girlfriend. You just getting here?" she said with a curious smile.

I nodded and put my purse down on the counter while I washed my hands. "Yeah, I had a little trouble getting out of bed this morning." I was smiling so hard my face hurt. Coco didn't miss a beat.

"I know that's right. If my man was as fine as yours, I wouldn't have gotten out the bed either. I saw him at the picnic. Gurrrlll, where in the world did you find him?" she teased.

I so wanted to tell her about when we first met and how good Chauncey treated me. I've known Coco since I started working at the clinic. We've hung out a few times, and she had always been someone I could talk to about my problems with Miasha's deadbeat daddy. But I knew the moment I opened my mouth and got to talking, I wouldn't be able to stop and my ass would really be late. The last thing I needed was for my boss to be trying to write me up. All I could do was suck my teeth and say, "I didn't find him. He found me." There was so much excitement in my voice. I just couldn't deny how I felt.

Coco leaned against the wall and gazed at my reflection in the mirror. "I'm really happy for you, Candace. You deserve to be happy."

"Thanks. I'll talk to you later. If you want, we can go to lunch." She worked in the WIC office across the hall, but we both had lunch at the same time.

"That sounds like a plan."

I reached for a paper towel and dried my hands. Coco was still standing there and I could tell she wanted to say something. "What's wrong?" I asked.

Coco leaned in closer and whispered, "I don't know what you did to Gloria, but she was hating on you. I heard her in the bathroom whispering about you to this bald-headed chick this morning. As soon as she saw me, she shut up."

I rolled my eyes. "Probably because I'm late."

She shook her head. "No, I think it's more than that. You might wanna watch your back with that one."

I learned a long time ago, Gloria wasn't someone to be trusted. I looked down at my watch. "Thanks for the warning. I better get in there." I grabbed my purse and hurried down the hall and entered the clinic. The second I walked in, I saw Gloria, who was on the phone, drop her head, whisper something, then hang up. The lobby was already filled with folks coming in for birth control and whatever else. I went to the back and felt like everybody was looking at me. Damn, I know I'm late, but it ain't like none of them haven't ever been a few minutes late before.

One of the nurses was sitting in the break room when I went to clock in. She smiled, then went back to reading her book. I reached for my time card, clocked in, and moved to the front desk. Gloria was whispering with Claudette, our medical coder. Jealous asses. *They're just mad because their men ain't nowhere near as fine as mine.*

Claudette struck a pose and smiled my way. "Hey, Candace. You must have left the picnic early because I came looking for you."

No, the person she was looking for was Chauncey. "We had other plans."

Gloria looked at Claudette, then started smiling. "Where did you say you met him again?"

"I didn't." I rolled my eyes and headed to my desk. I would be damned if I told that skank where he worked because I guarantee you before the day was out, she would have scheduled an appointment to get her feet done. Evidently, she was single again; otherwise, she would be sweating me and mine. As soon as I slipped my purse under the desk, I checked in the next patient, then logged in to the computer.

Brenda came up front to get the next patient's file. She glanced nervously over her shoulder, then whispered to me, "Sylvia wants to see you in her office right away, but you might wanna check your e-mails first." She then called back the next patient to see the doctor.

I gave her a puzzled look, then opened Microsoft Outlook and scrolled through my e-mail, looking to see what was so important. I noticed an office-wide e-mail that had been sent out this morning from a Tameka Dash. The name wasn't familiar, but since it was sent to the entire office I figured it had to be important. I clicked on the link and read the subject line: Do you know this man? She definitely had my attention. I clicked on the hyperlink below and was navigated to a different Web page. What appeared on the screen caused me to gasp. *Hell no!* There was no way. It had to be some kind of mistake. But sure enough, there he was. Chauncey. Several years younger, but still just as fine, even on the Internet. As much as I wanted to think it was some kind of joke, there was no denying the proof that was right in front of me on a legitimate Illinois government Web site.

Chauncey was a registered sex offender.

32

Chauncey

Smiling, I rose and went to retrieve a towel and caught a glimpse of someone coming through the door and cringed.

"Hey, Chauncey! I'm your ten-o'clock appointment."

"Whassup, Octavia! Go ahead and have a seat in the second chair. I'll be right with you." I smiled and waited until my back was turned before I groaned. Octavia weighed a good three hundred pounds and came in every two weeks for a pedicure. She was a loyal customer with a beautiful personality. The problem was her feet had a smell that no amount of soaking could cure. Even with gloves on my hands, that scent somehow found its way onto my skin and I could still smell it lingering in the air even hours after she was gone. I wonder how long I could hold my breath today? Damn! I guess there was a flip side to all jobs. There was no getting around it. I would just have to cuddle up close under my girl this evening. That smell would be the last thing on my mind. Candace had a natural scent I couldn't get enough of.

Tonight, I planned to tell Candace something she had a right to know about me. I had tried several times over the weekend, but things had been just too damn perfect to ruin the mood. But I couldn't wait any longer. I was ready for us to take our relationship to the next level, but if we were ever going to have a real chance together, I had to first keep it real.

I swung around and was heading to take a seat in front of Octavia's smelly feet, when I spotted Candace walking into the shop. I stopped and grinned, only she didn't return the smile. Instead, she gave me an evil look and moved in my direction.

"Hey, Candy," Tiffany called out, but Candace dismissed her with an open palm, not once taking her eyes off of me.

My smile fell from my lips. I didn't like her body language at all. She moved like a female on a mission.

"Hey, baby," I said, hoping it would soften her mood. Only it didn't work. When she stopped in front of me, her eyes were practically bulging out her head.

"Are you a . . . a registered sex offender?"

She might as well have punched me in the chest, because that's how I suddenly felt. Someone had gotten to her. "I, uhhhh . . . Who told you that?"

"Answer the got damn question!" she screamed. I kid you not, the entire salon went on pause. Not even a hair dryer was humming. Someone had even turned off the radio.

"Baby, can we talk about this in private." I was practically pleading with her. Everyone was looking at us and I was busted not only with my girl, but in front of my coworkers as well.

Candy's teeth clenched. Her fists were balled at her sides. "Answer me, dammit!"

It was clear she had no intention of keeping this situation private. Okay . . . here goes nothing. "Yes, baby, I am. But it's not what you t—" Before I even had a chance to explain, she punched me in the mouth. And it wasn't a bitch slap either. She hit me the way a dude would have, and if it had been a dude, right now, he'd been fighting for his life.

She backed away and it hurt me more to see the look of pain on her face than the throbbing at my bottom lip. "I can't believe this shit. When were you gonna tell me?"

"Candace, please . . . I was gonna tell you. I was just waiting for the right time."

"Really? And exactly what were you planning to tell me? That I was screwing a convicted rapist!" Her tone was confrontational. I couldn't believe this was happening. When she said convicted rapist it made me sound like I was dangerous . . . someone who had done something unforgivable. Only I wasn't that person. She should know that. We spent hours, days, weeks, months getting to know each other. All the time we been together, had that meant nothing to her?

"Baby, it was a mistake. You gotta believe me." I was doing something I had never done before, begging, yet I didn't care.

"You promised to keep it real with me." She looked so angry I didn't know what to say, because nothing would be the right answer. If only I could go back a week or even just the weekend. If only I had been honest with her in the beginning, then none of this would be happening. "Why didn't you tell me?" she demanded.

"Yeah, why didn't you?" mumbled some twig sitting to my right.

I ignored the questions and shook my head. There was nothing I could say to make this right. Not with all the women in the room shaking their heads and making *tsk* sounds with their lips. Tongues were gonna be wagging tonight. Octavia even gave me a nasty look before she reached for her shoes and slipped them back on her feet. She just didn't know it, but she was actually doing me a favor.

"I didn't know how to tell you. I was afraid that if you knew before you had a chance to get to know me, you wouldn't have given me a chance."

Now her head started moving as her neck twisted and her hands flew to her hips. "So you decided to lie to me instead and pretend you were something you weren't. I deserved to know the truth!"

"If I told you, would you have still gone out with me?"

Her silence told me everything I needed to know. She gave me a look of disgust, then turned on her heels and stormed across the salon and out the door. As soon as the door closed it was like someone had put the needle back down on the record, because everyone was talking at the same time. The only good thing that came out of the situation was Octavia had gotten up and left.

I glanced over at Tiffany and as soon as our eyes met, she gave me a look that said she was disappointed. She wasn't the only one. I was mad at myself because I loved Candace with everything I had. I saw a future with her that I thought would have lasted a long time. If things had continued to be good between us, before the year was out, I had planned to make her my wife. Now the only thing she wanted was for me to bend over so she could kick me in my ass.

I cleaned up my area and tried to figure out who ratted me out. *Don't let me find out who ran their mouth,* because when I do, they were going to have hell to pay for ruining my relationship with my girl. Was it Tameka? Maybe she had gotten to Candace. I stood there draining the foot tub and thought about banging on Tameka's door and demanding to know why she told. But I didn't have anyone to blame but myself. I should have been honest with Candace in the first place. Keeping secrets had lost me the best thing to have ever happened to me.

33

Candace

Today had not been my day. Before I could get out the office to find a gun and shoot Chauncey's ass, my boss called me into her office. Don't you know that bitch had the nerve to fire me? Not only because of the office-wide e-mail that was sent out, but because Kimbel had filed a complaint and threatened to sue the clinic. That herpes-infected bastard had told on me. I couldn't be mad at Sylvia, because she was right. There is this thing called the Privacy Act, and I had shared personal information with Tiffany. But truth be told, if I had a chance to do it over, I wouldn't have changed a thing, except telling my girl about her man sooner.

Sylvia ordered Brenda to watch me while I packed my stuff, like I was gonna try and steal patient files. I grabbed my things and held my head high as I strolled out the building. I didn't start crying until I reached the bus stop. It was one thing to lose my job for something I was guilty of, but it was an altogether other thing to find out the man I loved had been convicted of rape. I was a block away from the apartment before I got off the bus, hopped on another, and headed to the salon. I needed to see Chauncey, hoping that what I had found out wasn't true. Only it was. Even after he was busted, he still hadn't wanted to tell me the truth. And that hurt like hell.

I left and caught the bus back home. During the ride, I had to struggle to remain calm. I couldn't believe Chauncey had tried to make a fool of me when all this time his ass was a got damn rapist. He'd had sex with an underage girl. How in the world could I have been that stupid, letting a perfect stranger around my daughter? There was no telling what had been running through his sick mind. How many times had he told me how pretty Miasha was? I was so close to crying again, I was glad when the bus got within a block of my neighborhood. The driver couldn't open the doors fast enough. The moment he came to a complete stop, I jumped out my seat and hustled down the street. I had a feeling that after I stormed out the salon, Chauncey was going to head to my place.

I hurried up to my apartment. Usually I stopped first to get my mail, but not today. I didn't have time to waste. I opened my door, locked it behind me, and went to my bedroom to get comfortable. And to think I had just bought a brand-new suit last week. You better believe I was taking that sucker back tomorrow, because without a job, I needed every dime I could get. I shrugged out the peach suit and chocolate heels, and put on white capris and a blue shirt, then went into the living room and flopped down on the couch.

Now what was I going to do? I could barely pay my bills as it was, and now things would only get worse for me. I sat there feeling sorry for myself and contemplating my next move but didn't have long to think before I heard a knock at the door.

"Who is it?" I yelled.

"Yo, Candace, it's me. We need to talk."

I got up from the couch, walked over to the door, and shouted, "Go away before I call the police. I'm sure they'll love to hear that a registered sex offender is banging at my door!"

"Candy, would you please open the door so I can explain," he begged.

"There's nothing to talk about." Ignoring him, I moved into the kitchen, but Chauncey started knocking and shouting my name. I figured if I ignored him long enough he would take his ass home. Unfortunately for me, all my neighbors were at work, so there was no one around to call the police. Finally, it got quiet. *Did he leave?* Part of me was disappointed that Chauncey was leaving already, while the rest of me was glad he was walking out my life once and for all. I moved over to the window and looked down, waiting to see him walk away from the building and onto the sidewalk, but before he appeared, my phone rang. I waited until the third ring before I reached for it. "Hello?"

"Candy . . . open the door so we can talk."

"Talk?" I paused long enough to move to the door. When I glanced through the peephole, Chauncey was standing on the other side. He had on my favorite pair of shorts and looked so good leaning against the wall with a Bluetooth on his ear. I hated myself for still wanting him. "We have nothing to talk about."

"I called your job and Gloria told me you were fired."

Ooh, that bitch had a big mouth! "I got fired because of you. Someone sent the link to the sex offender's Web site to my entire office. Do you know how embarrassing it is to find out my man was convicted of rape?" I hated myself because now I was crying. The last thing I wanted was for this bastard to know how much he hurt me. "I trusted you. We promised to keep it real with each other and you didn't do that. You lied to me."

"I know and I'm sorry. I should have told you."

"Yes, you should have." I dried my eyes and cleared my throat. There was no way I was falling apart, at least not until he had gone down the street somewhere. "But it's too late now." I hung up the phone. Did he really think I was going to forgive him? I guess he did because Chauncey started banging on the door until finally I yanked it open. Don't you know he had the nerve to smile?

"Baby, let's go grab a bite to eat and talk."

"What the hell could we possibly have to talk about? I don't know you. All this time I've been with a man that I obviously know nothing about."

"I'm still the same person you fell in love with."

"Who said I'm in love?"

"You did."

It took everything I had to hold the tears back. "I lied. I was caught up in the moment, but I'm definitely not in love. So you listen carefully to what I am about to say 'cause I ain't gonna say it again. It's over between us, and if you bother me again, I'm calling the police."

I guess he finally realized I was serious, because Chauncey's shoulders dropped in defeat. "Yeah . . . a'ight." He then turned and walked away.

After I closed the door I rushed back to my bedroom and cried my eyes out.

34

Noelle

Shopping at the mall with an infant was no easy task. Thank God for strollers. I was on a mission and I needed Sierra with me to pull it off effectively. Luckily, she was wide awake and enjoying the ride. Whitney dipped off into a maternity store while I headed to the other end of River Oaks Mall to JCPenney. I didn't tell my best friend the reason for our sudden trip to the mall or what I was about to do because I didn't want her trying to change my mind, or even worse, instigating the situation.

I headed over to the women's department and searched the aisle looking for Gina. I had spent the week snooping around Scott's bedroom and last night I found her phone number tucked inside his Algebra notebook. The little girl who answered the phone told me where Gina worked. One call this morning and I was able to confirm not only the department, but that she came in at one o'clock.

I searched the entire section of the store and was

about to ask a sales associate for assistance when I spotted Gina over near the swimsuits. She was a little heavier than I remembered, yet still wore thick glasses and her hair up in a ponytail.

"Hey, Gina," I said, and pulled the stroller up beside her.

She looked at me like a deer in headlights before a slow smile curled her lips. "Hello. Mrs. Gordon, right?"

I nodded. "That's right. How have you been?"

Her eyes traveled down toward the stroller, where they lingered for several moments before she met my eyes again. "I've been good. Can't complain."

I looked down at Sierra and smiled. "This is Scott's daughter, Sierra."

"Really?" Her eyes traveled nervously to her left and right.

"Yes, she is." I gave her a hard look. And as shy as she was, her eyes dropped to the string bikini in her hand.

"How is Scott doing?" I didn't miss the bitterness in her voice.

"He's doing okay, considering the excitement of discovering he's a father. Someone came over and left this little girl on my porch."

Her brow rose from beneath her glasses. "Really?" She still refused to look me directly in the eyes, but then she never could before. It was hard to tell if she was hiding something or just plain shy.

"I heard you had a baby, too."

In a blink of the eye I swore she practically jumped out of her skin. Her bottom lip quivered. "Who told you that?"

"To be honest, I saw you in the mall several months

ago." By the way she was acting, it was the only way to get her to realize I knew the truth.

"Oh . . . yeah, I did. Well, nice talking to you, but I've gotta get back to work." She then turned and walked over to the next rack.

No she didn't just dismiss me. I followed her.

"What did you have? A boy or girl?"

There was a long pause. "A girl."

I leaned against the stroller. "A girl? Wow. I would love to see a picture."

For the first time, her gaze hardened. "I don't have any with me."

"That's too bad. I figure her to be about Sierra's age."

Gina's lower lip quivered again, and she reached up and wiped the corner of her eye. Was she crying? "Yeah, she's only a couple of months old." She turned her back to me and pretended to be working.

"Are you and the father still together?"

She swung around. "No, I'm not. Listen . . . I really need to get back to work."

"Okay, okay . . . Gina, I'm going to be honest. The reason why I am here is because I wanted to know if you are Sierra's mama?"

"Me?" She looked from me to the baby and looked dumbfounded.

"You *did* have a little girl."

"Yes, but after her father refused to claim her, I gave her up for adoption." Her voice cracked.

"I'm sorry." I hated to ask the next question, but I had to. "Scott wasn't the father, was he?" I tried to be as gentle as I could, but I had to know.

"What?" She started laughing. "No way. How should I put this . . . I wasn't Scott's type."

By looking at that mustache she was growing over her top lip, that much was a given. "True, I will agree with that, but that doesn't mean, well, you know . . ."

"Oh, I know quite well what you mean. You wanna know if we slept together? Yes, we slept together. Your son made me think he really liked me and that we had a chance of being together. But all he was doing was using me so I could help him keep from flunking math."

It was my son who treated her bad, yet I was the one who felt ashamed. "I'm sorry."

"So am I. What was the worse was that instead of just telling me it was over, he decided to rub his new relationship in my face."

"I hate to say this, but he dates a lot of girls."

"Girls?" she barked. "When I said I wasn't his type, I meant he likes older, mature women who have the financial means to take care of him. He rarely ever dated anyone his age for long. Serious, what high-school student could buy him a car?"

The more she talked the more I listened, and what she said made perfectly good sense. How come I never thought about that before? The clothes, money, expensive gifts, and the car, a high-school student couldn't have done those things unless she had money.

"Scott hurt me, but part of it was my fault. I shouldn't have followed him to that motel, but I had to know who it was he was seeing. I sat in the parking lot and waited ten minutes after he had gone inside the room before I found the guts to get out the car and go knock on the door. Only he didn't answer the door. Some cougar did."

"Cougar?"

She gave an impatient sigh. "Older women who

like younger men. She was standing there in this skimpy negligee and all I could do was think how beautiful she was. At that moment, I knew I never had a chance with your son. Scott moved over to the door in his boxers, grinning and apologizing at the same time. Then he lowered his head and stuck his tongue down that woman's throat. All I could do was walk away." She wiped her eyes and sniffled a few times.

"What did this female look like?"

Something behind me caught Gina's eye, then she frowned and pointed. "She looks just like that woman coming this way."

I snapped my head around and spotted Whitney walking toward me.

"Hey, I've been looking all over the . . ." her voice trailed off the second she spotted Gina standing next to me.

Anger boiled inside and I had to stop and take several deep breaths just so I could get the words out. "Please . . . tell me she's lying . . . about you sleeping . . . with Scott."

Whitney just stood there looking from me to Gina. When I was about to repeat the question, she finally sucked her teeth and spoke.

"Yes, and I'm carrying his baby."

35

Tiffany

"Make a right at the corner."

Candace had scooped me up for lunch and asked where Kimbel worked so she could run by his job and cuss his ass out. I felt guilty as hell for even mentioning the dude had herpes. If I had kept my mouth closed and hadn't tried to confront him at the strip club, maybe none of this would have happened.

"Candace, I am so sorry." And I was. "I had to confront Kimbel about his little issue, but the last thing I wanted was for you to lose your job because of me."

"It ain't your fault," she said, and I signaled for her to make a left at the next corner. "Hell, I would have done the same thing if I was you. Besides, I think everybody receiving that office-wide e-mail was what really did it."

I still couldn't believe Chauncey was a registered sex offender. He didn't at all seem the type. But then again, what should one look like?

We were just pulling up in front of the university's

athletic department when I saw Kimbel coming out of the building. "Candace, look, there he is."

She slowed the car to a crawl and waited to see which direction he was heading. Kimbel crossed the street and hopped into a candy apple red BMW.

"Who's that?" Candace asked.

I shrugged. "I don't know." But I was ready to find out. "Follow his ass."

As soon as the car took off, Candace pulled a few yards behind them. I know it sounds crazy to be stalking this dude, but we were on a mission. Candace had lost her job and her health benefits because of Kimbel, and I was willing to do whatever it took for her to feel vindicated. I tried not to think about who could be driving that car. It had to be a female, considering the car was definitely feminine. It also meant he had found him someone else.

"I hope it's not that chick I called over the phone."

"I doubt that anyone would be that stupid. I guarantee you it's someone else."

It was lunchtime and they pulled into Applebee's parking lot. A light-brown woman with long black hair climbed out the car. I ain't gonna hate; she was gorgeous and she looked at Kimbel like he was her knight in shining armor.

"Who's that?" Candace asked. She was starting to sound like a broken record. The last thing I wanted was to think about Kimbel being with another woman.

"I said I didn't know." I didn't mean to snap, but the fact he felt no remorse, hadn't tried once to call and beg me to take his ass back hurt. *Did I ever mean anything to him?* As far as I was concerned, he had no business getting on with his life that quickly because I still hadn't.

Candace parked the car and we sat there watching them go inside.

"You hungry?"

She was already opening the door. "Yep, you ain't said nothing but the word."

We walked in just at the hostess escorted the happy couple to a table to the far left. Kimbel sat down so that his back was to the door.

"Welcome, where would you like to sit?" she asked us when she returned to her podium.

"Over near the window." I wanted to be close but not too close. I didn't want Kimbel to know we were there until I was ready for him to know. I slid onto the booth so I wasn't facing them. "What are they doing?"

"Girl, she all up in his grill, smiling like he's the shit."

I tried to act like it didn't matter and reached for my menu and focused on deciding what I was eating for lunch.

"Ooh! Tiffany! She just got up and went to the bathroom."

"It's showtime," I mumbled, then finger-combed my hair. While Candace moved over to Kimbel's table to give him a piece of her mind, I went into the bathroom. Ms. Beauty Queen was at the sink washing her hands. I washed mine and glanced up into the mirror until I made eye contact. "That is a pretty shirt you're wearing."

She smiled down at her breasts. "Thank you. My boyfriend bought it for me."

I guess so since he bought me one just like it. "Your boyfriend? You wouldn't by chance be here with that guy in the black suit?"

"Yeah, as a matter of fact I am." She rolled her neck and had the nerve to have attitude.

I planned on taking it easy on her, but since she wanted to act all nasty about it. "You know Kimbel got herpes, right?"

Her jaw dropped. "What?"

"Don't let the smooth taste fool you. He plans to infect everyone he can. So just make sure you use a condom. See ya!" I turned and left her standing there. When I got back to the table, Kimbel and Candace were going at it. The manager was trying to quiet them down.

"Look, I'm out as soon as my date gets back," he reassured her, then gave an angry look when he saw me move up beside Candace.

Smiling, I brought a hand to my waist. "Your date? Isn't that her peeling out the parking lot?" Sure enough she was burning rubber. "I wonder why?" I then swung around and addressed the customers. "Hey everybody! We got herpes in the house!"

Candace took my hand and we raced out the restaurant, laughing our asses off.

36

Chauncey

"Dad invited Tommy and I over for dinner Friday night."

I looked over at my sister's smiling face. I wanted so badly to be happy for Linda, but it was hard when my own life had fallen apart.

Ever since Candace stormed down to the salon and called me a liar and a rapist, I had been trying to do everything that I could to get her to listen to me. But so far nothing seemed to be working. She wouldn't take my calls and when I appeared on her doorstep two evenings in a row unannounced, she refused to come to the door. I would have stood out there all night if her neighbor across the hall hadn't threatened to call the police. That was one thing I didn't need. Tiffany told me Candace had gotten fired from her job. I felt so bad. She reassured me that her boss finding out she was dating a registered sex offender was only a small part of it. Something else had triggered her termination. I wanted to be there to comfort her and listen to what was on her mind. It bothered me that I couldn't.

"Good for you. I guess that means Dad's okay with you dating a white man."

She nodded, "I think so. He always said don't bring no white man to this house; but the other night, Daddy told me after almost losing his son, he doesn't want to risk losing his daughter as well."

"I'm happy for you." My father and I had been talking off and on, but after losing Candace, I wasn't in the mood for conversating. I know he was trying to reach out to me and I needed to give the man a chance since it wasn't completely his fault; but right now having Candace back in my life was more important.

As soon as I left from having dinner with my sister, I drove over to the salon. It was almost nine, so I knew Tiffany was still there doing hair trying to make that money. Sure enough her car was in the parking lot. I pulled in beside hers and waited for her to come out. I pulled out a cigarette, something I hadn't done in months, lit it, and smoked three by the time Tiffany came out the building.

"Hey, Chauncey," she said, and looked glad to see me.

"Whassup?"

"Noelle ain't here."

After that outburst in the salon, Noelle had insisted I take some time off for an undetermined amount of time. "I didn't come to see her. I came to see you."

Tiffany unlocked her car and stuck her purse inside, then moved around and leaned on the hood. "Everybody's been asking about you."

"Noelle, still mad?"

She shrugged. "You know it's hard to read her at

times. She'll get over it. One thing I can say about her is she's fair."

That was yet to be seen, but I didn't say that. "How's Candace?"

"Miserable. Mad. Depressed."

"I know how she feels." I took another puff. "Listen . . . I need you to help me out."

Tiffany immediately started shaking her head. "I don't know. She's pretty mad right now. Maybe you should wait a couple of weeks." She looked nervous as she spoke.

"I can't." As far as I was concerned, I had waited long enough.

"Chauncey, she feels betrayed." She paused and gave me a weird look. "By the way . . . who's Tameka?"

A nerve at my jaw twitched. "My worst nightmare apparently. Why you ask that?"

"Because she's the one who sent her the e-mail."

I knew that scandalous chick was somehow involved. I guess that string-bean chick who worked with Candace had gone back and told Tameka she had seen me at the company picnic.

I dropped the cigarette butt on the ground and smashed it with my shoe. The entire situation had gotten way outta hand. "Serious, Tiffany, I need your help. All I need is for Candace to just listen to what I got to say."

She didn't look so sure. "You should have been honest."

"I know and I regret that I wasn't, but it's not at all the way it sounds." I knew I sounded desperate, but at this point what did I have to lose?

Tiffany glared at me with her arms crossed. "Okay . . . so make me a believer."

I took a deep breath, rocked back on the heels of my fresh white sneakers, and tried to explain. I knew if Tiffany didn't believe me, then neither would Candace.

"I didn't know she was sixteen until after I slept with her. I swear. She told me she was twenty-one and she looked every bit old enough to know better. I didn't find out the truth until it was too late. By then the police was waiting for me and her father was pressing charges."

"What did the chick have to say about that?" Tiffany asked, and I could tell she really wanted to believe I was telling the truth.

"She was so scared of her father, she cried rape. The rest is history," I said, and shrugged. My word was all I had left in the world.

She shook her head. "Damn, Chauncey."

"Tell me about it." Six years later, that night still burned in my head. I could still hear her screaming and crying and pretending I had forced myself on her. Even her friends who had left her alone at the club tried to act like I had kidnapped her. The second I stepped into the courtroom with a public defender, I knew I hadn't a chance in hell.

I leaned against the door of her car and told Tiffany everything. It was so easy talking to her. I don't know why I hadn't done the same with Candace, especially since we had spent so many evenings talking about everything. She knew about my relationship with my father and that my mother and I hadn't spoken in years, yet I hadn't the guts to tell her about being locked up.

When my phone rang, Tiffany looked at her watch, then slid off the hood. "I better go. I'll try talking to Candace, but I'ma warn you . . . she isn't the most forgiving person I know."

I pretty much figured that part out. "I appreciate any help I can get."

I watched her drive off, then looked down at my phone and frowned. It was time to handle that situation once and for all.

"It was you, wasn't it?"

Tameka answered the door in a skimpy green robe as if she had known I was coming over. "What are you talking about?" she said, and had the nerve to bat her eyes innocently.

I climbed her stairs and mean-mugged her ass. "Don't play dumb! Your girl, Gloria . . . you told her about me and she went back and ran her mouth."

She tried to fake like she was shocked and even cupped her mouth with her palm. "For real! Yeah, I told Gloria, but I never thought she would go back and say something to your girl." She was really trying to play the innocent role, but I had something for her ass.

"Yeah right. You knew exactly what was going to happen. She lost her job because of you."

Tameka gave me a silly smirk. "That's not what I heard."

"Oh, so you know more than you want to admit?"

She shrugged. "Gloria told me what happened. I bet Candace went off on you." Her eyes were sparkling with laughter.

"It's over," I mumbled.

"That's too bad," she said, then started smiling. "Why don't you come in so we can talk in private?"

I shook my head. I just couldn't figure out what would make this chick think I would still be interested in her. "Tameka, I don't have shit else to say to you."

"Chauncey, I can see that you're hurting, but I got something for that." She then loosened the belt on her robe and it gaped open. I stared down at her beautifully toned body in nothing more than a mint green bra and panties. Tameka was an aerobics instructor and had the abs and legs to prove it.

It took everything I had to turn and look away. "There is nothing you got that I want."

"Quit lying to yourself," she spat with a laugh. "I'm everything you could ever want and more. You might as well face it, with all the bad publicity sex offenders have been getting in the media in the last year, women just don't want to take the chance of coming up dead and buried in somebody's backyard. Me, on the other hand . . . I love a challenge," she purred.

"Whatever. Look . . . I don't want you no more. The thought of being with you makes me sick to my stomach. So do me a favor and leave me the hell alone." I gave her a dismissive wave and turned away.

"Don't turn your back on me! I already told you you would regret messing with me. Revenge can be so sweet." She started laughing hysterically. "When you change your mind, I'll be waiting."

I glared over my shoulder. "Get a life and stay out of mine."

Tameka struck a pose in the doorway. That crazy chick didn't give a damn who saw her half dressed. "Chauncey, I already told you, it ain't over until I say it's over."

"It's over." I was walking toward my car when I noticed the tow truck pulling out her neighbor's driveway. *Right on time.* "Yo!" I said and swung around. "Speaking of revenge . . . are you still hiding your Lexus in your neighbor's garage so the repo man doesn't find it?"

She gave me a suspicious look. "Yeah, why?"

"After that shit you did with my girl, I called Wholesale Connection and told them where they could find it." I pointed toward the tow truck as it drove past the house with her S300 on back. Tameka had been hiding that vehicle for over eight months. "Revenge can be so sweet."

"She's never taking you back!" she screamed after me.

For the first time in days, I smiled. "We'll see about that."

37

Noelle

I sat behind my desk going over the monthly expenses and couldn't help but grin. Although the economy was bad, Situations was continuing to make a profit. Not too many independent businesses could say that these days. In no way was I taking my good fortune for granted. I was definitely blessed for someone whose life was a mess.

"Can I come in?"

My head snapped up and I had to do a double take. *No she didn't bring her ass in my salon.*

"I don't have anything else to say to you." We both knew the only reason why I hadn't jumped across the desk and snatched them braids out her head was because she was pregnant.

"Fine, don't talk, just listen."

I cut my eyes at her. Whitney was trying to look scared and confused, but I wasn't buying that shit for a second. There was nothing naïve about her decisions.

She knew what she had been doing and played my ass in the process.

It had been a week since I found out my best friend seduced my son. The only thing that stopped me from whooping her ass was that baby growing inside her stomach. For twenty years, twenty long years, I had loved Whitney like a sister, and yet she stabbed me in my back.

Fine, she wanted to talk, then let's talk. "If you want to tell me anything, then tell me why? How could you seduce your godson?"

She gave me this solemn expression that made her look more pathetic than she really was. "It wasn't like that. If anything, Scott seduced me. He's been hitting on me for years. It's just that he finally got to me and I couldn't resist."

"I guess next you're going to tell me that the two of you fell in love?"

She paused and I could tell she was trying to choose her words carefully. "I've always loved Scott like he was a son. It wasn't until he started coming on to me that I noticed that he was a man, and a handsome one at that; but even then I was able to resist his advances. But after Landon and I split up and I was hurting, Scott came by to see me and when I told him about it, he comforted me, and one thing led to another and before I realized what was happening, we were seriously involved."

I glared across the desk, wanting desperately to claw her eyes out. "You just don't know how sick that shit sounds. I can do the math, and Scott wasn't even eighteen yet. You're nothing more than a pedophile!"

Grant had called last night and after talking nonstop about his job, I told him about Whitney and Scott. I didn't at all get the reaction I expected. It's amazing how if a man sleeps with a teenage girl, it's rape; but if a teenager sleeps with a grown woman, it symbolizes he's a man.

She held up her hands in surrender. "Noelle, I'm sorry that you see me that way, but I didn't initiate the relationship, he did, and once I was in it, I couldn't walk away from it."

Whitney is a prime example of a woman with low self-esteem. How else could she have allowed herself to be seduced by Scott? I'm clearly aware of my son's charm with women, but you would think a grown-ass woman with money and looks would be mature and confident enough to know game when it was being fed to her.

"All Scott did was use you." It wasn't a question, it was a fact. I knew how my son thinks. If I didn't give it to him, then he went and found someone else who would get it for him.

Whitney nodded in agreement, and if it had been anybody else's son but mine, I might have felt sorry for her. "You're right. To him I was an older woman, and after I bought him anything he wanted and made sure he never went without, he got tired of me."

I started laughing angrily at how ridiculous this whole situation was. "Scott has sex with anything wearing a skirt. How could you have been so weak?"

She shrugged. "I was lonely and Scott happened to be there when I was most vulnerable. I guess I confused my love for him as something else."

What else was new? In the years we've known each other, Whitney had been in love more times than I could count. She'd been engaged at least five times, and she believed every man who told her he loved her.

It was a vicious cycle with her. Was she ever going to learn she has to love herself first if she expected to be loved by someone else?

"I will never forgive you for sleeping with my son. There are some things we do and others we don't. You were my best friend, but you betrayed my trust."

"Noelle, I can't begin to tell you how sorry I am. I made a mistake. I'll give you some time to think—"

I held up a hand, cutting her off. "There's nothing to think about." I had already written her off like a bad debt. The only person I needed to discuss this situation with was Scott, but apparently Whitney got to him before I did because he refused to answer his phone when I called and all my messages have gone unanswered. I even texted the knucklehead the way he instructed and got no response. "Please, get the hell outta my office and don't come back."

She just didn't know when to give up. "Noelle . . . I hope in time you find it in your heart to forgive me." Tears were running down her face and her bottom lip quivered, but I was unmoved by both.

Was she stupid or what? Did she really think I would ever have anything else to do with her again?

Whitney started toward the door, then stopped and held on to her stomach.

I immediately became concerned. "What's wrong?" I wanted so badly not to care about her, but I wasn't made that way.

"I-I'm not sure. I've got a sharp pain here. Ouch!" She buckled over and used the wall to support her weight. "It really, really hurts!"

I rose and came around the desk and immediately noticed the blood trickling down her leg onto her white sandals. Whitney must have felt something warm because she looked down, saw the blood, and screamed. I caught her just before she hit the floor. Tiffany came rushing into my office.

"Is everything okay?" she asked.

"Call an ambulance!"

It felt like forever before they finally arrived. Blood was everywhere and, for a while I thought she might have lost consciousness. I rode in the ambulance with Whitney and held her hand while she screamed and cried all the way there. Her relationship with my son was the furthest from my mind. Despite how she betrayed me and my trust, I would never want anything bad to happen to her. If she died, I would be losing a piece of my life.

By the time we got to South Shore Hospital, the doctor was waiting and Whitney was hurried quickly into a room and examined. "Whitney, it looks like you're about to have a baby." The doctor forced a smile, but I could see the concern in his eyes.

"No, it's too soon!" she cried. "You can't take my baby yet."

She was right. The baby was barely seven months.

He shook his head. "I'm sorry, but we don't have a choice."

The nurses started rushing around getting the room ready for delivery. There was still blood and Whitney was screaming. I was ready to fall apart myself, but I couldn't do that. She needed me to be strong.

"Whitney, honey, you got to hang in there for your baby. Everything is going to be just fine," I said soothingly.

"No, it isn't!" she screamed. "Something is wrong with my baby. God is punishing me!" She was sobbing and becoming hysterical.

The nurse gave me a concerned look. "She has to calm down; otherwise, we're going to have to put her to sleep."

I turned to Whitney and took her arms firmly in my hands. "Whitney! Calm your ass down! Otherwise, they're going to cut your stomach open and take the baby and you're gonna have that ugly-ass scar like your sister Vicky for the rest of your life."

That got her attention.

Whitney sat up on the bed and her crying calmed somewhat. As vain as Whitney was about stretch marks, I knew that as far as she was concerned, having a cesarean section was worse than losing a limb. The nurse got the bed disassembled and the stirrups in place just as Whitney was hit with the next contraction. I held her hand and since I was supposed to have been her Lamaze partner, I showed her how to breathe. This went on for hours, with her squeezing my hand and pushing on the doctor's cue. And shortly after 9 PM, she gave birth to a four-pound eleven-ounce little boy. I was crying and laughing at the same time. He was so little, but he was perfect.

"Noelle, how many toes does he have?" Whitney asked as the nurse carried him over to the warmer. I didn't miss the desperation in her voice and tried to get as close as I could, but they were working fast to get his vital signs, and then they raced out the room with him and down to the neonatal intensive care unit. Whitney's eyes were closed and she was breathing heavily with exhaustion. "Noelle, is he okay?"

I watched as the nurses left the room, then moved over beside her bed and mopped her damp forehead. "Whitney, he's perfect. Five fingers, toes, and eyes to die for."

"That's . . . good. I wanna name him . . . Michael."

Her hand went limp and the machine next to her started beeping. I called Whitney's name, but there was no response. Then nurses came racing back into her room and told me to get out the way. I stepped outside just as another young nurse rushed in pushing a crash cart.

38

Tiffany

I parked at the corner, waiting for Kimbel to come out of his house. Can you believe that fool turned my cell phone off? Hell, it was his idea for me to give up my old wireless subscription and move to his plan, yet last night I tried to use my phone and it was dead.

Well, I'll show his ass.

At seven-thirty, Kimbel stepped out of his house in his black suit and tie. As usual, he looked luscious. He always had and to me he probably always would. Unfortunately, he played with my emotions and took my kindness for weakness. And I'm learning that everything that looks good doesn't mean it is good for you.

As Kimbel rounded his Jaguar to the driver's side, I held my breath and next thing I knew, he slammed his suitcase to the ground and started kicking the front tire. I started laughing my ass off. Kimbel was angry, which meant he wasn't too happy to find that at three o'clock this morning I had parked down the street, crept up to his car with a pocket knife, and carved HERPES along the driver's side. There was no way he could miss it. The words were the length of the door. There was also no way he was going to be seen driving his most prized possession to work.

I peeled away from his block, loud enough for Kimbel to see me leave. I even waved like I was a beauty queen. He-he! I was laughing so hard I had tears in my eyes and had to pull over. That will teach him to mess with me. By the time I got myself together, I had hoped to finally feel vindicated. Only instead, I felt just as miserable as I had the day before. Getting back at Kimbel no longer excited me as it did in the beginning. In fact, I was starting to feel like I had crossed over the line to stalker status, and I wasn't having any part of that. It really was time for me to finally just let go. But no matter how I felt, I wasn't a fool. Kimbel wasn't getting the ring back even after I made him pay for everything. The ring was my consolation prize. Nevertheless, I did need to close that painful chapter in my life, and I wasn't going to be able to do that until I took care of something first.

I was back at the salon working full-time again. I guess everyone had heard what happened because no one asked about my fiancé, which was a good thing. A couple of weeks ago, I probably would have gone off if anyone asked, but now I was in a much better place.

"Tiffany, you got a call!" the sales clerk yelled from the shop.

"Tell them to hold on." I finished wrapping my client's hair and stuck her under the dryer and headed to the lobby. "Brittany, go ahead and take a seat in my chair. I'll be right with you." I moved up to the counter and took the receiver from Claudia. "Hello?"

"Is this Tiffany Phillips?"

"Yeah, this is her. Who's this?"

There was a chuckle. "The pretty lady forgot about me already. My feelings are hurt."

Oh my goodness! I knew that accent anywhere. "Baughn! How you get my number?"

"You told me you worked in a beauty salon in Chicago, so I found you."

I turned away from the counter, grinning like a damn fool. "Damn, but there's over a hundred salons in Chicago."

"Yeah, mon. I discovered that," he replied with a chuckle.

I was definitely flattered by his determination. "I can't believe you're calling me all the way from Jamaica."

"I'm not in Jamaica, mon. I'm in Indiana."

"Indiana. W-What are you doing there?" I stuttered.

He laughed. "I'm a student at Indiana University."

What? I couldn't believe it. Baughn was here. In the U.S.A. When I left, I never expected to see or hear from him again.

"Why didn't you tell me you were a student?"

"You didn't give me a chance. After that night I called you and discovered you had left. My feelings were hurt."

Closing my eyes, I breathed, "I'm sorry. I just figured what happens in Jamaica . . ."

"Stays in Jamaica. I understand. Unfortunately, that wasn't at all what I was tinking. How about I drive down and take the pretty lady to dinner next Friday? That's if you are free?"

The thought of spending the evening with him was too tempting an offer to pass up. "I'd like that." I gave

him my new cell phone number and made plans for
him to call me later that evening. When I finally hung
up, I was tingling all over.

"Who was that?" Debra asked the moment she saw
me hanging up the phone. I cut my eyes at her.

"None of your business," I snapped. She was at it
again.

"Come on. You're not smiling like that for nothing,"
she teased.

The client sitting in my chair chimed in. "Uh-huh.
She look like she's about to get her some."

*Okay, I've had it with all these nosy-ass folks in this
place.* "Okay, listen up! My personal life is just that—
private. So quit asking about who I'm seeing or what
I'm doing. It's none of your damn business."

"Damn, Tiffany. We just playing."

I whipped around so fast I made that chick jump and
she almost dropped the hot comb from her hand.
"Debra, you play too damn much. I'm tired of you
eavesdropping on my calls and spreading my personal
business. You need to quit worrying about what I'm
doing and focus on trying to figure out who your
baby's daddy is." Yesterday I had heard her on the
phone saying the DNA results on the dude she suspected as her youngest child's father had come back
negative.

I waited for a quickie comeback and there wasn't
one. Debra just stood there styling someone's hair, trying to pretend she hadn't heard a word I said. She
heard as well as every other nosy female in the salon.
Maybe now she'd know to stay out of other people's
business. I went back to work, chuckling inside. *That'll
show her.*

Around three, I took a break, went out, and sat in my car while I made a call on my cell phone. "I would like to make an appointment with Dr. Clark."

"What are you being seen for?"

I swallowed before speaking. "I need to be checked for sexually transmitted diseases. I want to be tested for everything." If Kimbel gave me herpes, there's no telling what else he might have given me, and I needed to know before I infected someone else. *Game over.* It was time to get my life back.

While I waited for her to make the appointment, I closed my eyes and prayed I hadn't given anything to Baughn. Even though we used a condom, I had been reckless. Baughn hadn't given me reason to see him as anything other than a good guy and he deserved better. There was no way I could even think about having sex with him again until I knew for sure whether I had been infected.

39

Noelle

"Who's next?"

A young petite thing waved her hand, then moved out onto the floor. I'd never seen her before, which meant she was a new customer.

"Have a seat." I reached up and touched her hair, checking the texture. By the look of things, it had been a while since she'd last had a perm. "What can I do for you today?"

She shrugged. "I want just a wash and set."

"No perm?" I don't know how she expected me to roll up some naps.

Shaking her head, she replied, "I don't need a perm. I have naturally curly hair."

Curly where? "A texturizer would look really good," I suggested, hoping I could persuade her to do something to that mop.

She shook her head. "Uh-uh, no chemicals. Just a wash and trim."

All right, it was her hair, so I wasn't about to argue

with her. A lot of people were on that natural kick, but most folks either were locking their hair or keeping it braided. She was on some afro kick. A few inches, yes, but her shit had to be at least eight inches long, and that was patted down.

The music was thumping with Mary J. Blige's new beat, and I sang along while I washed and conditioned her thick course hair. As soon as I rinsed it out, I signaled for her to move over to my station and take a seat.

"Are you related to Mr. Gordon?" she asked, staring at me through the mirror.

I nodded. "Yes, that's my husband."

Her eyes lit up. "Ooh! He's the nicest man. I had him for senior English last semester and he knew how to make class fun."

"Yes, I hear that a lot about him." Just thinking about my husband made me smile. I couldn't wait for him to get back home next weekend.

"He also knew how to help you if you were struggling. He would go out of his way to do whatever he could to make sure we passed his class."

"Yes, that sounds like him."

She was sitting there grinning with this faraway look in her eyes. "He used to spend a lot of time with my friend Amber after school trying to tutor her. She was failing English. All she used to talk about was Mr. Gordon this and Mr. Gordon that," she chuckled. "I think she had a mad crush on him, but who could blame her. He is fine. You know . . . there was even a rumor for a while that he and Amber was secretly having an affair. Is that crazy or what?" She started laughing real loud and ghetto, expecting me to join in. When she realized I didn't see anything funny, she sobered real quick. "You know how folks be lying and starting rumors. Anyway, Amber ended up dropping out before the first marking period. Come to find out she was pregnant."

It took everything I had to hold it together. "Pregnant?" My voice cracked and I cleared my throat several times. "That's a shame. Did she end up going back to school?"

She shrugged. "I don't know. We stopped hanging out after that. I haven't seen her around, but I heard she had a little girl."

While I rolled her hair, I found my mind considering another possibility. Lord, forgive me for even thinking about my husband messing around with a student, but I was getting desperate, and at this point anything was possible. "I remember Grant talking about Amber. Said she was one of his favorite students. What's her last name?" It was hard trying to lie and asked a question like it was no big deal.

"Andersen . . . Amber Andersen, with an E."

That was easy enough. At least I had a name and a new lead to follow.

I couldn't get her hair done fast enough. I had this weird feeling, and one question kept going around and around in my head. Could my husband have fathered that baby? I just didn't want to believe it, but something just didn't feel right to me. Grant spent a lot of time with his students and took his career serious; however, I couldn't help thinking about one of his students dropping out. The school year began in late August and if she dropped out in October, that would have made her at least eight weeks pregnant. Meaning, she would have given birth in April, right around the time Sierra was born. I didn't want to believe it, but it was the only lead I had.

So far, I've called practically every student in the yearbook and Scott was pretty much MIA. He had sense enough to know that he had hell to pay. I was tired of him ignoring his responsibilities—little Michael and, until I found out otherwise, Sierra.

I was still having a hard time accepting that my best friend had given birth to my grandchild, but if I wanted to be a part of Michael's life, I had to find a way to get over it. Whitney was back at home, but Michael, although he was doing better, would stay in the hospital until he gained at least another pound.

After my last client of the day, I went back to my office, retrieved the phone book, and looked for every Andersen within a commutable distance. There were five. I ripped out the page and stuck it in my pocket. I planned to call or drive by each address until I found Amber and figured out what the hell was going on. My son wasn't cooperating and Grant was out of the country, which meant I had to get out there and find the answers on my own.

It was almost 7:00 PM. when I pulled in front of a small ranch-style house and climbed out. I had called earlier, pretending to be a friend, and asked for Amber. When I was told she was at school, I thought I had hit the lottery. I followed the directions I got on MapQuest and was surprised to be driving in a fairly decent neighborhood where folks actually watered their grass. That's just not something you saw too often in neighborhoods on the south side of Chicago. I pulled in front of a brick house with black shutters behind a Ford Focus. I moved up to the door and knocked. A few seconds later, a beautiful white woman with long blond hair and blue eyes came to the door. She was wearing purple scrubs, so I figured either she was a nurse or worked in housekeeping at the hospital.

"May I help you?" she asked.

I put on my best smile and asked, "Are you Amber's mother?"

She gave me a curious look from my eyes down to my toes. "Yes, I am. Who are you?"

I nibbled on my lip trying to determine the best way to proceed. "I'm sorry, this is kind of awkward. My name is Noelle Gordon; my husband, Grant, was your daughter's teacher last year."

The sparkle in her eyes told me she knew exactly who I was. "Yes, what can I do for you?"

"I was wondering if I could talk to your daughter?"

"She's not here. What is it that you need from my daughter?" She was starting to get a little testy with me and I couldn't fault the woman. I would have done the same.

Laughing, I tried to lighten an already awkward situation. "This might sound ridiculous, but around two months ago someone dropped a baby off on my porch. I heard your daughter was pregnant during her senior year and I was wondering if maybe . . . Amber was Sierra's mama." There, I said it.

The female smirked like she knew the answer to a secret before she even set her lips to speak. "Yes, as a matter of fact, Sierra is her daughter."

My jaw dropped. I couldn't believe I had finally found her. It hurt knowing the circumstances because discovering Amber opened a whole other jar of problems for me.

"Finally," I said, followed by a deep breath. "After

all these weeks of searching, I've finally found her. May I come by later and talk to Amber?"

Her mother shook her head. "She won't be here. She's going to school in South Carolina."

"South Carolina?" I was completely thrown for a loop by this entire situation. "No offense . . . but what kind of mother leaves her child on a doorstep, then leaves town?"

The woman folded her arms against her chest, then replied, "She didn't leave her on your doorstep. I did."

"But why? And what did you mean by . . . what's done in the dark?"

She smoothed her hands along the front of her shirt, then rolled her eyes in my direction. "No offense, but this is really none of your business. The person you need to be asking is your husband." She then slammed the door in my face.

40

Candace

Ever since I got fired, I'd been moping around feeling sorry for myself. I didn't have a job. My man was a joke, and I was the laughingstock of the neighborhood. I guess I could say life wasn't fair, but did it have to happen to mine?

"You can't keep feeling sorry for yourself. Isn't that what you told me?"

I opened my eyes and stared up at my best friend while she put a deep conditioner in my hair. If Chauncey hadn't been suspended, I would have never stepped foot in Situations again.

Tiffany gave me a sympathetic smile as she spoke. "You told me to let it go and be thankful I found out when I did; well, I am thankful you told me. I just hate that you lost your job for it."

I shrugged my shoulder. "I knew the consequences when I told you. But I just couldn't let you marry that fool without knowing the truth."

"And I thank you for it. I definitely would have been

making the worst mistake of my life." Tiffany leaned me back in the seat. I always loved the feel of warm water running through my hair. She waited until I was sitting over at her booth before she asked, "Have you talked to Chauncey?"

I glared at her. "For what? It's humiliating enough as it is."

"Candy, you should at least give the man a chance to explain," she scolded.

"Screw him," I said, sitting up straight in my seat.

Tiffany grew silent and had sense enough to know I was done talking about Chauncey. A couple of days ago, she told me he wanted to apologize to me in person, but I still couldn't forgive him. Just thinking about Chauncey hurt so much I wanted to punch my fist through a wall. I was crazy about him and I thought we really had something there, but it had all been a lie. To think I had wanted to spend the rest of my life with him. How was I supposed to forgive him after he lied and broke my heart? As far as I was concerned, things could never be the same again. The best thing he could do was stay the hell away from me.

After Tiffany hooked up my hair, I stopped at Church's Chicken for a two-piece, then headed home. I didn't have the guts to tell my parents I lost my job, so I kept dropping Miasha off in the morning and picking her up at five. Thank goodness Mama always contacted me on my cell phone, so I wasn't worried about her calling the clinic and finding out. The last thing I needed was for Papa to start worrying and insisting that Miasha and I move back in with them. I loved them, but they could be smothering and overly protective at times.

I was sitting and watching *The Ellen DeGeneres*

Show when I heard a knock at the door. I started to ignore it because not too many people knew I had lost my job. But whoever it was, kept knocking, so I went and answered the door and turned up my nose when I spotted Tyree standing there. He had been MIA for the past three weeks.

"What're you doing here?" I asked, and allowed my eyes to travel down his body. Tyree was standing there in jeans and a nice button-down shirt, wearing a belt, and was even smelling good.

"I dropped by the clinic and they told me you didn't work there anymore."

"What do you want?" I asked with a suspicious frown.

He scowled at my attitude. "I wanna talk to you about something."

I stepped aside and he moved inside. I'll admit I was a little surprised that he was out and about this early. Tyree was a night owl and spent most of his day in bed. He took a seat on the couch and I moved in the recliner across from him. Since I was depressed I had needed something to cheer me up, so I had taken my last bit of money to get my hair and nails done, which meant the rent-to-own company wouldn't get their money this week for my living room furniture.

"Where're you on your way to?"

He gave me a stupid grin. "I got a job."

"Hold up . . . a job? Since when do you work?" The last time I remember him working was flipping burgers, and that lasted all of two days.

"Yeah, I'm working at the Heinz plant in the packaging division."

"Okay, hold up . . . let's back this up a moment. You telling me you're punching the clock? Since when?"

"For about three weeks now," he replied with that same ridiculous smile on his face.

"Ain't that a bitch."

He chuckled at my reaction. "My supervisor made me a lead last night."

"You mean to tell me you're doing the damn thang?"

He shrugged like it was no big deal, but I could tell he was proud. "I figured it was time for me to get myself together if I was going to be a good father."

"I'm happy for you." And I was. "Does that mean I'll be getting my money on time now?"

"Yep, I get paid every week." He reached inside his pocket and pulled out a couple of hundreds and sat them on the table that unknowingly he just saved from being repossessed. "I also want to prove to you that I can be a good man to you, too." He rose and moved beside me and took a seat. "Candy . . . I still love you. Hell, I never stopped and I would like a chance to show you. What you think about us getting married and doing it right this time?"

"Married?" I looked over at him. For years I had waited for this moment, but he was too busy hanging in them streets. There was a time when I could have laid down butt naked in the middle of the road and declared my love to him. Tyree was still just as good-looking and was Miasha's father, but he wasn't Chauncey and that's what hurt. I loved that man and even though he played me, I wasn't ready yet to move on. "I don't know, Tyree."

The stern set of his lips said he wasn't ready to take no for an answer. "You don't have to say anything just yet, but think about it."

I nodded. "Okay, I'll think about it, but I won't promise anything." I don't know why I was hesitant. It wasn't like Chauncey and I were getting back together. Tyree was my daughter's father and if anything, Miasha deserved to have both her parents in her life. At least I knew what I had with Tyree. He smoked too many cigarettes and hung out too damn much with his boys, but it definitely beat a blank.

"I better get out of here so I won't be late for work."

"Damn, who would have ever guessed you would be saying those words?" We both had to laugh at that. He rose and I followed him to the door. "Thanks for the money, Tyree."

He swung around. "Anytime."

Next thing I knew he was kissing me. I opened my mouth and memories of our time together came flooding back, but then I found myself comparing his techniques to Chauncey's. Tyree didn't even come close, and that was enough to make me wanna scream. I pulled back.

"I'll talk to you later," he said with a confident smile, then headed down the stairs and out the door, leaving me with something to seriously consider.

41

Chauncey

"What are you doing here?"

I stared at my mama as she climbed the stairs to the three-bedroom, two-story home where I grew up. I had watched her coming up the street in her nurse's uniform. A Dodge Intrepid was parked at the curb, but she preferred to take public transportation and save on gas and parking.

"I asked you a question?" she demanded. A hand was at her thick waist just the way it always was when she was cussing me out for something I had done. "Did you lose your hearing while you were locked up? I asked what you're doing here?"

"I came to see you." I had hoped for my mama to have showed some sign she was happy to see me. That there was still some love in her heart for her only child, but it hurt me to say I saw absolutely nothing.

"I thought I told you never to set foot at my door again."

She still wore the same short afro. Only now it was

practically gray. "I was hoping after all this time you missed your baby boy," I replied with a smirk.

"My son's dead to me. He died six years ago." She could have stabbed me in the chest and it wouldn't have sliced me as bad as her words.

I moved closer and smiled. "We all make mistakes and I made mine, but I'm a better person because of that."

"So what do you want from me, a trophy or something?" She shook her head. "You raped a woman and there is no forgiving that."

Even after all these years, there was no point in arguing my case with her. It didn't matter to her if the girl was sixteen or forty or that I had been tricked. All that mattered to Wanda Wilson was her only son had been convicted for rape.

"At first I thought you hated me because of my conviction, but ever since I spoke to my father I discovered your hatred runs deeper than that."

"Your father?" she snarled.

"Yes, my father," I said, and she had the nerve to try and look angry and betrayed. *Ain't that some shit.* "He told me everything about how you wouldn't let me see him. All those times you had me sitting for hours waiting for him because you said my ol' man was coming to pick me up, when he had no idea where we even lived. How could you do something like that to your own son?"

"Why you think? Your father left us for another woman and had a child. He didn't care about us."

"That child's name is Linda. And yeah, he was wrong for having an affair, but you were the one who put him out. You were the one who told him to never come back."

"Of course I did! Do you think I would stay with a man after finding out he had been unfaithful!"

"I wouldn't expect you to, but no matter what he did to you, you had no right taking my father from me."

"He lost that right the second he walked out that door."

I stared down at the woman who barely stood five feet tall. "You are such a bitter woman. Thank goodness for Ms. Hattie. Did you know she used to let Dad sneak over and see me? He was there every day until she died." I could tell she didn't like hearing that because her beady brown eyes narrowed dangerously. "Tell me something . . . what did you do with all of my birthday and Christmas presents?"

Her bottom lip quivered. "I donated them to Goodwill."

My ol' man had been telling the truth. He hadn't been lying. Anger boiled inside and I felt ready to explode and scream at the top of my lungs. "Why?" How could a woman hate a man so much that she was willing to take my father away? "Mama, you tell me you can't find it in your heart to forgive me for going to jail, well, that's too bad. Unlike you, I blame you for nothing and forgive you for everything you've done to me."

She gave me a long look and silence past while I waited for her to say something, anything, to let me know that despite everything she still loved me. "Listen, I had a long day. If that's it, then please leave me alone so I can go in the house and relax."

I shook my head and tried to hold it together, but her rejection after all these years hurt me to the core. "I came over here because I had hoped that once you saw me you would forget the past and be happy to see me, but now that I'm here, I know that will never happen, and guess what? I am okay with that because I know it's nothing that I've done. It's just the type of person that you are. You're hateful and unforgiving and as hard as it is to say this, I know I don't need someone like you in my life."

I walked off leaving her standing there on the top step. I waited until I reached the corner before I looked over my shoulder and saw she was gone. I wished Candace was there so she would wrap her arms around me and tell me it was okay, but I ruined any chances of being with her. I lost the two women I loved; one for my own stupidity and the other due to no fault of my own.

42

Tiffany

"Tiffany! Tiffany, hurry and get your butt in here!"

There was no telling what Candace was getting ready to bitch about now. I rose from the bed and moved into the living room where she was standing in front of the television. When she swung around to face me, her eyes were so wide, they were frightening.

"Oh my God! Tiffany, you're not going to believe this!"

I glanced from her to the television screen that was showing the weather. She was scaring me. "Believe what?"

Tiffany started waving her hands wildly in the air. "They're gonna finish the story in a minute, but listen to this. King Funeral Homes is under investigation!"

"What?" I couldn't have possibly heard her right.

She nodded her head. "There were reports of a foul smell coming from the funeral home on 78th Street, so they sent the state out to investigate and they discovered a corpse in a body bag in a closet. Not only that, two other bodies were left decaying out on tables." She was talking so fast it took a few seconds for the words to register.

"What?" I couldn't believe it. "When?"

"Shhhhh . . . it's back on."

"Investigation began when two families complained they had not received the cremated remains of their love ones. One also reported that residents in the neighborhood started complaining of a strong odor coming from the location. King Funeral Homes at 7815 South Cottage Grove has temporarily been shut down until all violations have been corrected. Since the story was first aired, other families have come forward reporting jewelry being removed from their love one's possession."

All I could say was, "Wow."

"I know." Candace took a seat on the couch. "I guess we need to watch the news more often because for the last week, King Funeral Homes has been all over the news with reports of personal belongings being stolen."

I watched Kimbel's mother on television saying how they had fired staff members suspected of thievery and hoped to return the belongings to the loved ones. "The largest black funeral home in the city and we can't even trust our own people," I mumbled. It was pathetic, to say the least.

"I know. That's crazy."

I was still pissed at Kimbel, but his parents were good people and I felt bad for them. Here they were planning to open another funeral home and then something like this happened. When I got to work later that morning, I was still thinking about them and feeling bad, so on my break I decided to give Mrs. King a call. I was shocked she was even answering her phone.

"Hello?"

As soon as I heard her voice I started having second thoughts. After all, I was supposed to have married her son. I was probably the last person they wanted to hear from.

"Hello? Is someone there?"

So much for hanging up. "Mrs. King . . . this is Tiffany."

"Tiffany? Dear, it is so good to hear from you! I wanted to call you but I figured . . . it was better to just stay out of it. How are you?"

"I'm fine. The question is how are you holding up?"

She sighed heavily in the receiver. "We're taking it one day at a time. We made some careless management decisions. Now that we fired most of the staff at the Cottage Grove location, all we can do is hope that it will never happen again, and ensure loved ones are cremated in a timely manner. Now, if only we could find out where the valuables have gone."

"I'm sure they will surface."

"I'm sure they will. Kimbel is checking every pawn shop in the city of Chicago."

I frowned at the mention of his name. *Asshole.* "Well, you hang in there and I'll say a prayer for both of you." I'm sure Mama was already down on her knees praying enough for the both of us.

"Thank you, dear, and please drop by sometime and visit us. Even though you didn't marry my son, I'm sure you had your reasons and I respect that. Just don't be a stranger."

"I will." I hung up feeling good. I thought it would have been hard to listen to her voice. I had wanted so badly to be a part of their family.

I busted my ass the rest of the afternoon and was

dead on my feet by the time I got to Candace's that evening. Yet the second I stepped into her apartment, I grabbed a glass of water, then turned on the television to catch the late night news. They were talking about the funeral home again. It had also been the hot topic in the salon for the day.

"Candace! It's on again."

She came out of her room and took a seat beside me on the couch as the two of us listened. Things had gotten so bad families were talking about taking their business to the white man. Kimbel's parents were too ashamed to even show their faces and had hired a PR person to represent the family. But when the story shifted to the stolen valuables, a woman appeared on the screen standing in front of the funeral home, holding up a photo of her grandmother. "I've been asking the funeral home for months and got no answers. All I want is my grandmother's ring back." The camera zoomed in on the ring and I choked on my drink.

"What's wrong?"

"That's my ring," I said between coughs.

"You got a ring like that?"

I started frantically shaking my head. "No, that's my engagement ring. Now hush!" I listened to the woman say that the ring had been in her family for generations. A thousand-dollar reward was being given for information leading to the return. As soon as the weatherman came on I raced to the bedroom, rummaged through my jewelry box, and came back with the diamond and emerald ring. "Look!"

Our eyes met. "It *does* look like that missing ring. You don't think . . ."

She didn't need to finish the question. I already

knew what she was getting at—the same conclusion I had come to. "I don't think . . . I know. Kimbel stole this ring off a dead woman's body and gave it to me."

Candace brought her hand to cup her mouth. "I can't believe this shit! He stole jewelry from dead folks." She was shaking her head. My heart was pounding so hard I could barely speak. All I could think about was Mrs. King. I felt so sorry for her, but I had to do the right thing. I slipped my shoes back on my feet. "Where you going?"

Glancing over my shoulder, I replied, "I'm about to make Kimbel pay for everything he put me through. You know what they say . . . Karma's a bitch." I grabbed my purse and headed down to the police station. A thousand dollars sounded real good right about now.

43

Noelle

When Grant arrived home from the airport, I was sitting in the living room sipping a glass of wine, waiting. As soon as he had called me to let me know his plane had landed at Midway Airport, I put Sierra to sleep and had to make myself a drink to calm my nerves. *Sleeping with a student.* It was a wonder Amber's mom hadn't pressed charges; instead, we were gonna have to give her money. Money we'd have to pay to keep her quiet about the whole situation. Her mother hadn't said as much, but I already knew what it was going to take. Any other woman would have thrown her husband out into the street and made his ass beg for forgiveness, but not me. I planned to make Grant's life miserable. I was going to make my husband raise his child and have a constant reminder of what he did to us and our marriage.

I wiped tears from my cheeks. I deserved better and dammit, I was going to get it. And to think, all this time I thought Sierra belonged to Scott.

I heard Grant's car pull into the garage. I just sat there and waited for him to enter the room. As soon as he did, I rose to greet him. "Hey, baby." he said and looked happy to see me standing there waiting.

"Hello. How was your trip?" I asked while trying to count backward from ten. My eyes kept traveling to the letter opener on the coffee table. I wondered if I could stab him with it and win a temporary insanity plea? Grant walked farther into the room, then wrapped his arms around me. When our lips met all I could think about was him kissing that teenage girl.

Grant broke our kiss, looked at me, and smiled. "Man, it was an experience I will never forget!"

"I'm sure." *Probably like sleeping with teenagers.*

"You would not believe how much our visit made a difference for those kids."

I wondered if he'd slept with any of those Korean girls. I know I was letting my mind play tricks on me, but I couldn't help it. While he went on and on about his experience, I contemplated pulling off the perfect murder.

"Something sure smells good," he finally said.

I offered him an artificial smile. "I made meatloaf. Your favorite."

He grinned. "Yes, it is. Give me two minutes to change and I'll be right down."

I paced the room, punched the wall a few times, and waited until we were seated at the table before I finally felt calm enough to say, "I have a new client. She said you used to be her teacher."

"Really?" he said between chews. "Who is it?"

I reached for my glass. "Carmen . . . Carmen White."

Grant's face lit with recognition. "Sure. Bright girl. Has a lot of potential. I wonder what she's doing with her life?"

"I got the impression she was working and attending community college," I replied while stabbing my peas with my fork.

He shrugged. "Anything is better than nothing."

"Anyway . . . while talking to her I found out who Sierra's mother is."

His eyes snapped to me. "What? That's great news. Who is she?"

"Amber Andersen," I said slow and controlled, then waited for his reaction.

"Amber . . . my former student Amber?" His eyes shifted nervously.

I nodded, then leaned back in my chair. "I went by and met her mother. She had a lot of things to say, and when I asked her who was Sierra's father, she told me to talk to you."

"Me?" he held up his hands. "Listen, Noelle . . . what my students talk to me about in private is between me and them."

I cut my eyes at him. "I just bet. So did you know she was pregnant?"

Grant took a drink from his pop can before answering. "I suspected as much. After I heard she had dropped outta school, I went by her house to talk to her—"

"You went to her house?" I snapped, cutting him off.

He gave me a look like it was no big deal. "I'm a teacher and I was concerned. She hadn't been in class for days and I wanted to know why. That was when Amber told me she might be pregnant."

Did he really expect me to believe this shit he was trying to feed me? "Who's the father?" I asked as I started stabbing peas again.

He shook his head. "I can't say."

"What do you mean you can't say? Is it Scott?" I asked suspiciously.

He looked confused. "Scott? Hell no."

"Then who else could it be because Sierra sure looks a lot like your side of the family?"

A light suddenly went off in his eyes. "What are you trying to say?"

I was sure I had a crazed look in my eyes. "I'm asking . . . is Sierra your daughter? Is that why you're so adamant about getting her out of our house because you don't want your little affair in my face?"

Grant glared across the table. "You're sick, you know that? I am a teacher! I would never step over the line and violate a student's trust." I wanted to believe him. I really did, but how could I when all the facts said otherwise.

"What else can I believe? You won't tell me who the father is, yet you deny it's you. The baby looks just like Scott and Amber's mother dropped her off on our doorstep."

"Fine, if you don't believe me, then let's go over there." He sprung from the chair.

"Right now?" I challenged.

"Yep, right now. Since you don't believe me, I'm going to prove to you I'm not lying." He shook his head. "It's a shame my word just isn't good enough." There was sadness in his eyes and I know I hurt his feelings. Well, too bad. Grant wasn't the only one hurting right now. I guess my husband thought I was going to say forget it or call his bluff. *Not me.* I got up, went to my room, and slipped on a pair of jeans and reached for my sneakers. Grant followed, realized I was serious, and for the first time, he looked a little worried.

"Maybe we should just wait till tomorrow after we have cooled off. It's too late to be knocking on someone's door."

I glanced across the room at my alarm clock. It was almost ten o'clock. "I don't think so. We're getting this mess over tonight. So if there is anything you need to tell me, then you better do it now." As soon as I had on my shoes, I got the diaper bag ready, then removed Sierra gently from her crib and grabbed her car seat. Grant was still standing in the same place I left him. "Don't just stand there, let's go," I ordered. I was through playing games.

"Fine, but you're going to regret accusing me of messing around with a student. I can't wait to see your face when you find out you're wrong."

He climbed behind the wheel and was quiet all the way to Amber's house. Part of me was starting to have second thoughts. What if I was wrong? If I was, things would never be the same between us again.

On the way, Grant tried to act like he didn't remember where she lived. I had no problem giving him direction and when he pulled in front of the house, I turned to him and said, "You know I don't like surprises. If there is anything you need to tell me, now is the time." I was trying to give him one last chance to come clean because in about the next five minutes all hell was gonna break loose.

"I already told you I don't have anything to hide." He got out the car first and I started to have a bad feeling all over again. The house was relatively dark except for a light at the front of the house. I wasn't feeling anywhere near as confident as I followed Grant onto the porch and rang the doorbell. A few seconds passed before a light turned on and the door opened. A beautiful young woman stood there. Her eyes looked red and swollen like she had been crying. The second she recognized my husband, her jaw dropped.

"Mr. Gordon, what are you doing here?"

Out the corner of my eyes, I watched my husband shift nervously from side to side. "I came to speak with you and your mother."

Her eyes darted from me to him. "What about?"

"Sierra," I replied with a hint of attitude. I didn't have all night to be playing guess who. The sooner we got to the bottom of it, the better.

Amber's eyes grew wide. "You know where my daughter is?"

I wasn't buying her behavior for a minute. "Of course we do. Unlike you and your mother, we didn't leave her on someone else's porch. She's over in my car." Before I could get the words out, Amber pushed past us and raced over to the car and opened the back door. As soon as she held Sierra in her arms, she started crying. I had tears in my own eyes. You could tell she really loved her baby. What the hell was going on?

"Who gave you my daughter?" she demanded to know as she moved onto the porch, carrying Sierra in her arms.

Grant came around and stood beside her. "Your mother left her on our porch."

"What? Why? I've been crying my eyes out for two days. When I left for Army basic training, I signed my daughter over to my mom as temporary legal guardian while I was gone. When I got back she told me Sierra's father came and took my baby."

I rolled my eyes over at my husband. "She *was* with her father. Grant and I have been taking care of her."

Grant blew out a heavy breath, then smoothed a hand across his head. "My wife has this strange idea that Sierra is my child."

Amber gasped. "No way! Mr. Gordon? That's crazy. This is Shawn Williams's baby."

My eyes traveled from one liar to the other. They both looked nervous and scared. I was sick of the games. "I think it's time for everyone to stop lying. Dammit, Grant . . . you know that child is yours!"

Inside, I heard the shuffling of feet and someone coming toward the door. The porch light came on and the next thing I knew, Amber's mother stepped out onto the porch, wearing a skimpy pink gown. Does she have no shame? "Now isn't this sweet. One big happy family!"

Before I could tell the chick to check herself, Grant stepped forward with this stupid look on his face. "Lucy . . . is that you?"

"Hello, Grant," she said with a smirk. "I bet you're surprised to see me again."

"Y-You're Amber's mother?" he stuttered and looked seconds away from passing out on the porch.

She was nodding and grinning at the same time. "Yep, in the flesh."

I had to walk over to my husband and sniff him, because I swore he shit his pants the way he was staring at her. He had gotten caught and was stunned to silence. I was just glad that we were all there. No more lies. Before the night was over, everything was coming out in the open. Since the two of them were standing there looking stupid, I decided to get the conversation going again. "So Sierra *is* your daughter after all."

"Go on, Grant, tell her," Lucy said with a sly smile.

"Tell me what?" I said, and even Amber looked confused.

Lucy gave a loud, boisterous laugh. "Okay, since he's obviously still a coward, I'll tell you myself. Sierra's not Grant's daughter . . . Amber is."

Next thing I knew, everything went black.

44

Tiffany

I was so excited about my date with Baughn, I was messing up heads left and right.

"Damn, Tif! I said honey blonde. I look like fucking Carrot Top."

"Sorry, Sarah. I'll put some toner on it and lighten it a bit." It was like that all morning. I was so looking forward to my date.

I finished my last client by five, then hurried home and heated up the flatiron. While I was doing my hair, Candace came into the bedroom and took a seat on the bed.

"Tiffany, check this out. I was in the ladies' room at work. It's a pretty good size with about five stalls. Anyway . . . I went into the last one to take a dump. Of course, you know someone always has to come into the stall beside me."

I nodded as I looked away from the mirror. "Girl, you know that's how it always works."

"I know. Anyway, where was I? Okay . . . I'm one of

those who will wipe my behind when I'm finished until the tissue comes clean, but since I don't sit on any public stools, I squat. I was trying to balance and wipe my butt at the same time. I lost my balance and dropped the tissue, and it flew across the floor over onto the next stall."

"What? You lying?"

She giggled. "I'm serious. Dookey stains and all."

"Oh my God!" I was screaming with laughter.

"Tiffany, gurl, I was like, oh shit! Now what am I going to do? I waited for the female in the next stall to say something and when she didn't, I finally said forget it, then reached my hand under and retrieved it."

"Oh my God! Candy, no you didn't?" I said, even though the look on her face said she did.

She sucked her teeth. "What other choice did I have?"

"Not that."

Candace leaned back onto the bed. "What you expect me to say, uhhhh, excuse me, but can you pass that back over here?"

We were falling out. I was laughing so hard I had tears in my eyes.

"All that woman saw was this black hand sliding under her stall," she managed between chuckles.

"Yeah, but how many black females work in your building?" Candace was temping for a big law firm downtown and really liked her job a lot. The manager was so impressed with her skills, they were even considering keeping her on permanently. I was so happy for her because all that moping around had started to get on my nerves.

"There ain't but two black females in our department, so you know it won't be hard to figure out it was me."

My girl has no shame. I shook my head. Only Candace could come up with some crazy mess. "You are too much."

My cell phone vibrated. I put the flatiron down, then reached for it on the dresser. It was a text from Baughn: See you tonight. I smiled, then noticed I had one missed call. Not recognizing the number, I brought the phone to my ear and retrieved the message. *Hi, this is Marian at the Women's Health Associates. Can you please give me a call back?*

It was Dr. Clark's nurse! *Oh God! Oh God!* I moved into the bathroom and shut the door, then took a seat on the stool. My hands were shaking so hard I could barely dial the number. Hopefully someone was still there, because if I had to wait until Monday for my results, I was going to be a nervous wreck. While I waited for the receptionist to put Marian on the phone, I said a silent prayer. *Please, Lord. I'll never ask for anything from you again if you get me through this.*

"Tiffany?"

"Yes," I croaked.

"Thanks for calling me back. I just wanted to let you know your tests all came back negative; however, you do have a little yeast." I didn't hear anything else after the word negative. I didn't have it. Can you believe? *Yessss*! *Yessss*! Kimbel hadn't infected me with his germs. Hell, I hung up feeling so good about my evening with Baughn and what the future might hold for me.

I came out of the bathroom screaming and crying at the same time. Candace thought my mother had died. After I told her, we sat their hugging each other while I cried some more and started planning my future. Damn, life was good!

I had given Baughn directions to my house, and by eight I heard a car pull up out front.

"Tiffany, is that a Lexus convertible I see?"

We were both trying to peek between the blinds without him seeing us. "Damn, I guess it is." It was a far cry from the Toyota he had taken me out in in Jamaica.

Candace gave me a weird look. "What did you say he did for a living?"

"He goes to school and works at a hotel in Jamaica during the summer." I guess I didn't know that much about him after all, which was a shame. I spent an entire evening with him and I was more interested in talking about Kimbel's sorry ass than getting to know who Baughn really was. Tonight was going to be different.

"He must be making good money 'cause that car is about fifty G's."

The second he climbed out that car I don't know if it was me or Candace who sucked in a deep breath.

Her eyes snapped in my direction. "Damn, that negro's fine! You didn't tell me he looked like that."

"Probably because I didn't remember," I mumbled under my breath. Baughn was wearing a red T-shirt that fit snugly against his chest and a pair of jeans that hung low on his waist. On his feet was a pair of leather sandals. A gold chain was around his neck, and even from where we were looking I noticed a single diamond stud in his left ear. Oh, Baughn was definitely something to look at.

Candace had the door open just as he was coming up the stairs.

"Hello, pretty lady. You must be Tiffany's roommate."

She was grinning with a hand at her hip." Actually, she's *my* roommate."

Frowning, I pushed her aside and stared up into his smiling face. "Hi."

"Hello, Tiffany. I see you are prettier than I remembered."

He pulled me into an embrace like he missed me and I found myself squeezing back. It was hard to believe I was with him again. "And you're still looking fine as hell."

He escorted me to the car and held the door open for me. Something Kimbel had never done. The car was even more impressive on the inside—buttercream interior, heated seats. When he started the engine, it purred just like a kitten. Low and controlled. The smell of his cologne traveled over to me. It wasn't invading at all, just a hint of the masculine man that he was.

"What would you like to do?" he asked. He took his eyes off the road long enough to smile in my direction. He was such a cutie.

I shrugged. "I don't know, you're the one who asked me out."

"I was hoping you would want to see a movie and then go get someting to eat."

"Sounds like a plan."

Baughn treated me to snacks and afterward we headed to have dinner at a new club, All That Jazz, that had opened the weekend before. I had planned on going with Candace, but since tonight a reggae band was scheduled to go on stage, I thought Baughn might enjoy a taste of home. We had a seat close to the bar and both ordered a drink and catfish platters.

"How long have you lived in the States?" I asked.

Tonight I was determined to learn everything I could about him.

"I've lived here off and on all my life. I have dual citizenship. My father was in the military."

"Oh." I loved listening to his accent.

"He was killed when I was five and my mudda and I returned to Jamaica, but I always knew I wanted to get my education in the States. My father's parents live in Indianapolis. My grandfather's a lawyer and a partner at a large law firm. I hope someday to work for him."

A lawyer? I was definitely impressed. "I would have never guessed you as a lawyer."

"Yeah, mon. I've never wanted anything else." I had pegged him so wrong. "I was hurt that such a pretty lady ran off without saying good-bye," he said as he reached for his drink.

"I just assumed that what we had was just for one night." It wasn't the complete truth, but it would do.

Baughn shook his head. "You were dead wrong. Everyting was irie and I had hoped to see you again."

I leaned over the table and whispered, "I'm so glad you tracked me down."

"So am I." Our food arrived and we were enjoying our meal when I spotted Kimbel coming into the restaurant with another female. As soon as he saw me, I kid you not, he about messed his pants and took a seat near the back, making sure he was far enough away so I couldn't see his date, yet close enough he could see me. I guess he didn't want a repeat of last time. For the first time in weeks, I could honestly say that I wasn't thinking about him. Now that I knew I hadn't contracted herpes, I was ready to put him behind me and get on with my life.

I laughed and was having such a good time listening to a live reggae band and talking with Baughn that after a while, I forgot all about Kimbel. I excused myself and went to the restroom; on the way out, I found that asshole waiting for me. I pretended I didn't see him and tried to walk past him, but he blocked my path.

"I just wanted to let you know I'm taking you to court."

I decided to play dumb. "For what?"

"For half the wedding expenses," he said with a confident smirk. "You stole my wallet."

I crossed my arms over my chest. "Do you have any proof that I stole your wallet?" He was quiet. "Yep, take me to court, because that's the least of your worries. I can't wait to see what the judge says when I tell him why I canceled the wedding."

"You wouldn't."

"Oh, but yes I will; just watch me. I'll make sure it's on every blog, MySpace, Facebook . . . you name it. Maybe you don't have any respect for yourself, but at least show some for the women you are with. So please, do me a favor and take my black ass to court, because I'm about to put on a show for you." I paused for dramatic effect and looked him up and down in slacks and a crisp white shirt. I was no longer impressed. "Like I said, that's the least of your worries. I hear the funeral homes are in trouble and rumor has it you're about to go down."

"What are you talking about?"

"The *ring*, Kimbel. The ring you wanted back so badly. I was watching the news and I finally figured out where you got it from . . . you *stole* it from a dead woman's body."

I never saw a light-skinned man turn that white before. "What . . . what did you do with the ring?"

"What do you think I did? I gave it to the police. I'm hoping to be a thousand dollars richer any day now," I added with a smirk and noticed the muscle at his jaw tick.

"I still love you," he suddenly said, like I would be stupid enough to believe anything he said.

I laughed in his face. "Whatever I felt for you died a long time ago." With that I pivoted on my heels and walked away, making sure he saw how good I looked from the rear.

"Can we at least sit and talk about this?"

I swung around. "When I wanted to talk, you had some stripper bent over touching her toes. So, nooo, there's nothing you can say to me." I started to leave, then swung around again. "Oh, and by the way, I just want to let you know that I've been tested and I don't have the package."

What Kimbel said surprised me. "I'm glad, Tiffany. I'm glad you didn't get it. Do you think maybe we can go out to dinner and talk? I'd really like to start over."

Had he lost his mind? "No, not in a million years. I hope the *two* of you have a wonderful life together. And I'm not talking about that female sitting at the table either. Now, excuse me. I've got a real man waiting for me."

45

Noelle

"Would you like me to fix you something to eat?"

I stared at my husband, the man who had pledged to love, honor, and be faithful to me for the rest of my life, and rolled my eyes. "No."

He had been kissing ass for a week. But no amount of butt kissing was going to undo the damage he had done to our relationship. I still couldn't believe it. He had conceived a child with another woman. It was heartbreaking. I was angry and hurt at the same time. Nineteen years ago, when our relationship was at its worst, Grant had an affair with Lucy. Not once in all the years we've been together did he mention the affair or the baby that was a result of their time in bed together. It brought tears to my eyes every time I thought about my husband being with another woman. No matter how bad our marriage had been, I never once strayed.

"Noelle, we need to talk about this."

"No, we don't. You never wanted to talk before. Why start now?"

"Because I love you and I'm willing to do whatever we have to do to make things work."

"Then I guess you should have thought about that before stepping out on me. Tell me at least . . . did you wear a condom?" The blank look on his face explained everything loud and clear. Like father, like son. "Of course not. If you had, Amber wouldn't be here."

"How many times do I have to tell you, I never knew she had the baby. Last time we talked she was planning to have an abortion. I had even given her the money."

"Guess the joke's on you. She kept your money and had the baby."

"I didn't know."

Okay, I can accept that and probably look past the fact that he had a baby girl with someone else, but he had an affair. While we were separated, he was sleeping with someone else.

Lucy had confirmed that Grant ended the relationship the moment we got back together. But was that supposed to make me feel better? How am I supposed to know whether every time we had an argument he had run into the arms of another female? For all I know there might be some other babies running around. My life was a mess. My best friend had given birth to my grandson, and at some point I was going to have to come to terms with that so that I could be a part of my grandchild's life when he was finally released from the hospital. At the same time I had to decide if I could deal with knowing my husband had a child with another woman. It was sad enough Amber had taken Sierra back, but at least she had been nice enough to bring her by to see me and told me I can see her as often as I liked. Thank God for small favors. I love Sierra too much to lose her.

"Baby, please talk to me." I was so sick of his begging.

"Why? You weren't willing to talk to me any time during these last nineteen years about your affair, so why start now?"

"That was nineteen years ago. We've moved past that time in our lives. I love you. I have been committed to our marriage ever since." He sounded so sad, but there was no way I was caving in.

"How do I know that was the only time?"

"Because I have been faithful to you. Does my word not mean anything to you?" At one time he could have told me he created the sun and the moon and I would have believed him. Now I wasn't so sure. My life wasn't the same anymore. I needed some time and space to think.

"What's happening to our marriage?" he asked. I could see the fear in his eyes. Good. Let him be afraid.

I rose from the couch. "I'm not sure yet. All I know is I deserve time to think."

46

Candace

"Tiffany! Guess what? While you were sleeping, the cops hauled Kimbel's ass off to jail!"

She came racing to the kitchen wearing an oversize T-shirt and fluffy slippers. Her eyes practically bugged outta her head. "What! I just saw that fool last night." I got ready to tell her the story when she cut me off. "Hold up. Let me run to the bathroom first."

I laughed as she hurried back down the hall, then sat back in the chair and brought my coffee to my lips. Last night I told Tyree I couldn't marry him. The look on his face said he was crushed, but he was good with it. He broke me off a couple of hundred, promised to scoop up Miasha after church on Sunday so they could go visit his mother, then left. As much as I wanted stability in my daughter's life, I knew Tyree was not at all where my heart was at. I kept telling myself to take things one day at a time. *And all things shall pass.* At least I had a new job at a prestigious law firm with a heck of a salary that I truly loved. I would know by the end of the week if I was going to be offered a permanent spot. My life was slowly shaping up, yet I felt like there was a big hole in my chest.

"Okay, okay!" Tiffany waved her hands, grinning from ear to ear as she hurried into the kitchen. "Now tell me, what happened?"

Laughing, I shook my head. Thank the Lord for small favors. My best friend had come a long way in a few short weeks. "Well, it seems some female came forward with a necklace Kimbel had given her three years ago. I guess they've been slowly building a case against him. The police finally got a search warrant for his house and found all kinds of items he'd been stealing." I shook my head. "You lived with that man all that time and had no idea what was going on."

"I know. It's crazy!" Leaning against the counter, Tiffany told me about the exchange the two had outside the bathroom. I almost fell out my seat. Did he really think she would be stupid enough to take him back?

"That man is like a character off one of those soap operas. Thank goodness you weren't still living there, because the police would have gone through all your stuff." I guess herpes wasn't the only thing Kimbel was giving females. Thank goodness she didn't marry that fool. "Sooooo . . . how was your date with Baughn?"

"Our date was wonderful." Tiffany took a seat at the kitchen table across from me and gave the intimate details of her evening. I could tell by the smile on her face she really liked this Jamaican dude, and that was definitely a good thing. After that fiasco with Kimbel's STD-carrying ass, my girl deserved to be happy.

"When are you going to see him again?"

"I'm driving to Indianapolis to see him in two weeks." She was grinning like she had just won the lottery. "It's just hard to believe I flew all the way to Jamaica to meet a good man who lives right here in the States. He has no kids, a job, he's educated, and his family is rich. What more can a girl ask for?"

"I think you covered it all." I rose to refill my coffee cup. "You want some pancakes? I was gonna make some for me and Miasha."

She nodded. "Yeah, that sounds good."

I reached for the box of Aunt Jemima, then looked over and noticed Tiffany was looking at me funny. "What?"

"Are you ever going to forgive Chauncey?"

I frowned. Why did Tiffany have to ruin a wonderful morning by bringing his ass up? "Yeah . . . at the same time you decide to forgive Kimbel."

She gave me a don't-go-there look. "One doesn't have anything to do with the other and you know it. Kimbel lied to me in a different way. He put my life in his hands."

"And Chauncey put mine in his."

She shook her head like I was the one being ridiculous. "I bet you never bothered to even find out what really happened. Did you?"

"I already know what happened. I read the charge. Chauncey raped some teenage girl." Just thinking about it made me shiver. How could a man take something when there were so many hoochies out there giving it away for free?

"Candace, Chauncey had just turned twenty-one. He was out celebrating with his boys when he met this girl at the club. She told him she was twenty-one. It wasn't until he was arrested that he discovered she was only sixteen."

"And that's supposed to make it okay?"

Tiffany shook her head. "No, I'm not saying it does. But you know good and damn well how many times we used to sneak in the club with fake IDs and pretend we were legal. I remember that one time we met those college basketball players and they bought us free drinks all night. Yo hot ass even went back to the dorm with one of them. The entire time he thought you were legal."

I mixed the pancake batter and thought about what she said. Chauncey was starting to sound less like a rapist. If the girl had indeed lied, how was he supposed to have known? Why couldn't he have just told me that? I lowered my eyelids and sighed. I guess I hadn't given him a chance.

"Candy, just think about it, you could have ran home to Papa and told him ole boy raped you, and guess what? He would have been behind bars for sleeping with a minor. C'mon girl, it happens all the time. What's a muthafucka to do . . . ask every woman he meets for ID? And even if he does, how's he supposed to know if it's real?"

Tiffany's words hit me like a ton of bricks. The more I mixed the batter the worse I began to feel. Had I really made a mistake by ending my relationship with Chauncey without first giving him a chance to explain? Damn! He had tried so hard to get me to listen, but I refused to hear a word he had to say. "I guess I messed up."

Nodding, she agreed with me. "Yep, you did. And you better get it together quick. This light-skinned chick who just started at the salon last week has been on him something tough. I think they went out for drinks last night."

"What?" My head whipped around.

Tiffany sat back on her chair, the expression on her

face serious. "You don't want him and someone else does."

I rolled my eyes. I knew I was being selfish, but I wasn't ready yet for anyone else to have him. "I thought he was suspended?"

"Noelle let him have his job back. Not that she had much of a choice. Nobody does feet like he does," she added, with a suggestive wiggle of her eyebrows.

I hated to admit Tiffany had been right all along. I was going to regret letting Chauncey go. Here I was jealous; jealous because everyone was spending time with him but me. Now that I knew the truth, I was all set to track him down and tell him how sorry I was.

"He should be at the salon today." Tiffany rose. "Make me two pancakes. I'm going to go and start getting ready."

I watched her leave, then made breakfast. After I fed Miasha, I took a hot shower and got ready myself. Thank goodness it was the weekend, because I was on a mission. I dressed in a short pink Baby Phat dress, then slipped on white sandals and a matching white belt. Around ten, I dropped Miasha off at my parents. They were planning to take her to the zoo today, which was a good thing since I had something important I needed to do.

I stepped into the salon. It was loud in there as usual for a Saturday morning. Tiffany spotted me, smiled, then pointed to the back. It was now or never. I moved toward the break room. Noelle smiled and waved.

"Thanks so much for hooking me up with a babysitter. Your parents are wonderful!" she called over at me.

"No problem. They love doing what they do." I

kept it moving and stepped into the break room. Chauncey was sitting down and some tall chick was standing over him grinning. She had her chest stuck out and was puckering her greasy lips. Anybody could tell she liked what she saw. She might as well back the hell up because I came to claim mine.

Chauncey looked surprised, then disappointed to see me. "Whassup, Candy?"

Ol' girl must have heard of me because her head whipped around and she gave me a you-move-you-lose kinda look. There was no way I was letting her have what was already mine.

"Hey, Chauncey. Can I holler at you for a sec . . . in *private?*" In other words, hussy, you need to get to stepping.

"Sure. Heaven, can you give us a minute?"

She looked like she wanted to say no and had straight attitude, but she did the right thing and left us alone. However, once she was gone and we were all alone, I started getting all nervous and shit.

Chauncey rose and leaned back against the weight of the vending machine. "So whassup?" he said all nonchalant, like he no longer had feelings for me. I couldn't blame him. When he needed me most, I had turned my back on him.

I took several deep breaths before finally saying, "I came to apologize."

"For what?" Chauncey was acting like he had no idea what I was talking about. I guess I deserved that.

I didn't know where to start. "For everything. I should have listened to what you had to say. I shouldn't have been so quick to judge you." My voice was shaky and I hated sounding so weak.

He looked at me without an emotion in sight and

folded his arms. "You're right. You shouldn't have. I've been judged all my life. My mother turned her back on me the one time I needed someone the most, and then I try to start over a new life and yet I'm judged again."

I took a step forward. "I'm sorry. I shouldn't have done that. But I was scared. I have a little girl and just hearing sex offender with all the crazy stuff going on in the world, I panicked and ran, and I'm sorry for that." He just stood there looking hurt and there was nothing I could say to fix things. "That's all I wanted to say. In time, I hope you can find it in your heart to forgive me." I was hurting inside and ready to cry because I knew I had lost him forever. I swung around and headed through the door.

"It wasn't all your fault."

I held my breath, then slowly turned around and waited for him to continue.

"I should have been honest with you from the beginning and explained to you my past. My bad. I was wrong for that. If you're gonna be my wife, I have to learn to keep it real wit you."

"Your wife?" my voice cracked.

He flashed a gorgeous smile. "C'mere." He held out his hand to me. I took it and he pulled me against him. "I love you, girl." It was a long time before I stepped back and wiped my eyes. "I wanna build something solid with you."

"And I want to—"

Chauncey pressed a finger to my lips. "Wait a minute. Let me say something first. Candy, I was wrong. I should have told you the truth. I was nervous if you knew the truth about me you wouldn't have given a brotha a chance. I just didn't want to lose you."

I was shaking my head. Tears were rolling down

my cheek, but I didn't care. "It's okay, boo. I shouldn't have gone off the way I had. I should have given you a chance to explain in private. But now none of that matters. I love you. I never stopped loving you."

"I love you, too. And as soon as we both feel we're ready, I want to spend the rest of my life showing you just how much." He wrapped his arms around me and pressed his lips to mine, and there was no question how he felt. I was never letting him go and as soon as the time was right, you better believe I was marrying him.

"Chauncey, your eleven o'clock is here!" Tiffany called from the doorway.

His eyes never left mine. "I'll be out in a second. Right now, I'm handling my business."

Ooh! I loved the way that sounded.

47

Noelle

Seven months later

"Wait! I forgot something."

Grant put the car back in Park. "Baby, hurry up. I hate to miss the big occasion."

I playfully rolled my eyes. "Yeah . . . right." I knew good and damn well my husband hated weddings. I climbed out the car and hurried back into the house. I had forgotten Chauncey and Candace's gift.

It had been the buzz in the salon all week long. Candace and her wedding party came in for the royal treatment. I spent the past two days plucking eyebrows and doing body waxing. Tiffany was the maid of honor, so I had the luxury of doing her hair and the three bridesmaids, while she hooked up her best friend's hair and Miasha's for her big day. I had to lock Chauncey out the salon just to keep him away. Those two were so in love. They were the reason why Grant and I were still together.

With Chauncey, I learned something about forgiveness and second chances. Chauncey had it hard. His mother and so many other people turned their back on him because of a mistake he made in his past. I realized that I was doing the same thing to Grant. He made a mistake messing around with Lucy, and yes, it was hard knowing he slept with another woman, but it was during a time when our marriage had fallen apart. However, I was confident that when we got back together and found out I was pregnant with Scott, from that day forward we were totally committed to each other. I would be a fool to condemn him for something he had done in the past. Yes, he should have told me Lucy was pregnant instead of trying to hide her pregnancy by giving her the money for an abortion. It still hurt me to know that she had given him the daughter I would never have; but in the time I have known Amber, she had become everything I could have ever hoped for. She still hasn't forgiven her mother for leaving Sierra on our doorstep. But she has opened up her life to me and Grant. We get to see our granddaughter whenever we want. She is currently stationed at Camp Atterbury in Edinburgh, Indiana, which is about a four-hour commute. And we look forward to the drive. We had invited the two to spend the Christmas holiday with us, and the holiday would have been perfect if my son had been there.

Whitney and Michael had Christmas dinner with us. He was such a beautiful baby with those gorgeous gold-green eyes and that family birthmark. There is no doubt in my mind who his father is. Too bad Scott doesn't feel the same way. He had no intention of being a father to his child. According to him, he had been tricked, and since he hadn't wanted a baby in the first place, then he doesn't feel he should have to take any responsibility. It's so sad. Whitney is heartbroken that Michael may never have a father. Grant couldn't even talk any sense into Scott. Like I said before, the kid was spoiled. We decided since he wanted to be grown and make grown man decisions, then he could learn how to make it on his own. We cut him off financially and haven't spoken to him in over four months.

For the sake of my grandson, Whitney and I had worked on strengthening our relationship. I kept Michael for her whenever she needed a babysitter and she called me when she needed parenting advice. I don't know if our relationship can ever be the way it was, because betrayal is a powerful thing, but I have learned that forgiveness and second chances are important, especially when it involves the people you love most.

I grabbed the beautifully wrapped gift from my bedspread and hurried out the house to my devoted husband, who was patiently waiting in the driveway. "Okay, I'm ready," I said, and closed the car door.

"You sure you got everything this time?" Grant asked with that gold glitter in his eyes.

"If I forgot anything, I can buy it when we get there." I put the gift on the back seat beside my tote bag, then leaned over and pressed my lips to his. As soon as we leave the wedding reception, we're heading to the airport. Finally, we were taking that trip to Aruba.

In this thrilling new series, acclaimed author Lutishia Lovely dives into the scandalous heart of romantic obsession with a cunning, sexy seductress, and the object of her affections . . .

The Perfect Affair

Available June 2014 wherever books and ebooks are sold.

Turn the page for an excerpt from *The Perfect Affair* . . .

"Which suit should I wear?"

It was Tuesday following the three days Jacqueline had spent in New York with Randall. The symposium had proved too busy for them to have a second interview there so Randall had agreed for an interview at his company, PSI, Inc., which would also include a tour of his small yet impressive, news-making business. The time spent in New York had only solidified what had begun in LA. Jacqueline knew that between her and Sherri she was close to tipping the love scales in her favor and wanted to do everything absolutely right, down to the last earring and choice of purse.

Kris sat on the bed in front of her, having seen her in the tan suit and now eyeing the bold red choice. "I like that one," she finally answered.

Jacqueline looked down at the single-button suit, with its dipping cleavage and skirt that brushed her knee. "Are you sure it isn't . . . too much?"

"Not at all. That boring world of photogenes and chromosomes could use a dash of excitement, something exciting to wake up what I'm sure is a drab, tasteless office filled with men of equal flair."

"I'm not sure." Jacqueline continued to eye herself in the mirror. "I want to be taken seriously."

"Believe me, you will be."

"Okay. I'll wear the red." She flashed Kris an appreciative smile. "Thank you for being the best BFF a girl could ask for. You've always steered me right."

"And today will be no exception. Okay, next question. Have you been able to reach Phillip?"

Jacqueline flopped on the bed. "Finally, and yes he received my email and is studying the information I sent him. Thank God for that man. I don't know how I would have been able to pull this off without him."

"You haven't yet," Kris chided. "But I agree that Phillip will make it easier. Even though you've said he's not your boyfriend, Randall's wife has to feel better seeing him with you, knowing he's around."

"You're right about that!"

Kris cocked her head to the side as she watched Jacqueline pull her hair into a simple ponytail, pulling a few strands out to dance around her neckline. "How long do you plan to stay here, at Phillip's house?"

"Because he spends so much time with Marco he says it doesn't matter. But I'm thinking two, maybe three months."

Do you think that's enough time?"

Jacqueline eyed her from the bathroom mirror. "What?"

"Ninety days. Do you think that's enough time for your plan to work?"

"It's working already," she replied with a confident chuckle. "By the time we attend the expo in Vegas, Randall Atwater will be all mine."

* * *

Sherri paced the master suite where she'd retreated to make this call. After trying to talk herself off the ceiling, she'd decided to enlist a backup opinion. The first person she'd thought to call was Alexis, but given her single friend's low view of relationships in general and men in particular, she rang Debbie instead.

"Hey, Sherri!" Debbie's cheerful voice rang into a bedroom whose gloom was not only due to the morning rains.

"Girl, I need a second opinion because I'm about to get all worked up."

"Hold on, I'm driving. Let me put you on hands-free." Sherri heard rustling in the background. "Okay, can you hear me?"

"Yes."

"Talk to me, sis."

"So . . . I notice this morning that Randall is dressing differently than usual for a regular day at work."

"What does he usually wear?"

"Either jeans or khakis and a button down or polo."

"What is he wearing today?"

"Jeans, but paired with one of his nicer blazers and the nice loafers instead of his regular Jordans or other casual shoes."

"Okay."

"I asked him why he was dressed up. He said because of an interview he was doing with *Science Today*." Sherri paused after this declaration.

"So far, so normal," Debbie finally replied into the silence. "Why are you getting upset?"

"The freelance writer conducting the interview, their second in almost as many weeks. Her name is Jacqueline

Tate and . . . well . . . let's just say Halle Berry would become background standing next to her."

"A real average-looking sort, huh?"

"Exactly. A troll."

Debbie laughed. "You've met her?"

"At dinner during date night a week or so ago, she showed up with a man as handsome as she is beautiful on her arm."

"Her man?"

"It looked like it."

"So he has an interview with a pretty woman, who's involved with a handsome man, and spruces up a bit. Come on, Sherri. How long have you been married to that man?"

"We're celebrating our twentieth anniversary in August."

"Then you've known him long enough to know that this doesn't mean anything except that he is as normal as any other red-blooded male. He's like a peacock, trying to spread his feathers solely to impress. Unless the interview is taking place in a hotel room instead of his office, I wouldn't read too much into his actions."

"That's how I felt . . . at first."

"And then?"

"Then I heard him in his office, talking on the phone. When I walked in, something that I've done a thousand times, he stopped talking and asked what I wanted. I asked who he was talking to. He said he'd tell me later and then asked if I'd close the door on the way out."

"Okay, that's not cool."

"Exactly. When he came out and I asked again, he said it was a neurosurgeon out of LA. Why couldn't he tell me that right away? And considering how listening to the jargon in his world is like listening to a foreign language, why would he wait to continue the conversation until after I'd left the room?"

Sherri heard Debbie take a deep breath before responding, "I don't know."

There was silence, as Sherri walked over to the sitting area she'd redecorated just last year. She sat on one of two oversized chairs that faced the room's fireplace, and two of its three windows. The rain matched her mood.

"Sherri?"

"Uh-huh?"

"This is a personal question and you don't have to answer but has Randall ever been unfaithful?"

"Once, a long time ago."

"Oh."

"It was during the second year of our marriage. We were both young and stupid, not understanding that marriage was about compromise, not competition. I was the strong, independent sort focused on my own career. He wanted a doting wife. Let's just say there was a certain secretary at the place he worked who paid him the attention he craved. It lasted six months before I found out about it. He ended it immediately and Mom talked me out of getting a divorce. We finally got the counseling that should have preceded our marriage, learned to communicate better and basically just grew the hell up. We've had our share of challenges but he hasn't given me a reason to doubt his faithfulness in seventeen years."

"Then don't doubt it, Sherri. Trust your marriage, and trust your man."